"Paul Belden?" Gamadge asked.

"He's the fellow Cecilia Warren is going to marry, if they can ever afford to get married," said Benny Locke.

"They can afford it if she inherits Mrs. Gregson's money."

"What does that mean?"

"Mrs. Gregson has told me a very serious story, which begins with grease on the cellar stairs."

"Grease?" Locke frowned.

"And then poison in a mackerel."

Locke's ice blue eyes remained steadily on Gamadge's greenish-gray ones. "Oh." And after a moment. "Those accidents last summer. I don't know what you mean by 'poison'—the mackerel was bad."

"Very bad. Now she says that her gas oven was turned on one night, and last week somebody sent her a fruitcake seasoned with arsenic."

"What the devil are you talking about?"

"About the four attempts to murder Mrs. Gregson since last August," Gamadge said.

BANTAM BOOKS offers the finest in classic and modern English murder mysteries. Ask your bookseller for the books you have missed.

Agatha Christie

DEATH ON THE NILE
A HOLIDAY FOR MURDER
THE MOUSETRAP AND
  OTHER PLAYS
THE MYSTERIOUS AFFAIR
  AT STYLES
POIROT INVESTIGATES
POSTERN OF FATE
THE SECRET ADVERSARY
THE SEVEN DIALS MYSTERY
SLEEPING MURDER

Carter Dickson

DEATH IN FIVE BOXES

Catherine Aird

HENRIETTA WHO?
HIS BURIAL TOO
A LATE PHOENIX
A MOST CONTAGIOUS GAME
PARTING BREATH
PASSING STRANGE
THE RELIGIOUS BODY
SLIGHT MOURNING
SOME DIE ELOQUENT
THE STATELY HOME
  MURDER

Patricia Wentworth

MISS SILVER COMES TO
  STAY
SHE CAME BACK

Margaret Erskine

CASE WITH THREE
  HUSBANDS
HARRIET FAREWELL
THE WOMAN AT
  BELGUARDO

Margery Allingham

BLACK PLUMES
DANCERS IN MOURNING
FLOWERS FOR THE JUDGE
TETHER'S END
TRAITOR'S PURSE

Elizabeth Daly

AND DANGEROUS TO KNOW
THE BOOK OF THE CRIME
EVIDENCE OF THINGS
  SEEN
THE HOUSE WITHOUT THE
  DOOR
NOTHING CAN RESCUE ME
SOMEWHERE IN THE HOUSE
THE WRONG WAY DOWN

Jonathan Ross

DEATH'S HEAD
DIMINISHED BY DEATH

THE HOUSE
WITHOUT
THE DOOR

Elizabeth Daly

BANTAM BOOKS
TORONTO • NEW YORK • LONDON • SYDNEY • AUCKLAND

THE HOUSE WITHOUT THE DOOR

*A Bantam Book / published by arrangement with
Holt, Rinehart and Winston*

PRINTING HISTORY

*Holt, Rinehart and Winston edition published in 1942
Bantam edition / October 1984*

ISBN 0-553-24610-0

Published simultaneously in the United States and Canada

Contents

Doom is the House Without the Door—
'Tis entered from the sun,
And then the ladder's thrown away
Because escape is done.

'Tis varied by the dream
Of what they do outside . . .

From *The Poems of Emily Dickinson*
edited by Martha Dickinson Bianchi and
Alfred Leete Harapson. Reprinted by
permission of Little, Brown, & Company.

I

They Always Disappear

Gamadge hunched up his shoulders against the rawness of the November air, and peered from under his hat-brim at the little archway with its ornamental lantern. He asked: "But why does she live in a dump like this? Two hundred thousand dollars, and lives in a dump like this."

"Dump! My good fellow! We've made a very nice thing of it. It has atmosphere."

"That's what you brokers tell the clients, is it?" Mr. Gamadge was not in his usual state of amiability. He glanced about him, without taking his chin out of the depths of his upturned collar. His gloved hands were crammed into the pockets of his overcoat. His eyes were screwed up, full of resentment. "You get deaf people here, I suppose?"

"Deaf? Deaf? What do you mean by deaf?"

"Your tenants like to listen to the Third Avenue L?"

"Damn it all, we only ask forty-five a month for the front apartments. You can't pick and choose in New York for forty-five a month. When the elevated goes, as it certainly will, the prices are going to be higher. The flats in the rear are only fifty. People get used to anything; it's a good address."

"So it is, Colby." Gamadge favoured the tall, ruddy man beside him with a smile, and then gazed once more through the wrought-iron gateway. It was set in a high yellow-brick wall, which ran from the apartment house in question to its next-door neighbour, a brown-stone of the second period. Through the arch could be seen a paved walk, a low hedge, and evergreen shrubs.

Gamadge asked: "Mrs. Gregson's flat is on this alley?"

1

"This court, you mean. Yes, it is."

"I suppose she gets a ray of sunlight once a day, late in the afternoon?"

"She's only here now and then. I told you she had that house I got her in the country. You still don't seem to catch the idea, Gamadge; in a place like this you can be lost— absolutely lost."

"Absolutely lost." Gamadge repeated the words tonelessly. He turned, and walked past the wall and the side of the building to the street corner. This quiet residential block in the Seventies had preserved its gentility almost as far as Third Avenue, but ended there in sudden squalor. Papers blew along the pavement; cellar doors, protected by chains, yawned open; second-hand goods and kitchen-ware stood in front of their dingy shops. Surface cars clanked by, people with bundles in their arms waited for the lights to change, elevated trains roared overhead.

The double house had no atmosphere on Third Avenue, no distinction but a greater neatness than that of its neighbours. Its yellow-brick façade was reasonably clean, and there were Venetian blinds in its upper windows. The twin stores below were occupied by an electrician and a milliner; a fire escape descended from the roof to the second storey.

Gamadge walked back round the corner and rejoined his friend. It was only four o'clock, but the November afternoon had darkened; a dim yellow light suddenly glowed in the ornamental lantern above the archway. The two men went through into the paved alley.

"Very nice." Gamadge looked at a yellow housefront, at an open green door and two shallow concrete steps. They led to a yellow inner door and vestibule, with rows of shining name-plates and push-buttons and letter-slots below. "Very nice," he repeated.

"The tenants have privacy," said Colby. "There's a speaking-tube. The superintendent goes up once a day to collect the trash, and that's all you see of him unless you want him."

"I see; you're practically invisible." Gamadge went into the vestibule and peered at a card marked "Greer." He added: "Anonymous, too, if you're using an alias."

"Of course she uses another name. Would you believe me if I told you the super here has never laid eyes on her? Mrs. Stoner does all the talking."

"I believe it if you say so." Gamadge studied the red face of his friend. It was normally a cheerful, even a jovial face, but now it was downcast. "She was lucky to have you to look after her, Colby."

"The lucky thing was my being in the real estate business. That house I got for her up near Burford—the old fellow that owns it lives in California, and he doesn't care anything about references so long as his rent's paid. She didn't need a reference here, either, except from me; our firm owns this house. Of course she ought to be in a better one, but it was the only vacancy we had at the time, and she liked it and stayed on. She comes down for short visits, but most of the year she's up at Pine Lots. It's a nice old place, but lonely as the grave. That's why she wanted it."

"They always disappear," murmured Gamadge. "I always wondered where they got to; Mrs. Gregson didn't get far."

"She's hidden safe enough. She's never been traced to either place."

"You've done a lot for her."

"Not at all; it was strictly in the way of business. I hardly knew the woman; I only met her once in Bellfield before the trial. You know all that." He added: "The fools that most people are!"

"Am I strictly in the way of business too?" Gamadge looked at him, impressed by his vehemence. "Or am I being presented as a friend of yours?"

"I'm not asking any favours of you, and neither is she. She'll pay your bill, whatever it is." Colby was irritated.

"But this kind of thing isn't my business, as you know," said Gamadge mildly. "I avoid it. As for this case, it entails a huge responsibility, and I shouldn't touch it if I didn't wish to oblige you."

Colby looked anxious. "Of course it's a favour, Gamadge; sorry I was short with you. When you see her you'll want to do what you can. My God, her life's ruined; and now she has this other ghastly thing to contend with. If you can make anything out of it, perhaps she'll listen to reason and get away from all these people and play safe."

Gamadge said: "No need to be wrought up about it. Of course I'll do what I can, but from what you told me it doesn't look promising." He glanced along the alley to a cellar door.

"Nice little box hedge you have here; too bad there always have to be ash-cans, though."

Colby said: "Our super's a very reliable man, keeps the place very clean. Dare say he's been cleaning the things." A black face emerged from the cellar door, and he addressed it: "Hello, Wingate."

The black face gaped at sight of a member of the firm. "Mist' Colby! Anything wrong? They didn't tell me at the office there was anything wrong. I changed them locks, day I got the order to."

"Nothing's wrong; I'm just calling on a tenant. Mrs. Legge says you're entirely satisfactory, Wingate. How's the house?"

"Everything's fine, Mist' Colby, jam full except that party got exterminated out, second floor front."

"Brrr," said Gamadge.

"It's all right, sir, de place is fumigated and de party is comin' back."

"It happens in the best families," said Colby.

"Too bad I ain't allowed to sublet that Mis' Greer's place in summer," said Wingate. "She's away five or six months. I could sublet furnished for more than she pays."

"Stick to your job and let us worry about the renting."

"I could sublet easy, but that woman lives with her won't let me do it."

"Why should Mrs. Greer sublet, if she doesn't want to?"

"Seems too bad to have it empty. You'd think a lady couldn't pay more than fifty a month would be glad to save that, too."

"Very kind of you to think of it," said Colby, with a grin. "I'm afraid what you're really worrying about is there not being anybody in the apartment all summer to tip you."

"There ain't much tipping in a house like this, Mist' Colby, but that woman lives with Mrs. Greer, she tips. She won't let me put foot inside de do'; fire inspector couldn't hardly get in; but she tips."

"You see that the tenants get all the privacy they want." Colby pushed a button in the vestibule, and announced himself through a mouthpiece set in the wall; the door clicked, he opened it, and they went in. Gamadge looked with approval at fresh yellow-plastered walls and the black, rubberlike composition that carpeted the stairs. He said: "Nice job of work you've done here."

Colby turned on a switch and filled the hall with light. "Two apartments, front and rear, on each side," he explained. They went up the soundless stairs, Colby in front. As they reached the first landing Gamadge made a confession:

"I'm rather dreading this; it's a new experience. Do they look and talk like other people?"

"They?" Colby turned his head to frown at him. "Don't put her in a category."

"I must; she's a woman who was tried for murdering her husband, and acquitted. There have been others."

"Of course she was acquitted. She ought never to have been brought to trial. I wish you could have seen her before it happened. The nicest kind of plain little woman, rather shy. Of course she's changed now—if she hadn't changed she wouldn't be human. She looks very different, you know— she's tried to disguise herself, and I tell her nobody would recognize her. I don't think they would. She's not embittered, and that's a miracle. She had almost a year of it before the trial, you know—blasted routine."

"Routine?"

"What else was it—all the delay, when there wasn't a scrap of new evidence on either side, and they knew they were wasting time hunting for it?"

"Very odd case."

"Plain enough, unless you were looking for mysteries. Man committed suicide, of course."

They reached the second storey, and Colby rang at a black-painted door. It was opened a little way, and after a pause a pale, wrinkled face looked out at them. Recognition came into the faded blue eyes when they met Colby's, but the fear in them remained.

"Good afternoon, Mrs. Stoner," he said. "I've brought my friend Gamadge along, as I promised."

"How do you do." The eyes turned to Gamadge.

"How do you do."

She stood back. "Please come in."

As he followed Colby into a small lobby, Gamadge wondered whether she were as old as she looked; with her thinning grey hair, her lined forehead and colourless mouth, her taut, bluish skin, she might be seventy; but perhaps she was twenty years younger than that, old before her time. The hand which still grasped the doorknob was toilworn, but it was not a really old hand. She was a gentlewoman, neatly and unfashionably dressed in grey wool, with a little old pearl brooch at her collar. Three inches of ankle in woollen stockings showed below her ample skirt; she stood with her feet in their black, laced shoes firmly planted side by side. There was no expression on her face beyond the fear in it. She held a hat and a coat crushed together under her arm.

"Go right in," she said faintly. "Vina expects you."

They stood facing the door of a small kitchen, artificially lighted, and ventilated by a fan which hummed busily. Mrs. Stoner retreated into this cupboard, and Colby led the way to a large, boxlike room on the left. It was high-ceilinged and well-proportioned, with two windows looking across the alley to the dead wall of the next house; Gamadge thought that its boxlike quality proceeded from the fact that a builder had been allowed to tear out the original fireplace. Perhaps a certain type of modern furnishing would have suited the room, and made the most of its spaces; but Mrs. Gregson had evidently bought nothing new. Her possessions belonged to a Victorian house, and were of several periods; from the walnut of the seventies to the golden oak of the nineteen hundreds. The upholstery was of yellowish-brown velvet; the curtains matched it, and were lined with paler satin. There was a bronze clock, homeless without its mantelshelf, and looking impermanent on a walnut cabinet. There were two oil paintings framed in gold, a glass table-lamp with a yellow silk shade, a piano-lamp with a pink silk shade, a large and faded oriental rug of some value.

Colby followed Gamadge's look about the room. He said: "She just brought some things out of the Bellfield house."

"Apparently."

"She doesn't take much interest in fixing places up any more. She's hardly touched the house and grounds up at Pine Lots, and she doesn't bother with the garden there. She had quite a garden at Bellfield."

"She hadn't much scope here. You might have left her a fireplace, old man."

Colby was again irritated. "People don't want them.

They make dirt, and the wood has to be brought up. Besides, we needed the flues for our pipes."

"I bet you did."

"You're not in the real estate business."

"That's true."

"She doesn't really live at all, not what you and I would call living," muttered Colby. "She's out of it; out of it."

Gamadge looked at a round marble-topped table with spreading legs; he imagined a family seated about it, reading, sewing, playing draughts. He turned as a door in the north wall opened. Colby said: "Mrs. Gregson, this is my friend Henry Gamadge."

A medium-sized woman came forward and lighted the yellow lamp. Then, after a moment during which she stood silent, looking at Gamadge, she spoke in a rather high, monotonous voice. "I'm very glad you could come, Mr. Gamadge. Won't you and Mr. Colby sit down?"

She seated herself at the end of a velvet-covered sofa. Gamadge and Colby disposed of their hats and coats on a settee, and moved chairs to face her. There was a pause, during which Gamadge politely studied the woman who had been photographed so often two and a half years before. But those photographs had shown a conservative small-town matron, her clothes just escaping dowdiness, her personality obscured by rigid conformity to type. The features of the celebrated Mrs. Curtis Gregson had been commonplace, even under stress.

He was looking at a Mrs. Gregson transformed. She had indeed made an effort to change herself, and the effort had been a success. Her thick dark hair was dressed plainly and fashionably off her high forehead, her eyebrows had been shaped into a soaring line. Her straight mouth had been given form by a very slight application of colour; but her squarish face, which Gamadge had read or been told of as rosy, was now pale. She was perfectly groomed, her dark dress beautifully made and fitted. Her fine stockings and delicate shoes had not been bought in Bellfield, Connecticut. The bag she carried matched her shoes, and no doubt had been made to match them. Mrs. Gregson, in adopting a disguise, had forced herself out of the ranks into elegance.

But the squarish face, if no longer commonplace, was no longer anything. It was a blank, except for the look in her dark, well-shaped eyes. There was blankness in them, too, but it was not the blankness of mental vacuity; after three years they showed amazement; the shock of a great surprise.

"So this is how they look afterwards, is it?" Gamadge asked himself the question, and answered it: "They've looked into the abyss; it's all they see."

There were only two objects in the room that might be supposed to express her personal tastes; a woman's magazine, lying open on a table, and a book beside it. The magazine showed a full-page picture in colours of people feeding peacocks on a green lawn, with a lake and mountains in the distance; the book was Osbert Sitwell's *Escape With Me*.

Colby's voice recalled him to a second contemplation of his hostess. "So Gamadge is taking it up as a favour to me," Colby was saying. "He's had some great successes. It's good of him, you know."

"Not at all," said Gamadge. He thought: "Her skin's like satin. She has time to try all the lotions. She can spend weeks planning and ordering a dress like that. She's probably learned to do her own hair—she wouldn't go to hairdressers."

". . . don't know how I can thank him," said Mrs. Gregson.

"But I have no facilities, Mrs. Gregson," explained Gamadge. "I can only form opinions, and act on them to the best of my ability."

"If you'd only had him three years ago!" lamented Colby. "He'd have formed opinions then! The trouble is that he hadn't done any of this work three years ago. He didn't know he could."

"I am glad he knows now," said Mrs. Gregson.

Gamadge's eyes interrogated her quiet mask. It told him nothing; but if she had humour, and was being amused, he couldn't let her think him too conceited to see the joke.

"Satire," he said, "is called for. Colby exaggerates."

"Satire?" Her dark eyes questioned him. "What did I say?"

"Nothing; I'm always afraid people will think I take my investigating too seriously. You mustn't bank on me, Mrs. Gregson. I'm a bungling amateur. As I was saying to Colby, this case entails a tremendous responsibility on the investigator; I hardly dare embark on it."

"I must consult someone. I hoped you'd do what you could."

"Are you sure you won't consult the police? They have facilities, you know, and they can be discreet."

Mrs. Gregson was about to reply, but Colby spoke for her with some violence; his short, reddish moustache seemed to bristle as he said: "She's had enough of that! She wants a decent, intelligent human being to work for her, not a system that nearly wrecked her, or a cynical, hard-boiled lawyer!"

"Applegate is a bit tough," agreed Gamadge.

"I have plenty of money, Mr. Gamadge." The irony of the words had probably ceased to impress her, but they impressed her listeners. "I'll pay you whatever you ask."

"No results, no bill." Gamadge smiled at her. "If I can't help you solve this problem, I won't ask for anything."

She looked shocked. "You'll have expenses!"

"I'll keep a record of them." Gamadge leaned back, crossed his knees, and got out a notebook and a pencil. "Colby's given me an outline; will you fill it in?"

"One minute." Colby turned his head to frown at the open lobby door. "Do we want Mrs. Stoner in on this?"

Mrs. Gregson asked drily: "Do you think she's been stifling in that kitchenette all this time? She was just going out when you came. I wish you'd stop worrying about poor Minnie Stoner, Mr. Colby; really I do."

"I don't know how you have the nerve to keep the woman in the house with you."

"She doesn't sleep here," said Mrs. Gregson, smiling a little. "She sleeps in a boarding-house."

"You're not to take her back to Pine Lots with you, mind!" He got up, went into the lobby, looked about him, and returned, closing the door after him. "She's gone, all right," he said.

"Of course she's gone. I might as well suspect you, Mr. Colby, as Minnie Stoner."

"You don't want to suspect anybody."

"No, I don't. That's why I'm consulting Mr. Gamadge."

"You'd have the lot of them here with you if you had room for them, even now."

Mrs. Gregson glanced at her other guest with resignation. "Mrs. Stoner's in a dreadful state about it all," she said. "Mr. Colby doesn't know her."

"You let Gamadge be the judge of all that sort of thing from now on," Colby admonished her.

"As far as suspecting people goes," said Gamadge, "you'll find me no better than the police. Now, let's see: it was in July, wasn't it, that you got that letter?"

II

Four Is Too Many

"It wasn't the first," said Mrs. Gregson. "I've had one every year since they let me go."

Gamadge made a note in his book, and then looked up at her. She was leaning back against a cushion of old-gold satin with brown velvet corners; it was a well-preserved relic, and it made an excellent background for her pallor and the fine black of her dress. She wore no ornaments. Her ringless hands lay clasped loosely on her lap, her feet in their exquisite shoes were crossed. Gamadge thought: "That's where her calendar begins—'since they let her go.'" She had travelled a fearful road, and now she was resting beside a milestone; hoping, perhaps, that she might not have to go on. Resting physically, at least; but who knew whether there were mental rest in stupor?

"So this is the third?"

She picked up her bag and opened it. "Yes. I have it for you."

"Didn't you keep the others?"

"No, I thought they were from a crank. I threw them away." She handed Gamadge a greyish envelope, oblong, ugly, and crookedly stamped. The address was printed neatly in block letters.

"Did you get many crank letters?" Gamadge studied the envelope, opened it, and took out a single sheet of cheap paper.

"Yes, but most of them came before the trial. They weren't like these. The first two of these only said: 'Curtis Gregson's murderer is still at large.'"

The rather high, naïve, monotonous voice spoke the words as if familiarity had removed the horror from them. Colby mumbled something. Gamadge looked once more at the envelope. He said: "This is addressed to Mrs. Curtis Gregson, Bellfield, Connecticut. It's postmarked July 15th, New York City, Station Y—that's in the East Sixties. Was it forwarded to you as an enclosure?"

"Yes, Mr. Canning at the Mandeville Trust attends to all my affairs; he's the only one there that knows my new name or where I live now. He puts all my Gregson letters into envelopes, and sends them up to Burford."

Gamadge laid the envelope down and read aloud from the sheet of paper:

"'Curtis Gregson's murderer must remain at large no longer.'" He glanced at her. "These things must have frightened you very much."

"Well, I thought they were just from cranks. But this last one—I thought I'd better show it to Mr. Colby when I saw him. I hate to bother him, he's been so good."

"May I keep it?"

"Of course."

"It looks rather like a fixed idea, you know, and fixed ideas are pretty close to madness." Gamadge put the letter into its envelope, and the envelope into his breast pocket. "You received it on what date?"

"July 18th."

"Mailed to you on the 15th, reached Bellfield the next day, and the bank on the 17th. Colby's notes tell me that the first episode you wish to consult me about occurred on August 15th. Did you connect these three letters with it?"

"Not then. I did later. I didn't connect anything with the first episode. I thought the second one was an accident, too."

"Tell me about the first one. It and the second occurred in the country, I think?"

"Yes, we were up at Pine Lots. Minnie Stoner and I live together there. I've bought her a little annuity; she's quite independent, but she wants to stay with me. Pine Lots is about two miles beyond Burford, and the country is beautiful. We live alone—I never have servants. A farmer down the road takes care of the place, and sells us milk and eggs and things. He's the only other person on the road—between us and Burford, I mean; or rather, between us and the highway. Burford is farther down."

Colby said: "I never liked you to shut yourselves up there. Apart from all the rest of it, Mrs. Stoner is the last person you ought to be with; she's a constant reminder——"

"Who else is there, Mr. Colby? I can't face strangers."

"There isn't any chance that you'd be recognized."

"I'm afraid there is. I can't risk it."

"Well, all that's to be changed now. Mrs. Stoner is thick with the Warren girl and Benton Locke."

"She was always fond of them."

Gamadge's hand had gone automatically to his pocket, and had extracted a cigarette case from it. He was about to replace the battered silver relic, but Mrs. Gregson had seen it. She said: "Oh, I'm so sorry. Won't you and Mr. Colby smoke?"

There was no ashtray in the room, but Gamadge fetched a cut-glass bonbon dish from a table, gratefully lighted his cigarette, and watched Colby gratefully light one. He thought it very characteristic of Mrs. Gregson that cigarettes, tea, and afternoon refreshments should not be part of her daily scheme of life.

"My cousin Cecilia Warren comes up to see me, sometimes," she went on, "and so does my husband's adopted son, Benny Locke. They're too busy to come often, but they manage it two or three times a year."

Colby burst out: "I should think they would manage it!"

"Well, it's dull, you know, and they can't always get off. They sometimes come together, in Benny's car—they both live in New York. I suppose you've heard of them, Mr. Gamadge?"

"They lived with you and your husband in Bellfield."

"Yes. The night he died they, and Minnie Stoner, and the cook, were the only people in the house except me."

"They both gave evidence at the trial, I believe."

Mrs. Gregson said yes, they had given evidence.

"Good friends, are they?"

"They always got on well enough; she's older, you know. She's twenty-nine. Benny is only twenty-two."

"How old is Mrs. Stoner?"

"Sixty-five."

"She is no relation, I think?"

"No, she was a great friend of my mother-in-law's. My husband was fond of her, and when he realized that she was in poor circumstances he took her to live with us. She insisted on doing a great deal of housework. She's very conscientious." Gamadge made a note, and Mrs. Gregson paused for a moment, and then took up her story: "On Friday, August 15th, we expected Celia and Benny for supper and the week-end. Benny was driving up, but Celia had to come by train. She didn't know whether it would be the one that gets to Burford at seven-three, or the seven twenty-two. She is secretary-companion to an old lady, and her time isn't her own.

"At about seven I started for the cellar, to get some strawberry preserves that Minnie and I made in June. I slipped on the top stair, and fell all the way down the flight to the cement floor. Fortunately, my knitted skirt had caught on a splinter half-way down, and it broke my fall. I got a bump on my head, and I hurt my knee, nothing worse than that. I think I was unconscious for a minute or two, but I'm glad to say that I woke up in time to hear Minnie coming along the passage from the kitchen. Before she got to the cellar stairs I screamed at her—I remember how I screamed."

Gamadge asked: "Where exactly was this splinter that appears to have saved your life?"

"On one of the posts. There's only one rail, and the stairs are very steep. It's a dangerous flight."

"Did you and Mrs. Stoner investigate the top step immediately, or were you too badly shaken up?"

"We both looked then. It wasn't exactly the top step, Mr. Gamadge; it was the sill of the door."

"And you found that there was some kind of grease on the sill?"

"Yes. We couldn't make out what it was—butter, or lard, or floor wax, or what. Minnie had been waxing the floors, so we couldn't go by the smell. There wasn't much of the grease."

"Just enough. How long could it have been there?"

"Quite long. Minnie hadn't been down to the cellar since noon." She added: "Minnie thought *I* must have dropped it there, but I knew I hadn't. She isn't young, and sometimes she does drop and spill things; I thought it was an accident, and I was a little annoyed. Perhaps it was, you know."

"An accident?" Colby laughed.

"That first time."

"Four times is too much! They were none of them accidents!"

"Perhaps three of them were. Well. Benny came in his car a little after seven—it's an hour and a half by car from New York, you know. Celia arrived in a station cab about half-past seven; she had caught the six-seventeen from New York, and got to Burford at seven twenty-two."

Gamadge said: "I have several questions, but I'll reserve them. How did the evening go?"

"I had had such a shaking that I went to bed before supper. Celia brought mine up to me on a tray. She was a good deal disturbed about my fall, and she made Benny fix the broken post. He isn't very good at that sort of thing," said Mrs. Gregson, with her faint smile. "Celia talked to me again about having a younger woman in the house. She begged me to. But she doesn't understand how I feel about strangers. I don't know whether you do, Mr. Gamadge?"

"I think I understand very well."

"She didn't have my experience after the trial. She went away and was protected by that Mrs. Smiles she works for—nobody even knew where she was. And they wouldn't have cared so much if they had known; but I——" She paused. "I couldn't stay in Bellfield even one night; I couldn't stay in a hotel anywhere. The newspapers—you don't know what it's like. I've been worried about having Celia and Benny come up together, for fear they'll be connected with me and followed. You know I'm still in the papers, sometimes, and somebody's put me in a book. I'm often," said Mrs. Gregson, with an odd movement of her head from side to side, "in the magazines."

Gamadge thought: "She'll always be in some book or some magazine—*Problems Unsolved. Great Murder Cases. Who killed Curtis Gregson?*"

"I felt better on Saturday," she went on after a moment. "All right, in fact, except for my stiff knee. Minnie Stoner rubbed it. I came down for breakfast after the others. We had mackerel—those little ones. About an hour after I'd eaten mine I began to feel sick, and then I had an awful pain. We had no doctor up there, but I'd seen a sign in the village, and Benny went for him—a young man, Dr. Roder—very nice. He wanted to take me to a hospital, but Minnie wouldn't allow it. She thought it would kill me."

"Kill you?"

"To find myself in a strange place among strangers. She wouldn't let me go, and he—I thought *he* would kill me," said Mrs. Gregson, with her shadowy smile. "The things he did to me!"

"I can imagine."

"He said it must be fish poisoning."

"But hadn't the others eaten mackerel too?"

"We each had one—I told you they were quite small. At least, Minnie didn't; she had an egg. She never eats fish. By late evening I felt better, and I was all right the next day."

"Did Roder take specimens for analysis?"

"Oh, no. He thought it was the fish, and it may have been."

"He didn't even take the fish?"

"The fish?" Mrs. Gregson was surprised. "I had eaten it!"

"Did he take the remains of it, I mean?"

"No, he didn't."

"Fish poisoning isn't too common, you know."

"It wasn't the fish!" insisted Colby.

"Let us keep our minds open while we can. What next, Mrs. Gregson?"

"Nothing for a long time. Benny left early in the afternoon, when I began to feel better; Celia stayed all night, and the next day the man she's engaged to—a man named Belden—called for her in his car and drove her home."

"Where does Mr. Belden live, and what does he do?"

"He lives in New York. He's an architect and landscape designer, or something. They've always known each other. She was his stenographer before—before the trial."

"And now they're engaged. Where does Mr. Locke live, and what does *he* do?"

"I told you he lives in New York. He's a dancer."

"I remember now—so he is."

"That's all he ever wanted to be."

"Is he engaged, or married?"

"No, I don't think he is. He used to go around with a girl

in Bellfield, but she wasn't—I never thought he wanted to *marry* Arline Prady. She worked in a drugstore." There spoke the Bellfield matron, dormant but still alive beneath her disguise. Mrs. Gregson did not sound as if she much approved of Miss Prady.

"Well," said Gamadge, "we now skip two or three months, don't we? There's a change of scene."

"Yes. I come down to this little apartment in the autumn. I go out a little. I wear a veil."

"You aren't afraid that Mrs. Stoner will lead people's attention to you?"

"No, her picture wasn't in the papers much, and she doesn't go out much, herself. She likes the movies, though. She doesn't think people notice her in the little dark ones."

"Who takes care of your country house while you're away?"

"Mr. Hotchkiss, that farmer."

"You're sure *he* doesn't know who you are?"

"Oh, no. He hasn't a notion of it. There are only six people—seven, now, counting you—who know I'm Mrs. Gregson, unless Celia has told Mrs. Smiles. The ones you know already, and Dr. Goff—he used to be our doctor in Bellfield."

"Yes. I remember."

"We drove down here on the 11th. This is Tuesday, the 25th, isn't it?"

"Tuesday, the 25th."

"We came two weeks ago. I have a car, and we both drive it. On Wednesday evening Minnie Stoner went to this little place—the moving picture theatre. She went quite late, after we'd done the supper dishes. We said good night—she was going from the picture show to her boarding-house. It isn't far."

"You apparently don't mind being alone, Mrs. Gregson."

"No, I like it. I always felt so safe here."

Colby made a growling sound. She turned to him, apologetic at once. "You couldn't help it, Mr. Colby—nobody could." Her hand, lifted in an indescribably hopeless gesture, fell to her lap. Then she faced Gamadge again. "My bedroom's there, Mr. Gamadge, through that door in the north wall; and the bathroom's behind it. There's no way to get to them except from this room, and the only way into the flat is through the front door. My bedroom windows look out on the street; I don't mind the noise from the avenue, it's cheerful. I lock the front door, and I always felt so safe. The only trouble is that when I'm in bed I can't hear much that happens out there in the lobby."

"Do you read much, Mrs. Gregson?" Gamadge looked at the Sitwell book.

"Yes." She also glanced at it. "Especially travel. I always wanted to travel."

"You'll travel some day," muttered Colby.

"A week ago Wednesday," said Mrs. Gregson, "I was reading in bed, and I thought I heard the front door close. It closes with a snap. I thought Minnie had come back, and I called out: 'Is that you?' But the door had shut, and whoever it was had gone. Nobody answered. Being rather nervous, I thought I'd get up and investigate."

Colby said: "I wish I had nerves like yours!"

"They're not as good as they were. I got up, and I went into the lobby. The door was shut and latched—nobody but Mrs. Stoner and myself has a key, not even the superintendent; so I wasn't frightened. But I thought I'd look into the kitchen. The door was shut tight. When I opened it, there was a strong smell of gas; then I was frightened, terribly frightened, because of the pilot."

"By Jove," said Gamadge.

"It's always burning, you know, a little tiny flame under the stove lids. I don't know how I had the presence of mind, but I rushed over and pried up a lid and blew the flame out."

"Good for you."

"My knees were shaking. I looked at the taps, and the oven tap was full on—the gas smell was coming through the oven door. I shut off the tap, and then I went and opened all the windows."

Colby said heavily: "These pilots—there have been accidents."

"Accidents! Explosions and wrecks, you mean," retorted Gamadge. "By Jove, Mrs. Gregson, you had your nerve with you. Most women would have dashed out of the flat and out of the house, and left the pilot to blow up the firemen. The oven door being shut would make the bust-up worse when it came. Your bedroom is just behind?"

"Yes."

"Whoever turned that oven tap on," said Colby, "hoped she'd be in the kitchen when the explosion came."

"No accident about that, Mrs. Gregson." Gamadge stated it as a fact. "I know those oven taps—we have one, and I saw it when it was installed. You have to push the thing in to turn it on."

"Yes, you do." Her pale face turned to his. "But what frightened me most of all was the idea that somebody could get into the flat. I thought of those letters, then. I thought of them right away."

"Naturally you did."

"Minnie was in a dreadful state when I told her next morning. She went and made the superintendent change the locks; at least, she made him change ours. He wouldn't change the street door one, of course, until we rang up Mr. Colby. I was so sorry—all the tenants' keys!"

Colby said: "Don't bother about that. As for anybody getting in, it's just a matter of being able to get hold of your key for ten minutes. There's a locksmith on every other block up and down Third Avenue. Two minutes to reach a hardware store, five to get a key cut, two more to be back in the flat, with the original returned and the duplicate in your pocket."

"I know," said Mrs. Gregson sombrely.

"Who'd been calling on you here, the Tuesday that you came, and the next Wednesday?" asked Gamadge.

"Celia, and Paul Belden, and Benny Locke. They came on Tuesday."

"And of course Mrs. Stoner is always with you. Well: I suppose you did at last begin to count up your accidents?"

"Yes. I mean, I began to think about the letters. I didn't think about the first accidents until the fourth thing happened, six days later; just a week ago."

She rose, went to a little desk in a corner, unlocked it, and from the well of it took a cardboard box eight inches square. She brought it to Gamadge, and then sat down and watched him open it. He first contemplated the inside of the cover with affection.

"Good old Boone," he said. "There's no better cake than his on earth."

"I always did love Boone's fruit cake."

The box contained half a loaf of black fruit cake, heavily

iced. The icing had been marked off into generous slices, and three slices had been cut and removed from the box.

"It was delivered by hand last Tuesday," said Mrs. Gregson, in her dry way. "The superintendent told Minnie he found it hanging by its string to the front-door knob; lots of packages are left there if people are out, and nobody seems to steal them."

"We live in a maligned city. Have you the wrapping paper and the string?"

"No, Minnie opened the parcel while I was out—she thought I'd bought the cake. But she remembers that it was addressed to 'Mrs. Greer,' at this address. Boone's doesn't remember who bought it."

"At this festive time of year they wouldn't."

"Minnie says the address was printed."

"I rather wish we had it. Print tells not much, but it's useful for comparison, and I should have liked to compare that specimen with the letter in my pocket."

"When I came home Minnie brought me the box, and I was delighted." Mrs. Gregson's jaw set; after a moment she went on stonily: "I thought Celia had sent it. She knows I love fruit cake. Minnie doesn't eat sweets at all."

"And how did you happen to find out that the cake wasn't as nice a present as it appeared to be? I suppose you did find out something of the sort?"

"Minnie cut three slices. She's very careful about food, and she noticed that some grains like sugar had gone down into the cake through the icing. Then she saw tiny little holes in the icing, several to each slice."

Gamadge peered at the cake. "I see none."

"They were only in the first slices—the ones you have to cut off, you know. People usually buy only a half a loaf, it's so expensive."

"And Mrs. Stoner wouldn't let you eat your cake?" Gamadge was gently poking at it with his forefinger.

"No and I decided to send the slices up to Dr. Goff, in Bellfield. He's always been awfully kind, Mr. Gamadge."

"I remember that he tried to be."

"At the trial, you mean? He couldn't do much, but he was very good to me. He had the slices analysed, and the confidential report came yesterday. So I consulted Mr. Colby, and he consulted you."

"Was the stuff white arsenic?"

"That's exactly what it was."

"Dr. Goff must have been somewhat upset."

"He was. He telephoned, but I told him I was consulting Mr. Colby. How Mr. Colby can suspect Minnie Stoner after this!"

"Perhaps you didn't explain to him that Mrs. Stoner saw the holes in the icing before you did."

Colby said: "Oh—she may have lost her nerve for some reason."

"I'm sure I shouldn't have noticed anything wrong about the cake," declared Mrs. Gregson.

"Have you Goff's report?" asked Gamadge.

"I have it," said Colby. "About six grains of arsenic, approximately two to a slice."

"Much more care was used than in preparing Mrs. Gregson's mackerel; this time there was a lethal dose in every slice." Gamadge again peered at the Boone cake. "Even though I see no holes in the rest of the icing, I don't recommend your eating the rest of your cake, Mrs. Gregson. Nor do I advise putting it into the garbage; some hungry creature might find it. Just smash it up and shove it down the drain."

"You aren't keeping it?" Colby was surprised.

"Well, no; we have the report on what was undoubtedly the dangerous part of it, and this part can't be traced." He placed the box on the table, and lighted another cigarette. "Well, let's face up to it. You're willing to face up to it, Mrs. Gregson?"

"I must." She leaned back against her yellow cushion, and her eyes wandered about the room. "It isn't just because I'm afraid. I can't explain—not yet; and I won't let you or Mr. Colby tell anybody anything. But I must find out who's been doing these things if I can."

"You needn't explain." Gamadge also leaned back, and he smiled at her. "I think I know. But first let us dispose of the evidence, what there is of it. Very clever of somebody that there isn't more."

III

Gregson Dependents

Colby had been looking puzzled. He said: "I don't know what better reason there can be for getting to the bottom of these attempts than saving Mrs. Gregson's life from a would-be murderer."

"She will tell you that there is a better reason." Gamadge's eyes were very green as they met Colby's blue ones. "So good a reason that she won't mind plain speaking on my part for the sake of the cause."

"I don't mind anything." She folded her hands and waited.

"Good. I'll begin by saying that this anonymous letter" —Gamadge took it out of his pocket—"was not of course written by an illiterate person. The paper is cheap, and could have been bought at a five-and-ten-cent store; but the style is correct, literary, even grandiose. No ordinary crank wrote it. We are expected to infer from it that the writer is a self-appointed avenger, who thinks that there was a miscarriage of justice in Connecticut two years ago."

Colby shifted in his chair. Mrs. Gregson said: "Of course the letters meant that."

"They were followed by four extraordinary episodes," continued Gamadge, "and we should be fools not to see a connection, of course. But we must not assume that the episodes were attempts actually to kill you."

Colby protested: "What on earth do you mean? What else were they?"

"None of them did kill Mrs. Gregson."

"But any of them might have killed her!"

"What were the chances, Colby?"

21

"If that splinter hadn't caught her dress she might very well have broken her neck!"

"People do fall downstairs without breaking their necks."

"Those symptoms she had after eating that fish—I'm no doctor, but didn't they show arsenic poisoning?"

"I don't doubt it, not for a moment; but the dose wasn't fatal."

"She had treatment within an hour."

"If she'd had a proper dose she probably wouldn't have responded to treatment."

"How about that gas oven?"

"There the chances were even greater that she'd escape with her life."

"I'd not care to take those chances, I can tell you!"

"But her death wasn't even reasonably certain unless she had gone into the kitchen itself at the very instant that the gas reached the pilot. As for the cake, Mrs. Stoner saw the holes in the icing as soon as she had cut the slices."

"Very clever of her!" Colby was heavily sardonic. "Mrs. Gregson might not have seen the holes in the icing."

"The fact remains that none of these four attempts succeeded. This is a very ugly affair, you know, and we must expect to find depths within depths; let us begin by arguing, for the sake of eliminating possibilities, that the attempts were all fakes. The perpetrator evidently didn't mind killing Mrs. Gregson, and may indeed have meant to kill her and been unable to bring it off; but let's argue that the motive was to frighten her, to punish or to persecute. Can you think of anyone in your immediate circle who might want to do that, Mrs. Gregson?"

She said calmly: "You mean, does any of them think I killed my husband."

"And cherish a longing to serve the ends of justice, as he or she imagines it."

"I don't think so. If I thought so, would I have them come to stay with me?"

"Let me put it another way: which of them had a great devotion to your husband?"

Mrs. Gregson looked down at her clasped hands. "Minnie Stoner was very grateful to him."

"But you think that she is fond of *you.*"

"I know she is."

"How about the adopted boy—Benton Locke?"

"I never thought Benny Locke cared for anybody but himself."

"Miss Cecilia Warren?"

"My husband took very little interest in Celia. She was there because she was my cousin, and had nowhere else to go."

"Let's drop the persecution motive, then, which is getting us nowhere, and try another. What if four faked attempts at murder were arranged in order to throw suspicion on some one person?"

Mrs. Gregson looked up at him. Colby said: "Good Lord, the ideas you get!"

"I never thought of such a thing," said Mrs. Gregson.

"Suspicion," continued Gamadge, "could only fall on somebody who had access to Mrs. Gregson or her house at the proper times. We'll tackle that later. Who profits by your death, Mrs. Gregson?"

"Minnie has her annuity, and I haven't left her anything in my will. I give Celia and Benny a small allowance, all I can afford. I've left them everything I have in my will, in equal shares."

"Have you, really?"

"Celia is my only relation, and I thought my husband would want me to look out for Benny Locke."

"Well, we must assume that Miss Warren's, and Mr. Locke's next friends would also be interested in their financial prospects. If you were convinced that Miss Warren or Mr. Locke were trying to put an end to you, would that affect your last will and testament?"

"Of course it would. I'm not sentimental enough to leave money to somebody who wanted to kill me, Mr. Gamadge."

"Let us hope not. What would you do about the legacy of such a person?"

"I never thought. I suppose I'd leave all my money to the other one."

"Perhaps somebody supposes so too. Now for opportunity: and we must begin with the grease on the stair. Was the house open that afternoon, Mrs. Gregson?"

"It's always open if we're there."

"What's the approach to it?"

"The road from the highway is very lonely; there's only

the Hotchkiss farm, as I said. You pass a stump lot on a hill, and a belt of pines, and then there's a narrow side yard."

"Trees in the yard?"

"Evergreens, and some bushes."

"Where were you and Mrs. Stoner that afternoon?"

"Minnie was in and out of the kitchen, and upstairs. I was upstairs too, getting the spare rooms ready."

"Is there another back entrance besides the kitchen door?"

"There's a side door as you approach the house; it leads to a passage."

"And where's the entrance to the cellar?"

"Off that passage, before you get to the kitchen."

"Very convenient. Suppose Mr. Locke had come a little earlier than he seemed to come, Mrs. Gregson; or suppose Miss Warren had arrived by an earlier train? I suppose there are plenty of afternoon trains to Burford?"

"Yes, there's one that gets there a little after six. But——" She was gazing fixedly at him, her eyebrows drawn together.

"Miss Warren could have come up on that train, walked to Pine Lots, put the grease on the stair, and walked back to the station. There she could have waited, and taken the cab that met the seven twenty-two. Couldn't she?"

"She could walk the distance."

"As for the mackerel; you came down last to breakfast. How do you know what happened to that fish between the time it was put on your plate—in the kitchen, I suppose?"

"Yes."

"In the kitchen, by Mrs. Stoner, and the time it was eaten by yourself? It's a long time ago, and none of these people can be expected to remember where they and others were that morning, and who went into the kitchen, and who was alone in the dining-room. Where *was* the fish when you came down?"

"I called down that I was coming, and I found it at my place at the table. The others weren't there."

"As to the affair of the gas oven; all these people have had access to your keys at one time or another, I suppose?"

"I supose so."

"Men's pockets are as it were a part of themselves, but women's handbags are always lying around. Mrs. Stoner's bag, and your bag, for instance. As Colby explained, it wouldn't take long for somebody to get hold of a duplicate key to this flat, and to the front door of this building. The cake—anybody on earth could have got that cake to you; anybody, of course, who happened to know that you liked fruit cake. One thing emerges from this void: no outsider engineered these four episodes, Mrs. Gregson. You know that as well as I do, and I won't insult your intelligence by discussing the point. It *is* a void, you know; perhaps we'll never find out what lies at the bottom of it."

"Don't say that, Gamadge!" begged Colby.

"I'm no magician, Colby. I can't pull the rabbit out of the hat unless the rabbit is there. But I can offer Mrs. Gregson two or three pieces of advice, which amount to solemn warnings. And I can talk to the parties."

Mrs. Gregson said: "That's what is worrying me so. I don't want to be unjust, and they'd never forgive me——"

"I'm very tactful; am I not, Colby? Here's the advice: First, you really must send Mrs. Stoner back to Pine Lots. I'll see her there, away from your supporting presence. You're best away from her just now, Mrs. Gregson."

"If you say so." She was still frowning at him.

"Second—and most important: Change your will."

"Change my . . . ?"

"Your will. Change it now, this afternoon. Colby and I will witness it for you, and it will be as good as if it had been done by a firm of lawyers. Leave your money temporarily to anybody—shall we say to a cats' home? That has a contemptuous implication, but I hardly know why? I have a cat myself."

"It would be so frightfully unjust to—to the others; if I should die!"

"How do you know, Mrs. Gregson, that they're not all involved in this?" He added: "I'll break the news to the ex-beneficiaries. Leave it to me."

"I can't do it to-day! I must think." She looked at Gamadge desperately, and his heart sank. "I don't think I realized how awful it all was until now!"

"It's a nasty situation, and must be met with what weapons we hold."

"Excellent suggestion, I call it," said Colby.

"I might die suddenly. I *can't* cut them both out like that. I can't risk it. Can't I pretend I've changed it?"

"Much better to have it a fact; facts are more effective than fictions. But if you're determined against the idea I'll tell them you've changed it, or are about to change it. Have you told Miss Warren or Locke about those letters, and the four attempts?"

"No, not a word. Minnie Stoner knows."

"Let's hope she hasn't told them."

"She's had no chance to tell them."

"She may have seized a chance, but let us hope not. My third, and I hope a more acceptable piece of advice: I want you to go up to a nice little place I know of near Cold Brook—that's about a dozen miles up the line north of Burford, you know. It's more a rest cure than a sanatorium, and it's very comfortably run by two nice women of my acquaintance, trained nurses. It's expensive, but you get your money's worth."

Colby was delighted. "That's a brilliant idea of yours, Gamadge! You'll be right out of it all, Mrs. Gregson; best thing in the world for you in every possible way."

She said: "I'd love to go, but I told you—I don't go among strangers."

"Don't you worry about that. These two women that run the place will protect you fully and ask no questions. One of them is a nice, quiet, efficient girl, and the other's a jolly old war horse—a good sort. She took care of me once when I had a broken ankle, and she introduced me to her partner and told me their plans for this sanatorium. I helped them write the prospectus, and I sent them some patients, and—er— that kind of thing."

"Bought a little stock in it?" Colby laughed.

"Well, that's neither here nor there. The point is that I know the place from the ground up. It's called Five Acre Farm, or Five Acres; nice little property up the road two or three miles from Cold Brook. It's been done over with a sun parlour and a lounge and I don't know what all. It's been a success. They even have a visiting physician, and the guests can have all kinds of treatments and foolishness. Mrs. Tully and Miss Lukes only take desirables, and the patients live in clover. None of those people would know you, Mrs. Gregson, and I dare say none of them ever heard of you."

"It sounds very nice."

"You needn't appear downstairs at all unless you feel like it. You can take walks—lovely scenery, even at this time of the year. I could call up to-night—they probably have room for you so late in the season—and drive you up there to-morrow myself."

"You take my breath away." She gave him the faint, difficult smile.

"Send Mrs. Stoner up to Burford in your car. I wouldn't rush things, you know, if I didn't think there was a rush."

After a pause she said: "You're very kind; I'll go."

"Good. I'll make all arrangements. This is one place," and he grinned at Colby, "where *my* reference gets you in. Could you be ready at half-past nine, say?"

"I must go to the bank first."

"I'll come here and wait for you. And now I want the addresses of those young people, and I want to know how to get to Pine Lots."

"It's the second road to the left beyond Burford. I'll give you the number of Benny's rooming-house, and the telephone. Celia lives with a Mrs. Smiles." She went over to the desk in the corner, and sat down at it. While she wrote Gamadge and Colby stood waiting with their overcoats on and their hats in their hands. She turned, with a slip of paper in her fingers; Gamadge went over to her. Looking down into her eyes, he felt as if he were looking at the windows of a deserted house.

"Mrs. Gregson," he said, "I know why you never ran away from all this."

"Do you?"

"Yes." He took the paper and folded it. "I know why you have brought yourself to tell me this story; I know why you're willing to pursue this investigation, although it may mean raking up the past; may even mean publicity for you, and the end of your privacy."

"I wondered if you would guess."

"I have guessed. You think that Gregson's murderer is at work again."

Colby exclaimed. Mrs. Gregson kept her eyes on Gamadge's. He went on: "You hope I'll find evidence that his murderer, having failed to get you killed by due process of law, has been using methods more direct. Your husband's money is the motive now, as it was then."

Colby advanced. He said fiercely: "I never saw it. You'll get proof of this, Gamadge." And as Gamadge doubtfully shook his head, exclaimed: "You're not giving up before you begin?"

"I must warn Mrs. Gregson not to bank on my finding proof of it. I know that the hope means more to her than life itself, and I implore her not to risk her all on it. For a man or woman who sacrifices everything to a fixed idea is risking too much. What shall you do if I fail you?"

"I must face that." She sat rigid.

"You've brooded on it too long. Take your money, leave this place and the house at Burford, cut loose from Mrs. Stoner and from the others, give up the quest. Make yourself a life; stay in cheerful hotels, meet people, teach yourself not to care whether they recognize you or not. Get away from your dependents, and there will be no more letters, and no more stories of attempts against you. Believe me, it will be worth it!"

She had listened to his urgent voice attentively. But she in turn shook her head. "You can't conceive what it means to me. I must go on with it."

"Then I'm off." Gamadge suddenly regained his natural ease of manner. "See you in the morning, and be sure to bundle Mrs. Stoner out of town before we start for Cold Brook. She's not to know where you're going; nobody's to know."

She stood up, grasping the back of her chair with a firm hand. "I won't tell. Thank you both. Thank you, Mr. Colby, for bringing him—I know he'll find out something."

"He'll do the trick. Look at him—the man's on the hunt already!" For Gamadge was half-way to the door. Colby followed him.

As they reached the stairs they met Mrs. Stoner, slowly climbing. She wore the crushed grey hat that she had carried under her arm at their first meeting, and the long grey coat. Her fur neckpiece had seen many winters. There was a little veil tied about her hat-brim which partly obscured the upper part of her face. Her eyes were wide behind it as she looked up at the two men; but they shifted like a nervous animal's.

"Good night," said Gamadge cheerfully.

"Good night."

Colby did not greet her at all. He said, as they went downstairs, "I hate leaving those two together."

"They won't be together long."

"Thank goodness you persuaded Mrs. Gregson to go up to that place; but I wish you hadn't sounded so doubtful of the outcome."

"Do you really think I shall find out who put grease on those cellar stairs, or poison in that mackerel? Or solve the problem of the gas oven and the fruit cake?" He glared malevolently at Colby.

"You ought to be able to dig up something." Colby, following him out of the house and along the alley, looked unhappy. "You're in the deuce of a hurry, anyhow. Have you an idea?"

"I'm in the deuce of a hurry to get home and get to a fire." Gamadge strode out from under the archway, and looked up and down the street for a cab. "You coming? Clara'll be glad to see you."

"I must get to Bellfield. I'll just make my train."

"Good luck to the huntin' and fishin', not to mention the ridin'. Pretty soon you'll be makin' a snow man."

Colby refused to respond to this childishness. He hurried off to get a cab on Third Avenue; Gamadge, after a long look after him, turned and walked towards Lexington.

IV

Gregson Laughed

Gamadge entered the library of his old house in the Sixties, and found himself walking on a sea of papers. Furniture stood up from among them like reefs at low tide, and an island in front of the fire contained a tea table and Gamadge's old coloured servant Theodore. He was clearing the tea tray.

"I'd like some of that before it goes, if you don't mind." The master of the house lifted his right foot from a pile of autograph letters signed.

"Right away, Mist' Gamadge, sir; get you some fresh."

Theodore hurried out, ignoring the activities on the other side of the large room where Mrs. Gamadge sat cross-legged on the floor, her hands full of manuscript, and Harold Bantz, Gamadge's young assistant, prowled on all fours among documents. Martin the cat, devoted to paper in any form, lay at full length on a bed of parchment, occasionally putting out a paw to make it rustle; when it did so he rolled over and slapped at the noise with an air of reproof. Sun, the chow, sat near his mistress and seemed to supervise her labours. He paid no attention to Martin; he had learned to forget him.

Mrs. Gamadge raised her ingenuous face to her husband. "Isn't this nice?" she inquired. "I thought it would be so cosy to do the Bendow correspondence up here."

"Well: the trestle tables in the laboratory are practically ideal for sorting papers," said Gamadge mildly. "That's why I bought them."

Harold, a youth of short stature and morose countenance, stolidly and silently continued to crawl among documents. Clara's face fell. "Oh, dear," she said, "I know you hate a mess. I made Harold do it. I thought it would be fun to work up here; where there's a fire."

"Bless you, darling; it was a very sweet idea. You shouldn't be working at all . . . oh, God!"

He sprang forward. Martin, tantalized beyond endurance by the crackling of a stiff glazed bit of notepaper, was chewing a corner of it and fighting the rest of the sheet with his hind legs. Gamadge fell upon him, pried open his jaws, and saved all but the fragment which Martin, with closed eyes and much jerking of the head, was hastily swallowing.

"This is too bad!" Gamadge inspected damp remains. "The Honourable Mrs. Norton's shopping-list. *One red velvet smoking-cap, 30 shillings.* That was Lord Melbourne's Christmas present, I know it was, and I was going to write an article proving something or other. Damn it all."

Clara got to her feet. "Oh, I'm so sorry."

Harold was scrabbling papers together and stuffing them into files. He said: "That ain't Mrs. Norton's list."

"How do you know?" Gamadge studied it irritably. "There are letters of hers here, and one of them's to Melbourne, I bet anything it is."

"This list ain't in the Honourable Norton's writing."

"You decided that after viewing it with the naked eye?"

"No; you viewed it with the naked eye and decided that it was."

During this colloquy Clara stood dejected. Gamadge skated to her across reaches of slippery correspondence, and clasped her in his arms. "It was sweet of you, my darling. You ought not to have bothered with the things at all. You ought to have been out having some fun."

"I like it at home." Clara had been a principal in a murder case not long before, and was still shy of society.

"I ought to take you out more myself. We could have gone south and played some golf, but Colby's tied me up to a brute of a case. You and Harold have to help me solve it."

They sat down on the chesterfield sofa. Theodore, coming in with hot water, remarked: "Mis' Gamadge and Harold, they're young; can't expect 'em always to think old."

Harold's rage was very great. He said: "You keep your condescension to yourself. I know what I'm doing."

Gamadge winked at him behind his wife's shoulder. Harold had strict orders to allow her to assist in the laboratory and, if necessary, to wreck it; but she had not wrecked it, and really did assist.

"What's this case Mr. Colby is making you work on?"

"Before I tell you what it is I want you both to listen to a strange story. I have a lot of notes Colby prepared for me, and some newspaper clippings. But first I want my tea."

He disposed of it in large swallows, punctuating them with bites of muffin. Harold went downstairs and returned with two notebooks; one, his own, considerably battered; the other new.

"Mrs. Gamadge can practise her shorthand," he said.

"I can try to." She accepted the notebook and a pencil. "Thank you, Harold, but I'll never learn how."

"Yes, you will."

He sat down facing them. "All set?" inquired Gamadge, through muffin. He swallowed, put down his cup, wiped his fingers on a doily, and got a sheaf of typed pages and a bunch of newspaper clippings out of his pocket. "Ever hear of the Gregson Case?"

There was a pause. Harold said: "You mean the Gregson murder case? Certainly I have."

"I have too," said Clara. "Everybody heard of it. It was only a couple of years ago."

"Two years last June. You're right," agreed Gamadge, "everybody heard of it. Our friend Colby lives in Bellfield, you know, and he knew Gregson slightly, and he met Mrs. Gregson once before the trial. Now he's taken her under his wing."

Harold stared. "I thought nobody knew where she was, nobody at all."

"Colby does, I do, and soon you and Clara will. Colby, I must explain, although he lives in Bellfield, isn't a native; he bought a place on the outskirts, and he's a country gentleman—when he isn't dealing in real estate. He commutes."

"I like him ever so much," said Clara.

"He attended the Gregson trial through some pull or other, and decided that it was a complete miscarriage of justice; not her being acquitted, you know; her having been brought to trial at all. Many people thought the acquittal was the miscarriage of justice; and the fact is that she got off by the skin of her teeth. I verily believe that in Scotland the verdict would have been 'not proven,' and that in England the judge would have looked very pinched under his wig. But the jury had gazed long upon Mrs. Gregson, and heard her speak; and it took them forty-five minutes to come back and say 'not guilty.'

"As a matter of fact, it's a case that has kept the experts guessing ever since; and I'm supposed to solve it: alone, unaided (unless you and Harold aid me), and with no material to work on but Colby's notes."

"Who wants you to solve it?" asked Clara. "Mr. Colby?"

"Mrs. Gregson. I met her this afternoon."

"You did?" Harold was impressed. "What's she like?"

"She's like a woman who had a shock from which she's never recovered."

"I don't wonder," murmured Clara.

"But she's not the woman whose picture you can see among those clippings; she's not the Mrs. Gregson the jury saw. She has adopted a new physical personality, but in spite of it I could tell why she was acquitted against the evidence and the summing up. I'd better give you an outline of the case.

"Curtis Gregson's family settled in Bellfield a long time ago, but they didn't preserve their presumably nice old colonial house; they tore it down during the 1870's, and built a new one which they improved into a fine old Victorian monstrosity with gables, bay windows, a cupola, and stained glass over the windows and around the front door. Here's a picture of it. Admire the pin-cushion flower-beds on the lawn, and the gabled carriage house turned into a garage. The house is painted a mustard yellow, so I'm informed, with chocolate trim.

"The Curtis Gregsons were quiet, stay-at-home people. Gregson played golf, and he went to all the town meetings, but he and his wife didn't patronize the club dances. He was a lawyer, in the reputable firm of Banks & Styles, and commuted to New York. Played a poorish game of bridge on the train, didn't care for poker. Colourless man, physically and otherwise—sandy-haired, clean-shaven, just under medium height, eyes light grey. Not much of a mixer, but not disliked. At the time of his death he was forty-three.

"Mrs. Gregson was forty. She was an outlander—from a little up-state town near Utica. You won't believe me, but the name of that town is Omega."

"Why shouldn't we believe you?" asked Clara.

"Because it's such an extraordinary mixture of the classical and the early American. It sounds as if somebody must have misunderstood the Indians. However: the ladies of Bellfield are said to be very much of a clan, proud of their town and jealous of their privileges therein. Mrs. Gregson did her share of sitting on charity committees, and hauling flowers and eatables to the bridge drives and bazaars, but she was not *haute* Bellfield, and never in all the twenty years of her married life did she make intimate friends there. She seemed not to require them. The fact that she had no children may have helped to keep her out of the main current.

"But when her catastrophe arrived, no man or woman in the place had a word to say against her, or would listen to the theory that she had poisoned her husband. They won't listen to it now.

"Colby met her just once, about two years before the tragedy, and he won't listen to it. He met her in her own house. It was Gregson's turn to preside at some kind of golf meeting, and those meetings were always held at the club, but the club happened to be undergoing repairs. So he had the meeting at his residence, and Mrs. Gregson was on hand to greet the committee. Colby says he barely noticed her at the time, but that afterwards he remembered what she was like perfectly well. A slightly dowdy, rather nice-looking woman, with lots of wispy brown hair and red cheeks. Nothing to take the eye of Colby, a very worldly man. She had a pleasant way of talking, but nothing to say. Colby describes her as 'countrified'; he probably means provincial, but would consider the word an affectation.

"She disappeared, and wasn't on hand when the men went into the dining-room for refreshments. Everything was laid out ready, there were no servants, and they helped themselves to whisky, sandwiches, and coffee out of an urn. He saw her once or twice afterwards in the street, but not to speak to; he says that when the news broke he couldn't have been more astounded if they'd arrested *him*.

"He knew vaguely that the Gregsons had two young people living with them—relatives, he supposed; but only one of them was a relative. Miss Cecilia Warren, aged twenty-six, was a cousin of Mrs. Gregson's, also from Omega. Benton Locke, aged nineteen, was the son of one of Gregson's oldest friends. Locke's father and mother were dead, and Gregson had taken him in some years before. I may say here that Miss Warren was Mrs. Gregson's only living relative, the daughter of Mrs. Gregson's father's sister. Mrs. Gregson's maiden name was Voories, and her family had christened her Vina. What do you think of that?"

Clara said, surprised, that she didn't know what she was expected to think of it.

"You like alliterative names? You like the name of Vina?"

"Well, Mr. Colby's right—it's a little countrified, perhaps."

"Don't go through life understating things out of politeness, Clara; don't, I beg of you. It's a hell of a name."

"What does it matter what her name was, or is?"

"It matters a lot; it gives you a slant on her background. And she never altered it, mind you; I bet that helped with the jury! You know, Mrs. Gregson's faculties have been sharpened by what she's been through, but she's really quite a dull woman."

"That makes it all more horrible."

"Yes, it does. Well: the aunt who married this Warren died long ago—twenty-odd years ago. Warren died in 1931, seven years before the Gregson trial.

"There was a third dependent in the Gregson household, a widow named Stoner, Minnie Stoner, a friend of Gregson's mother's. She was a kind of lady-help, and now she lives with Mrs. Gregson. In 1938, when the tragedy happened, there was only one other person in the house, the cook, Martha Beach. I know nothing about her, except that she wasn't a young woman.

"There's a certain peculiarity about the status of the two young people in the Gregson circle. Cecilia Warren arrived there when she was sixteen, in 1930; but nothing was done for her socially—Bellfield knew her not. She was put straight into a business college, where she learned stenography and typewriting, and as soon as she was qualified she got a job. She had several jobs, and ended in an architect's office as a kind of secretary to one of the firm, a young man named Paul Belden. He comes from Amsterdam, New York, and he and Miss Warren have known each other for years—since childhood. They're now engaged to be married."

Clara said: "If Cecilia Warren had to earn her living, I don't think there's anything so queer about all that. You say Mrs. Gregson didn't go out much herself."

"The peculiarity comes later—you'll see. Her existence, however, seems to have been none too merry. Young Locke arrived at the Gregson home when he was fifteen, went to high school, did very badly there, and was put to one and another job—in vain. He insisted on dancing. Dancing is the only thing that he has ever taken seriously, so far as I know, and dance he would. Gregson seems at last to have let him go his way. Locke's father was a brilliant man; by profession an accountant, but by nature a musician. He didn't work at much except music, and died penniless. The boy was brought up to sleep on the floor and live on bananas—so Colby seems to think; but he was devoted to his father.

"Well, we now come to the celebrated night of June 5th, 1938. It was a very warm evening, unusually warm and sultry, which fact has everything—practically everything, as you will see—to do with the case. Gregson came home on his accustomed train, which arrives at Bellfield about six-thirty; Colby remembers seeing him on it. It's the express that most of the Bellfield men commute by. Cecilia Warren and Locke arrived on their local at about seven. I should mention that the Gregsons had no chauffeur, and that Mrs. Gregson taxied

Gregson to and from his trains; Miss Warren and Locke
walked in all weathers. The house is between half and a
quarter of a mile from the station, and is approached by a fine
road that runs between elms and maples—uphill."

"Quite a walk, on a bad winter's night," observed Harold.

"Or even on a rainy summer morning. On that hot June
evening dinner was eaten at seven-thirty; Miss Warren and
Locke wouldn't have been in time for it if it had been earlier,
but as a concession to the servant problem in Bellfield
Martha Beach was allowed to go—presumably to the movies—
after she had cooked it. It was served, and the dishes washed
afterwards, by Mrs. Stoner.

"Immediately after dinner Gregson complained of a slight
indigestion. He said that it had been dogging him all day, and
he attributed it to the heat. I will say here that there was
nothing seriously wrong with his digestive apparatus; except
for a bilious tendency he was what you might call a well man.
He decided on this occasion to take bicarbonate of soda and
go to bed early, and he went up at about nine.

"You are now to take careful note of the arrangement of
rooms in that house. It has a wide front hall, with the parlour
and the library on the left, and dining-room, pantry, kitchen,
and so on to the right. Mrs. Gregson's bedroom was over the
parlour, and Gregson's over the library. There's a bath between."

"I thought people like Mrs. Gregson never had a room of
their own," said Clara.

"Mrs. Gregson had one, and I dare say that the prosecution at her trial hoped that the jury would disapprove of that
fact. The bathroom had once been a store cupboard; Gregson
had had it piped—his parents never dreamed of more than
one bathroom in a house.

"On the other side of the hall, opposite Mrs. Gregson,
there is a sewing-room and sitting-room combined. Behind it
are linen cupboards, a large bathroom, and the guest chamber This last, just opposite Gregson's quarters, had at some
time or other been fitted with what is known as a summer
door; shuttered, you know, and to be used in hot weather
when the regular door had to be kept open for air.

"On the third floor we find Martha Beach, the cook, over
Mrs. Gregson, and Locke over the sewing-room. Mrs. Stoner
behind Locke, Miss Warren behind Martha Beach. Bath

between Locke and Stoner, trunk room between Miss Warren and the cook. Get it?"

"I get it," said Harold. "The help and the non-paying guests were all up on the third floor together."

"And the help's room was by no means the least desirable of the lot. Miss Warren had the one with the sloping roof, the peephole window, and no cupboard; her clothes hung on hooks behind a curtain. It came out in evidence that the top rooms were pretty cold in winter—the cook had a gas heater, by the way. And in summer the whole top floor was an oven. They gave Martha Beach an electric fan."

Clara said: "Murder trials do bring out the queerest things."

"That's what makes them so fascinating," said Gamadge. "We hear of mutton soup for breakfast in the dog days, fly-paper soaking in saucers for the ladies' complexions, chloroform on the mantelpiece. Nobody, in court or out of it, seems to remember how funny their own little ways would look if brought out at a trial."

"We might come out very funny at a trial, Henry," said Clara.

"We might indeed. It would sound funny if we had to admit that we had no idea who Harold is, or where he came from."

"But I do know where he came from," said Clara.

Gamadge stared in astonishment at his assistant, who muttered: "We get to talking."

"You do, do you?" After another moment devoted to a wondering survey of the taciturn Harold, Gamadge returned to his notes. He was totally incurious, except in the way of business.

"As I said, Gregson went upstairs at nine. Mrs. Gregson prepared the dose of soda for him, and the whole family was in on it; there was none in the Gregsons' bathroom cabinet, so Miss Warren got the large tin of soda that was in the third-floor medicine cupboard. Mrs. Stoner brought a tumbler of boiled water upstairs, and a silver spoon. Locke stood in the hall and talked to his benefactor, while that gentleman, at the open door of his bedroom and in his shirt sleeves, tossed off the mixture. Locke was asking permission to borrow the family car—he wished to take a friend to the movies. He did not specify what friend, but the Gregsons knew very well that it was a Miss Arline Prady, who worked in her father's drugstore in the village.

"Permission was reluctantly granted—the Gregsons did not much care for Locke's best girl. Then Gregson closed his door, and after that no member of the household admits to seeing him again, alive. Mrs. Gregson came downstairs and listened to the radio until ten, when she also went to bed; quietly, so that she need not disturb her husband. Mrs. Stoner washed the dishes, played patience, and went up just after Mrs. Gregson. Miss Warren usually disappeared as soon as dinner was over; she went out, or read in her room; on this occasion she went upstairs, but she did not read. She said afterwards that the night was so hot she simply lay on her bed in the dark. She heard the cook come in, a little after ten.

"Locke got home at eleven-thirty, garaged the car, saw or noticed no lights in the house, and went in. He locked the front door after him. Mrs. Gregson had already made the rounds for the night and fastened all other doors and all downstairs windows.

"Next morning Miss Warren and Locke came down as usual for their early breakfast, prepared for them by Mrs. Stoner, and then walked off to catch their early train. Mrs. Gregson came down at eight, the Gregson breakfast hour; she told Mrs. Stoner that her husband's door into the bathroom was shut, and that she wasn't going to wake him. At nine, however, she did go up; she was afraid he might not want to sleep longer. She found him dead. The doctor, a Dr. Goff, got there in a few minutes and said that he had died of an overdose of narcotic—probably morphia. The 'probably' seems an excess of caution, since there was one of those little brown-glass tubes beside the tumbler on the night table. The label said that it had contained twenty-five quarter-grain tablets of morphia; it was now empty. There was a trace of morphia in the tumbler, with dregs of soda bicarbonate. At the post-mortem they found that he had swallowed at least three grains, perhaps more.

"Goff, and the entire Bellfield community with one exception, supposed that it must be suicide. The inquest was to be a mere formality, and everybody hoped that the jury would bring a verdict of accidental death, to save Mrs. Gregson's feelings. Let me repeat here that there had never been the faintest breath of gossip about her, and assure you that spotless moral reputations weigh heavily in favour of women who are being tried for murdering their husbands."

"Why shouldn't they weigh heavily?" asked Harold.

"No reason; but sometimes there is a reason why the contrary shouldn't weigh heavily against them. However, we're not at the trial yet, we're at the inquest. Studbury, the medical examiner, had known Gregson slightly, and had not known Mrs. Gregson at all; he employed the man who worked on the Gregson place, and he learned from him a curious fact: Martha Beach had told him that when Cecilia Warren got home on the evening of Gregson's death, and first heard of it, she exclaimed (to Martha Beach, who told her the news): 'But he can't have killed himself, I heard him laugh in the middle of the night.' She never repeated the statement, nor did Martha Beach—except to the hired man.

"Studbury could not of course be sure that Cecilia Warren had ever said any such thing; but he saw Gregson's law partners, who were in a state of incredulity and bewilderment over the idea of Gregson killing himself, and from them he got two additional pieces of information; Gregson was worth at least two hundred thousand dollars in paying stock and insurance, and his first and only will left every penny of it to his wife.

"Studbury then discovered from Goff and others that Gregson had no physical reason for ending his life. He was fussy about his health, had regular examinations made by the medical department of his insurance company, and paid semi-annual visits to his oculist and his dentist. As for the possibility of his having led a double life and found it too much for him, his partners exploded it. They solemnly assured Studbury that Gregson's time had been fully occupied in New York by his business. He was in the office all day, lunched there, and only left to catch his commuters' special. He had had no more chance to lead a double life than he would have had if he had been in a condemned cell.

"Studbury began to think that it was very unusual for a suicide to leave no farewell letter; and he worked up such a case in his own mind against Mrs. Gregson that at the inquest he played a terrible, if legitimate, trick on her. He called her first, and took her sworn statement that she had seen and heard nothing of her husband after nine-thirty on the night of June the fifth. Then he called Miss Warren, and asked her to repeat her statement to Martha Beach about hearing Gregson laugh.

"Miss Warren was a reluctant witness, staggered by his question and at first unwilling to answer it. Then she told a very queer story indeed. It seems that she didn't after all stay up in that attic of hers on hot nights. For years she had made a practice of creeping down to the guest-room after everybody was in bed, and staying there until early morning. It had that shuttered door, you will remember, and it has windows north and west. Personally, I don't blame her."

"You mean nobody in the house knew she slept down there?" asked Harold.

"Not a soul. She slept on top of the bed, and remade it carefully every morning. Locke could come in late and go upstairs without noticing the shuttered door at all."

Clara asked indignantly: "Why did she have to sneak around the house like that?"

"Mrs. Gregson, recalled, said that she *didn't* have to, and that if she had dreamed the girl was uncomfortable she would have done something about it. A general impression got about that Miss Cecilia Warren was a reserved, if not secretive, kind of young woman, and she certainly made that impression on the jury—then and at the trial."

Clara said: "Some girls in her position wouldn't like to ask a favour."

"The impression got about that Gregson was the master of his house, and made the rules in it. As he was undoubtedly a miser too, one could see that no great confidence may have existed between him and the people he was sheltering."

"If I was in that position," said Harold, "I wouldn't ask a favour."

"You wouldn't anyway," replied Gamadge. "Is your room by any chance too hot or too cold for you, may I ask?"

"No, it ain't."

"I'm relieved to hear it."

"I wouldn't ask a favour either," said Clara, "if I were in Cecilia Warren's position. She may have been sensitive."

"She may. Well on the night of June the fifth she had come down as usual, opened the windows, closed the lattice, and lain in the dark. She heard Benton Locke come in and go upstairs—as I said, the guest-room is at the rear of the hall, and she wasn't afraid that he'd notice anything. Pressed by the M.E., she said that she knew he wouldn't give her away if he did find she was using the guest-room. You'll remember that she was now opposite Gregson's bedroom, across the hall.

"She didn't know exactly when Gregson laughed, but she said it couldn't have been long after twelve, because she had heard Locke come in not very long before. She said that it had not been a loud laugh, just a low kind of chuckle, but that it was Gregson's. It's a fact that if you're on the bed in that guest-room, with the regular door open and the shuttered door closed, you can hear a laugh through the door of Gregson's bedroom; you can hear a laugh when you wouldn't hear low voices. An ordinary laugh would sound like a 'low kind of chuckle'; that house was built solidly and tight. Here's another fact: she couldn't have heard anything short of a stentorian guffaw from the other rooms in the house, if their doors were closed; and their doors were closed.

"She woke about six; from long habit she always woke at that hour. She heard nothing of Gregson's death until the cook told her the news that evening, and had made the statement about the laugh more to herself than to Martha Beach. She had never repeated it—and the M.E. had to drag this out of her—because she was afraid it would make trouble for Mrs. Gregson.

"Her fears were justified. Mrs. Gregson swore that she had heard no laugh, and that she could only suppose him to have laughed in his sleep, or coughed, or something; but by that time Gregson must have been in coma; and heavy breathing doesn't really sound much like laughter.

"Dr. Goff was called; a most reluctant witness, with a strong bias in favour of Mrs. Gregson. The trend of the inquiries had startled the life out of him. He deposed, however, that when he first saw the morphia tube a corner of the label was missing—had been torn or scraped off; and it happened that that corner was the one that contained the serial number of the tube. He also deposed (in agreement with Studbury) that the tube must be at least twenty years old; because such tubes held twenty-five tablets twenty years ago, but since then they have only held twenty."

"I never knew that," said Harold.

"Nor did I. Laymen aren't as a rule familiar with tubes of morphia tablets; a layman only gets possession—legitimate possession—of one through a doctor, for some special purpose; to treat a drug addict in the family, or to use in the family for the alleviation of some painful or incurable disease; cancer, gall bladder, that kind of thing. At any rate, two grains of morphia are fatal to most people, and this tube had contained six and a quarter and nobody knew where it had come from.

"Well, imagine the state of mind of the local jury. They all knew that quiet, dowdy Mrs. Gregson, or had seen her driving herself about on mild errands in the family sedan. She was as ordinary as the clothes she got from the village tailor, and the hats she wore for three years. They announced that Gregson had died of morphia, they didn't know how or why. Studbury, was disgusted, Bellfield declared that he was a most officious, disagreeable little man, and Mrs. Gregson was arrested that same night on a charge of murder in the first degree. That you, Theodore? If Mrs. Gamadge is agreeable we'll have cocktails now."

"I'm agreeable," said Clara.

"I has 'em," said Theodore, coming forward with a tray.

V

The Gamadge Gambit

Gamadge put down his empty glass, and rustled his notes. "The People of the State of Connecticut," he said, "rejected the suicide idea—rejected it, through the mouth of the prosecutor, with irony and with contempt. Why, they wanted to know, should Gregson—whom nobody accused of having been a raving maniac—why should he laugh quietly to himself in the middle of the night (they saw fit to accept Miss Warren's story), scrape the serial number from a twenty-year-old-at-least tube of morphia tablets, and gulp a round dozen of them down; for no ascertainable reason, and without leaving a letter to his wife? They said that a suicide doesn't take pains to make the source of the poison he uses untraceable, or go out of his way to leave suspicion upon his household.

"Accident, they maintained, was out of the question. No man mistakes morphia tablets for bicarbonate of soda in powdered form, or takes three grains of morphia at once unless he's an addict; and Gregson wasn't an addict. Murder was the alternative, and who had motive, opportunity, and the necessary information but Mrs. Gregson? Information was necessary: morphia is a poison which murderers don't use— the prosecution knew of only one case in which it had been used—because it's a tricky drug; everybody doesn't react to it in the same way. It puts some people into a coma, but it excites others—makes them noisy and unmanageable. Poisoners look up the effects of their drug, and Mrs. Gregson would know Gregson's reaction to morphia; know that he wouldn't react to it by waking the house. She'd either seen him under the influence of a small dose of it or she'd asked him whether or not it put him to sleep. Cold-blooded, no doubt; the horror of poisoning is the cold-blooded premeditation which goes with it.

"Applegate defended. He cited six well-known cases of suicide for which no motive had ever been found, and he talked at some length about the mysteries of the human soul, and the solitude of human suffering. He quoted Maeterlinck— something about people smiling in the family circle and weeping in the dark. All true and all good. He then said that twenty-year-old tubes of morphia may very well lose bits of their labels; but I personally have never seen labels stick as those labels do—tighter than the bark of a tree. He said it would be shocking indeed if this poor woman sitting here in danger of her life should lose that life because a corner of an old label, which happened to contain a serial number, should happen to have been lost. He said the serial number was lost because it was *on* a corner. Perhaps he was right.

"He then laid great stress on the fact that the morphia couldn't be traced to the possession of Mrs. Gregson. Gregson had been as likely to possess it as anybody else in the house. Anybody else, he repeated sternly, in the house.

"Then he tackled the laugh in the night, and in his cross-examination of Miss Cecilia Warren he tackled it for hours. When he had finished with the laugh in the night, I can assure you that he had come within about a sixteenth of an inch of accusing Cecilia Warren of the murder."

"I wondered if he wouldn't," said Harold.

"Oh, he did."

"But *can* they?" asked Clara. "Is it allowed?"

"The defence in a murder trial is given great leeway. Applegate knows the game, and he knows how to instruct a jury by implication, innuendo, and inference. A good deal of his speech was stricken from the record, but the jury got it first. He pointed out that Miss Warren's word was uncorroborated; he took a high moral tone about poor relations, living on the bounty of their cousins, who sneak into guest-rooms and listen at doors; and he reminded the jury that if Mrs. Gregson had motive, Miss Warren also had had one—a reversionary interest in Gregson's money, since she was Mrs. Gregson's only living relative.

"He then introduced the theory that the laugh, if there was a laugh, had come from outside the house. On summer nights, he explained, people drift off pavements into the shade of trees, and those trees are often on the lawns of big houses. He said that sound carries oddly at night, especially to people who are dozing, half-asleep. And he wound up by hoping that that was where the laugh had come from, if there was a laugh, if Miss Warren had actually heard a laugh, if she was not actuated by malice, and if, in fact, she had actually spent one single night, in all her life, on that bed in the guest-room.

"He ended with a short, effective, and really touching tribute to Mrs. Gregson's blameless life and spotless reputation. Mrs. Gregson doesn't like him, perhaps he showed her that he didn't care whether she was innocent or not; but he did very well for her.

"The judge was old Bligh, a learned and a fair-minded man. He summed up without bias, but he didn't do the defence any favours. He said that if people committed suicide there was always a reason for it, whether that reason could be discovered or not, but that it was unfortunate that the morphia couldn't be traced to Gregson. He reminded the jury that Miss Warren's evidence, whatever else it did, completely cleared Locke and Mrs. Stoner and the cook, since none of them could have gone into Gregson's room without waking or disturbing a person behind a shuttered door, on the guest-room bed; and that Miss Warren had put herself voluntarily, if impulsively, in the position of a material witness. I think he was pretty well convinced that Mrs. Gregson was guilty—she had a financial motive, and her opportunity was overwhelmingly greater than that of the others. He apparently believed Miss Warren's story; the question was, would the jury decide to believe it?

"They stayed out less than two hours, and came back with a verdict of not guilty. There she sat, you know, in one of those Bellfield tailor suits, and one of those amorphous felt hats, with wisps of hair coming out from under the brim. Here's a picture of her taken during the trial; doesn't she look bludgeoned? Knocked into a daze? Colby said she made a good witness. The jury no doubt remembered how she'd taken Cecilia Warren in, years before, practically off the street.

"Colby was absolutely convinced of her innocence. Banks and Styles were furious at the verdict, and many other people thought the acquittal a farce. They were angry at the thought of her living in comfort on Gregson's money, but they needn't have worried. She hasn't had much of a time; she hid herself away, and she won't show her face. She'll never live a normal life again until she's been completely cleared."

"Is that what Mr. Colby wants?" asked Clara. "For you to clear her?"

"Well, he didn't give me such a large order as that; he's hopeful, though."

"I don't know how you could do it without knowing more about it than all this," said Clara. "We don't know anything. We don't know what the people are really like—Cecilia Warren, or Locke, or Mrs. Stoner."

"We know that unless they were all in a conspiracy, Mrs. Stoner and Locke had no motive—they lost free board and lodging by Gregson's death. Or at least Mrs. Stoner may have thought she was going to lose it; as a matter of fact, Mrs. Gregson has given her an annuity, and gives the others allowances."

"Perhaps they all loathed Mrs. Gregson," said Harold, "and deliberately put her on a spot."

"Then the motive on Cecilia Warren's part was pure loathing, seldom an adequate motive at her age; for if Mrs. Gregson had been convicted she wouldn't have inherited

Gregson's money, and Miss Warren wouldn't have inherited it from her."

Clara asked: "What does Mr. Colby want you to do?"

"He called me up this morning to tell me that since August there had been four attempts on Mrs. Gregson's life."

"What!" Clara bounced on the chesterfield, and even Harold gaped at the information.

"She told me about it this afternoon. She won't consult the police; but if my investigation means publicity, she'll face it. Do you know why?"

"I should think anybody would know why!" Clara stared. "She naturally doesn't want to be murdered, and I don't wonder that she prefers publicity to losing her life."

"Not at all. Gregson's murderer is undoubtedly at the bottom of these new phenomena; and Mrs. Gregson hopes that I may discover evidence in connection with them which will clear her reputation for ever."

"You'll simply have to!"

"Well, as a matter of fact I advised her to drop the whole thing and clear out."

"Drop it? Drop it? I shouldn't drop it if I were in her place, I can tell you!"

"You don't realize that she's now a woman of one idea; if I don't get the results she hopes for I believe she may actually lose her wits. She's no longer the Mrs. Curtis Gregson of those photographs, Clara; gone are the Bellfield tailored suits, the six-dollar hats, the wisps of hair. She is now Mrs. James Greer, perfectly turned out and dressed. She puts in her endless spare time striving for physical perfection."

"I never heard anything so pitiful in my life."

"Meanwhile the inner woman has been marking time; she has been doing nothing else since the trial. She lives for one thing only—to be able to convince the world that she is innocent of her husband's murder. Now she thinks there's hope of doing so, and Colby has persuaded her to enlist me. I don't like the responsibility involved; I don't feel equal to it."

"You didn't refuse to take a stab at it, though," said Harold.

"No, I didn't; it seems to me that there would be one thing worse than taking this case: not taking it. Well, you'll both have to help me. First I want to show you something." He got the anonymous warning out of his pocket. "Mrs.

Gregson tells me that she got two letters after the trial from the person who sent her this last one; obviously it *is* the same person. The first letters merely said that Curtis Gregson's murderer was still at large."

"How ghastly!" breathed Clara.

"This one is more ghastly still. It says: 'Curtis Gregson's murderer must remain at large no longer.' A month later somebody put grease on her cellar stairs. Then came a dose of arsenic in her food, the strange history of an escape of gas, and a Boone fruit cake that might have killed three Mrs. Gregsons."

Harold said: "Somebody means business."

"Somebody means business. The other letters were printed, like this one: and the printing is very characteristic. The lower loop of every S bulges, as you see; every G is slightly askew; the middle horizontal of every E is as long as the top and the bottom one; not a single O is closed at the top, and the R's have long tails. But how are we to get other printed matter to compare with this? What *do* people print besides anonymous letters?"

"They're told to print their names on their tax returns," said Harold.

"And how would you go about getting a look at somebody's tax return? The police might be able to manage it, if they showed cause; but I couldn't, and I have no time to try. I'm hurried, worried, and driven."

"Are you?" Clara looked at him anxiously.

"Very much so. Harold, I'd like you to transcribe the notes that I took when I interviewed Mrs. Gregson this afternoon; then you and Clara can read them and get an idea of what we're up against. Clara, your job is going to be a dull one. You're to get up bright and early and go down to the public library. Get all the newspaper accounts of the Gregson case from start to finish—the *Times* will do—and write me a short history of all the principals in the case. Include a certain obscure Miss Arline Prady, who worked at that time in her father's drugstore, and don't neglect a Mr. Paul Belden, now a resident of this city, but I think a native of Amsterdam, New York. I'm not so sure you'll get anything on Belden, though; everybody connected with the affair received attention from the press, no doubt; but he wasn't engaged to Miss Warren at the time."

"Mr. Schenck always knows everything about everybody," said Clara.

"Excellent idea. Call Schenck up, and see if he'll work on Belden; I want to know what he's like now. Harold, your job is a sinecure. You need a rest and a change, and you're going up to get it at Five Acre Farm."

Harold said: "That Tully woman."

"Most competent, agreeable person."

"She's very nice," said Clara, "but she does eat such lots of things out of paper bags, and she smokes cigarettes with perfume in them."

"When she's off duty she's entitled to a little relaxation; let her enjoy herself in her own way. I telephoned up there on my way home this afternoon, and she's taking Mrs. Gregson in on my recommendation—under the name of Greer, naturally. Nobody is to know where she is except Colby and the firm of Gamadge & Co. Harold's going to look after her, and his name will be Thompson."

"Tully and Lukes know me, all right."

"The patients don't, and neither does Mrs. Gregson. I wouldn't have her think I think she needs a chaperone for anything. I want her calm, not nervous; but I want her looked after."

"How am I to look after her?" Harold's face had assumed a lowering and doubtful look.

"Don't bother her; but I don't want her going off on long drives by herself, and that kind of thing. Best to be on the safe side—that's why I made her give Mrs. Stoner her car. If she wants to drive, you get them to let you drive her."

"Will Tully and Lukes know who she is?"

"Certainly not, and they won't tell her who you are. She's just supposed to be a lady friend of mine in need of a rest. I don't know why you look like that; you'll enjoy yourself very much. I'll get them to give you one of those rooms on the back terrace; then you can do a little night watching under Mrs. Gregson's window. You can sleep late in the mornings; that ought to suit you."

"If I'm to hang around windows at night, you'd better make an arrangement with Tully. She'd have the skin off my back."

"She won't know anything about it. I wish you'd co-operate."

"Who's to know she's up there? Colby won't tell."

"You do what I ask you to. Anyhow, you'll get some decent food for a change."

Harold frowned. He would not be persuaded to eat with the family because he preferred to absorb strange nourishment at counters, in the company of the drifting population. Seeing his gloom, Gamadge said casually: "You'd better take my dressing-case."

This magnificent object had been a wedding present from Clara's aunt; Gamadge had faithfully lugged it about with him on their honeymoon, but had never opened it; and it was an object of admiration and respect to Harold, who could often be seen admiring it in its seclusion on a cupboard shelf. He dimly smiled. "I'll have to put my initials over yours," he said. "It will take me quite a while."

"Don't forget that you're Thompson now. You'd better do some shopping to-morrow; take Clara with you, for goodness' sake. She'll know the kind of shirts to get—I don't want you startling the patients up there. Early, now; you'll have to take a morning train to Five Acres."

"Nice long day you're planning for us."

"I'll want a report from you every day; and you won't have to use code, because they have a telephone booth, and the patients can't switch in. I don't care to hear any complaints from the firm; I fully expect to be out and about half the night myself."

He went into the hall and got Benton Locke's boarding-house on the telephone. A foreign voice gabbled at him, and after a pause a weary masculine one asked who was talking.

"Henry Gamadge. I'm a document man—examine manuscripts, that kind of thing. Now and then I do a little private investigating; criminology, you know. Give you references, if you like."

The voice asked: "What are you calling *me* up about?"

"I'm a little worried about a Mrs. Stoner—Mrs. Minnie Stoner."

The voice asked, after a pause during which Harold winked at Clara: "What about her?"

"Can't talk over the telephone. I thought I might consult you this evening after dinner, if you can give me half an hour."

After another pause Locke's voice came over the wire, no longer in a drawl, but hard and sharp: "Who are you investigating for?"

"Explain when I see you."

"I'd like the explanation now." The voice added: "I'm too busy to waste time."

"I have been consulted by a Mrs. Greer."

Locke coughed. Then he said: "About Minnie Stoner?"

"Not specifically."

"I'm dog-tired; been working all day, and I'm giving a lesson to-night."

"I strongly advise you to discuss the situation with me, and as soon as possible."

"I don't know what Minnie Stoner—can't imagine what it's all about. I go out to meals; I can't be here until eight-thirty."

"Half-past eight will suit me very well."

"I can't give you more than half an hour. I'm working on some choreography, and if I put off this lesson I'll be up all night."

"Half an hour ought to do."

"If you hadn't mentioned Minnie Stoner I shouldn't have seen you at all. What's this party—Greer—investigating, for Heaven's sake?"

"I'll tell you when I see you."

Gamadge came back into the library. "Mr. Locke is very uppish," he said.

"What's he uppish for?" Harold was gathering up the last of the Bendow correspondence, playfully assisted by Martin the cat.

"He's a serious dancer."

VI

Serious Dancer

Benton Locke lived not far south of Mrs. Gregson's apartment, but his street ran between elevated railways, and had long given up the struggle against shabbiness. Nor had his boarding-house atmosphere. A coat of fresh paint had lately been applied to its vestibule and double front door, but its high porch was grimy. A small place of business—lamp-shades, Gamadge thought, peering through the gloom of the area—was established in the basement. The combined smells of anaesthetics and antiseptics billowed from a pet-hospital across the way.

Gamadge rang the bell. An amiable foreigner in a long black house dress and comfortable slippers opened one of the doors and peered at him through gold-rimmed glasses.

"Mr. Locke?" Gamadge spoke through an ascending blare of radios; there must be several, he thought, on every floor.

"Yes, third storey, rear."

Gamadge came in, and she closed the door. "Ma'am," he inquired, "do you ever feel the need for a silence like death?"

"Is it not dreadful?" She shook a flaxen head. "Half de time, I can hardly hear my own radio."

"What a shame. Is yours the quite loud one coming from the back parlour?"

"Yes. We must not be selfish; people must have deir pleasure."

"So they must." He climbed two steep flights of red-carpeted stairs, and knocked at a door. A resonant baritone voice told him to come in.

He obeyed, and found himself confronting a young man of magnificent physique, who had discarded his coat, his collar, and his tie. He wore slacks and sandals, and a blue shirt tucked in at the neck. He was a young man with no claim whatever to good looks, but Gamadge thought that he would make up strangely and effectively. He had a small head, flattish pale features, tow-coloured eyebrows over chilly blue eyes, and tow-coloured hair. He was quite ready for Gamadge.

"Have a seat," he said carelessly, indicating a hard chair. Gamadge sat in it, and Locke fell rather than sank upon a studio couch against the wall. This, which was upholstered in faded blue, the hard chair, a dresser, and a table, were—with the exception of a radiogram near the window—the only furnishings of the room. There was no floor covering, and the windows were fitted with dun-coloured shades.

"I'm dog-tired." Locke settled his head against the blue cushions.

"Your work must be very exacting." Gamadge spoke respectfully.

"Exacting? I teach ballroom dancing, I work at summer resorts, I practise at my own work every day, and now I've just landed a job with the Diehl ballet."

"No, really? Congratulations."

"You like dancing?"

"I'm a fan."

"You fan don't know what the work is. If I hadn't the strength of a horse I'd have given up long ago. Of course all this, even the Diehl, is preparation; I'm working up my own choreography, and when I have capital I shall dance alone."

"Really alone? No partner?"

"I want no partner for my dance." He turned his head, and gazed into some dream of the future. Against the blue of the pillow, under the light of the unshaded bulbs, his face in profile looked like a modern plaster cast; ugly, interesting, all flat planes and rough modeling. "I have the hardest part of it done," he said. "A friend in an art school has designed costumes for me, and I know a girl who plays the piano. She'd tour with me. She has a first-rate sense of rhythm."

"You're ambitious, Mr. Locke—admirably so."

"Dancing is all I ever cared about, but you can't even dance without money. Not if you want an audience."

"I suppose you're not telling what your dance is going to be like; descriptive, symbolic, classical? I haven't the knowledge to put my question intelligently."

"It describes a personality, and its development throughout the ages."

"This is very tantalizing."

"You won't see it unless I raise some money," said Locke, sombrely. "This war is going to set me back, and by the time I get going I may be too old to do my stuff. Dancing isn't a thing you can drop and pick up again. I ought to have had my chance five years ago."

"Too bad Gregson wasn't interested."

Locke was immediately alert. He sat up, got a packet of cigarettes out of his pocket, and offered it to Gamadge before he replied. Gamadge declined the cigarettes, and lighted one of his own. Locke pushed a brass dish towards him with his toe, and said airily: "I didn't expect any help from Gregson while he lived."

"Bellfield probably wasn't highly aware of the arts. I dare say you didn't get much encouragement in your art while you lived there."

"I never lived in Bellfield."

"Didn't?"

"No; Gregson's house was the place where I ate and slept."

"A dour household, perhaps."

"It never seemed so to me; I wasn't part of it. Nobody in it cared about me, or I about them—except poor old Minnie, of course, and she loves everybody." He leaned back against the cushion, and for a while his archaic profile looked motionless as stone. Then he said: "Gregson wasn't the kind of person you like or dislike, and I felt no particular gratitude to him; he took me in because he was fond of my father. He ignored me, after he found that I was determined to dance. He would certainly have thrown me out, only my father was his best friend. I don't know how Father put up with him; but Gregson used to come to our place, and he liked it. He was lucky—you don't meet people like my father every day. Gregson would never have come within miles of knowing him if they hadn't gone to college together."

"Didn't Gregson recognize the obligation?"

"We didn't beg of him, if that's what you mean. My father died of pneumonia; we didn't exactly roll in luxury, and he never did take care of himself."

"So Mr. Gregson adopted you—and let it go at that."

"He didn't adopt me legally, and he certainly let it go at that. I couldn't have borrowed money from him. I think poor old Minnie Stoner is the only person I ever did borrow money from; but she was a human being, you know."

"Wasn't Mrs. Gregson a human being?"

"I didn't know her well; she was just an uninteresting woman to me, and of course she had no money of her own to give away."

"Miss Warren?"

Locke turned his head and lifted an eyebrow. "Cecilia Warren hadn't a penny; and besides, she'd had all the humanity killed out of her. She was for herself, first, last, and all the time. You don't know much about poor relations. You don't know what it's like to be a hanger-on." Locke smiled. "Minnie used to go down to the cellar in the middle of the night in midwinter and stoke up the old hot-air furnace so we shouldn't freeze to death next morning in the attic. Gregson was sure to make a row, too, if he thought the consumption of coal seemed abnormal. Minnie used to make sandwiches for us and hide them in our rooms so that we could have a snack when we came in late. When she lent me that money to pay for my lessons, all she had on earth was some few hundreds she'd saved from her husband's insurance. I'm glad that the poor old girl has that annuity, and a snug berth with Mrs. G."

Locke apparently had no intention of asking questions. Gamadge said: "Mrs. G. seems to think more of you than you do of her."

"Oh—she's told you that she gives Celia and me allowances?"

"She's left you and Miss Warren all the Gregson money in her will."

"She'll live for ever."

"Well, let us hope so; but it's a compliment, at least." Gamadge studied him with a certain amusement.

"Why shouldn't she leave us the money? Celia's her only relative, and she knows Gregson expected her to look out for me—if anything happened to him."

"You're sure of that?"

"She told us so. But I appreciate the compliment, as you call it; I go up to see her at that dreary place near Burford— go up two or three times a year in my old wreck of a car. For a busy man like me, that's something."

"You go up to see her because she's promised to leave you money?"

"About a hundred thousand; do you know any better reason for paying a visit?" Locke's thin mouth widened. Gamadge also smiled, as he said: "Is that why Miss Warren goes?"

"I assume that it is."

"Mrs. Gregson certainly did very little for Miss Warren in a social way, while you were all living in Bellfield."

"The Gregsons did very little for themselves in a social way. Gregson grubbed for money and played golf; Aunt Vina, as I was supposed to call her, grubbed in the garden and sat in on ladies' charity committees. Neither of them cared for amusement."

"How did Miss Warren amuse herself?"

"I'm sure I don't know. She was lot older than I was, and I never had much to do with her. She was more or less of a sphinx, you know. We just tramped back and forth to and from those damnable trains, and that's all we saw of each other."

"And she didn't dislike Mr. Gregson, either?"

"Dislike him? No, I don't think she did. As I said, there was nothing much to dislike about him; we didn't expect him to give us money. Certainly Cecilia didn't expect it; why should he? She was Mrs. Gregson's responsibility, not his."

"Somebody must have disliked him actively." Gamadge looked at his cigarette, and dropped the ash from it into the brass dish at his feet.

"Why do you say that?" asked Locke, glancing at Gamadge from half-closed eyes.

"Well, somebody murdered him."

"Oh, that wasn't murder."

Gamadge, admiring the extent of Mr. Locke's preparedness, asked mildly: "Wasn't it?"

"Certainly not. I never could see what all the fuss was about. It was an accident." He went on, as Gamadge said nothing: "A hell of a defence Applegate put up! I could have done better for the poor woman myself. Gregson was a hypochondriac, always dosing himself; I bet he had morphia for his first earache—why, my grandmother used to give me laudanum for a sore tooth! She'd put a drop on cotton, you know. Nobody thought anything of it."

"Well, but those tubes of morphia have never been handed out for family use as laudanum used to be."

"I bet he'd had that tube all his life. I bet he woke up that night—the night he died—with that stomach-ache he'd been having, and got out the old tube, and dumped what he thought was one tablet into the soda glass; but he was in a hurry, and it was dark, and he dumped them all. That's what happened."

"Most interesting suggestion; why didn't you offer it to the lawyers for the defence?"

"I told the only lawyer who interviewed me for the

defence, and I told the police. Nobody paid the slightest attention."

"Of course I shouldn't myself expect the jury to swallow all those morphia tablets."

"Easier to swallow them than to swallow the idea of Mrs. Gregson murdering anybody."

"Or Miss Warren murdering anybody?"

"Cecilia Warren is as hard as brass tacks, but not as hard as all that. Did you ever know anything funnier than that story she told about making herself comfortable all those years in the holy of holies—the guest-room, you know? Wish I'd thought of it myself. Did you ever hear why she slept up in the attic instead of in the guest-room?"

"No, why did she?"

"Because she smoked, and Gregson said it gave him asthma and headaches. Nobody ever smoked in that house, except in the attic. Nobody ever murdered anybody in that house." He said at last, looking sleepily at Gamadge: "Are you digging into the past for Mrs. Gregson?"

"Gently poking into the past."

"Rather late in the day for that. What did you mean by saying that your investigation had something to do with Minnie Stoner? It's the first I ever heard of anybody dragging her into it. She was out of it from the first, absolutely out of it."

"She lived with the Gregsons then, and she lives with Mrs. Gregson now."

"I wish she didn't. Celia and I are always trying to get them both to come out of that hole of a place up there and live some kind of life. Paul Belden could get a place for Mrs. Gregson."

"Paul Belden?"

"He's the fellow Cecilia Warren is going to marry, if they can ever afford to get married."

"If Mrs. Gregson dies, perhaps?"

Locke slowly raised himself to a sitting position. He asked: "What does that mean?"

"From what Mrs. Gergson tells me, it means something. She has told me a very curious story, which begins with grease on the cellar stairs."

"Grease?" Locke, gazing fixedly at him, frowned. "Grease?"

"And then poison in a mackerel."

Locke's ice-blue eyes remained steadily on Gamadge's

greenish-grey ones. He said: "Oh." And after a moment: "Those accidents last summer. I don't know what you mean by 'poison'—the mackerel was bad."

"Very bad. Now she says that her gas oven was turned on one night, since she came to New York; and last week somebody sent her a fruit cake that had been seasoned with arsenic."

"What the devil are you talking about?"

"About the four attempts to murder her that Mrs. Gregson seems to think have been made since last August."

"I never heard such nonsense. Those things in August were just happenings, and the gas oven, whatever you mean by it, sounds like a happening too."

"The cake was analysed; it contained at least six grains of arsenic."

There was a long pause. Locke sat forward on the couch, his hands hanging between his knees and a cigarette burning unregarded in the fingers of his left one. At last he said: "It's crazy."

"You can see that Mrs. Stoner has had the best opportunity to engineer such attempts."

"That poor old soul." Suddenly the young man rose to his feet, towering above Gamadge like a colossus. He asked loudly: "Has Vina Gregson hired you to try to scrape up evidence against the three of us?"

"I didn't scrape arsenic out of that cake; it was done in a laboratory, by a toxicologist. For goodness' sake sit down," said Gamadge irritably. "What would you have done if these things had happened to you? Laughed them off?"

Locke hesitated. "I feel like throwing you out of here," he growled. "Minnie Stoner!"

"Do use your head," begged Gamadge. "I'm not police; I'm not trying to do worse than prevent a crime. You three are the only people who were on hand at Pine Lots last August; I want you to think back to those two days—the 15th and the 16th."

Locke sat down again on the studio couch. He said: "I don't remember much about them."

"Do you remember when you left New York that afternoon—Friday, the 15th?"

"We started soon after lunch, about two."

"We?"

"I took a friend along with me for the ride. We stopped at a tavern near White Plains, and had drinks. I don't use alcohol myself—I had a lime squash, and my friend had a gin and lime fizz. Does that interest you?"

"Everything interests me, even the name of your friend."

"Her name's Prady. We've done a little dancing at resorts, but she isn't much good yet. We sat under the trees a while, and then we went on up to Burford. The mileage from New York to Burford is about thirty-five miles along the route, no detours. We got to Burford too late for my friend to catch the train she meant to take back to town, I think it was the six-forty."

"Your memory is excellent."

"For trifles, it is. She had the deuce of a long wait, until nearly eight o'clock, I think; I had to leave her at the station. I drove to Pine Lots—got there about seven."

"You must have taken plenty of time out at White Plains."

"We did. We let the time go by—you know how it is. A hot day, and there didn't seem to be any rush. I don't use the trains back and forth, so I don't know 'em; she ought to have kept me reminded."

"Three hours for refreshments; well, as you say, the time goes by. Could I check up on this with Miss Prady?"

"If you care to waste your time on it. She lives here."

"In this house?"

"In this house. She used to work in Bellfield, but she quit when I got her a small dancing job."

"You say you reached Pine Lots about seven?"

"And found Aunt Vina nursing her bruises. She looked pretty green, and Minnie was all of a twitter over the accident. I took a look at the cellar stairs, but by that time Minnie had of course wiped up the grease—if there ever was any grease. I thought Aunt V. had probably caught her foot, or stumbled, or something. People don't like to admit that they stumble for nothing, so I thought she had imagined the grease for reasons of pride."

"You are a sceptical turn of mind, Mr. Locke."

"Oh, I am."

"And you mended the balustrade for them?"

"You ought to be telling me the story; I'd forgotten that.

I mended it—by sticking the splinter down with adhesive tape."

"Do you think that anyone could enter that house up there, and put grease on the top cellar stair, without being seen or heard by Mrs. Stoner or Mrs. Gregson?"

Locke considered. "They could, if Minnie and Mrs. G. had been in the kitchen or upstairs."

"How about a secret approach in a car?"

"You can approach as far as a belt of trees—it screens the road from the house. You can scoot across the side yard, I suppose; the upper windows are curtained, and they belong to the guest-room."

"Would *you* take such a chance?"

Locke's mouth widened in a smile. "In an emergency I should."

"Then, as I understand it, Miss Warren came along—in a station taxi."

"Yes; she hasn't the use of the old lady's car for personal trips. It's a big affair with a chauffeur attached. Poor old Cecilia is still in the parasite class, you know."

"I know. Next morning came the mackerel episode; I suppose you can't help me by remembering who was left alone with Mrs. Gregson's individual mackerel before she came downstairs?"

Locke scowled at him. "Minnie had it in the kitchen, keeping it warm, I suppose. We were all back and forth, in and out of the kitchen; self-service, you know. Nobody can pin it on Minnie, if there's anything to pin."

"You don't admit the seriousness of the situation, Mr. Locke?"

"It's damn serious, but it's also grotesque."

"Did you wonder at all what could have caused Mrs. Gregson's illness? Did you immediately attribute it to fish poisoning?"

"I attributed it to the fact that Minnie's as blind as a bat, and I thought that she'd got bug powder or cleaning fluid or something into the cooking."

"Into Mrs. Gregson's portion only."

"That didn't worry me at the time. Minnie Stoner wasn't born to be a cook, you know—she was born to rock gently back and forth and crochet tidies. She's too old for the job now, anyway."

"To sum up: these occurrences were accidents to you, and have remained accidents in your mind ever since?"

"Certainly."

"Now we come down to New York, to Mrs. Gregson's flat."

"These hide-holes of hers are unspeakably dreary."

"Perhaps because they're hide-holes."

"I suppose you're right. Extraordinary thing, human justice. The law sends a man or woman out into the world without a blemish on his or her reputation, and the miserable creature is ruined for life."

"Not always; don't lose hope."

"Me? The question doesn't bother me much. Well, we're back in New York, thank goodness."

"With Mrs. Stoner sleeping at a boarding-house, and spending the rest of her time with Mrs. Gregson or at the moving pictures. Mrs. Gregson says that she saw you all the very day she arrived."

"She saw me the day she arrived. As I explained, I owe her civility."

"She saw Miss Warren and Mr. Paul Belden; and then she had what sounds like a nearly fatal accident with her gas stove."

"Did she or Minnie Stoner leave a tap on and almost suffocate her?"

"The pilot light would have caught before she died of suffocation."

"Oh."

"And the tap—the oven tap—has to be pushed before it can be turned."

"I see. Was Minnie Stoner in the flat all this time?"

"She had gone for the evening."

Locke said thoughtfully: "That's a trifle grim, I must say."

"It all comes down to the problem of who had an extra key to the flat—besides Mrs. Stoner, of course. If there had been an extra key cut——"

Locke said drily: "Don't labour the point. Somebody could get in if they had an extra key, and turn on the gas. Minnie Stoner didn't need an extra key."

"But Mrs. Stoner called Mrs. Gregson's attention to the fact that an anonymous present of fruit cake had been doctored."

Locke sat fingering his cigarette. Presently he said: "The

cake's the pay-off, and it lets Minnie out; why do you consider her at all, then?"

"Mrs. Gregson also got an anonymous letter—the third, so she tells me, of a series. Would you like to see it?"

Locke silently took the letter from Gamadge, and silently handed it back; his face had become profoundly thoughtful.

"This letter," continued Gamadge, "is a threat; or that is what it seems to be on the face of it. What if all those other happenings could also be interpreted as threats? Might we ask ourselves whether they could be attempts to frighten Mrs. Gregson into suspecting one of her immediate circle?"

Locke met Gamadge's eyes. He said: "Which one?"

"The one most open to suspicion, naturally. At any rate, the letter and the following occurrences are not to be ignored or taken humorously; you'll agree with me on that. In the light of what you have learned this evening, are you willing to confide to me any incident, no matter how trifling, which seems significant to you? Don't worry too much about incriminating anyone; I won't make irresponsible use of the information, and unless I'm forced to use it, I'll keep it to myself."

"I could make a story up, you know." Locke smiled.

"You could; but sometimes there's no better evidence than false testimony."

"I don't agree with you there; and you'll have to give me time to concoct something, true or false."

"There is no time."

Locke, startled, glanced quickly at him. He asked: "Are you trying to make my flesh creep? You sound very sure of yourself."

"Glad to give the impression."

"Tell you what; I'll go over to the flat to-morrow and confer with Aunt V. and Minnie Stoner."

"You can't."

"Why not?" His face was again lowering.

"Mrs. Stoner is driving up to Pine Lots, and Mrs. Gregson is about to disappear. To-night, if she has any sense at all, she will be incommunicado."

Locke, regarding Gamadge with a strange smile, said that caution did seem to be indicated.

"I've recommended another precaution; Mrs. Gregson is thinking of changing her will."

"Change her——" Locke drew his feet under him.

"Leave her money to cats, or some other deserving charity; temporarily, she hopes."

Locke sprang up. This time his face was so convulsed with fury, and his attitude so threatening, that Gamadge rose too; but a possible crisis was averted by a knock at the door. Locke paid no attention to the timid rap; he was still glaring at Gamadge when it was repeated. He said, without turning his head: "Come in, come in; what are you waiting for?"

A tall, thin girl entered, and hesitated meekly on the threshold. She had a plain face, ardent dark eyes, and a mass of curly brown hair. She wore a pull-over sweater of once violent but now faded pink, and pink cotton shorts; the laundress had creased these sharply at the sides, so that they stood out like an inverted Japanese fan. Her long, bare legs ended in socks and tennis shoes.

She said in a tinny voice: "I'm sorry."

"All right, Mr. Gamadge is going." He added, with a grin: "I think he has some questions to ask you though."

She turned large, timid eyes on Gamadge. "Ask me?"

"You are Miss Arline Prady?" Gamadge spoke gently, but she did not do more than glance at him; her eyes, eager and worshipful, were again on Locke. She said: "Yes. Are we going over those steps, Benny?"

"When Mr. Gamadge gets through with us." Locke went with long, noiseless strides to the radiogram, and turned a switch; the room was instantly filled with an odd, halting tune.

Gamadge said, laughing, "I won't interrupt the lesson."

She looked wonderingly at him. "Did you want to ask me something?"

"No; as Mr. Locke said, it would be a waste of time."

He went without more ado out of the room, and down the crimson stairs.

VII

Hobby of Mrs. Smiles

When Gamadge reached home he found his wife and Mr. Robert Schenck playing chess. Clara was gazing at the board and biting a finger; Mr. Schenck's rather foxy face had a thin smile on it as he watched her.

"Go ahead and take it," he said.

"You have to give me fifteen minutes; I'm entitled to fifteen minutes," mumbled Clara. Mr. Schenck was not the kind of person she had been brought up with, but she did not seem to be aware of the fact; she liked him very much.

"Whatever man he's offering you," said Gamadge from the doorway, "take any piece on the board but that one."

Schenck rose. "You better look out," he said, "leaving Mrs. Gamadge home for young fellers like Harold and me to entertain."

"Harold's working on the dressing-bag," said Clara.

"You seem very cosy here." Gamadge went over to a coffee-table, on which had been set out whisky, glasses, a siphon, and a container of ice. He poured himself a drink. "Schenck, has Clara asked you to look up a Mr. Paul Belden for us? I don't know what firm of architects he's with."

"Jones, Hammond, and Green. Do I go this blind, or do I get to know why you're interested in him?"

"He's engaged to a young woman I'm interested in—a Miss Cecilia Warren, secretary-companion to a Mrs. Smiles."

"Smiles?"

"She lives up on the corner of Park; here's the address."

Schenck went into the hall and consulted the telephone book. He emitted a low whistle. "Mrs. Joseph Smiles," he said, coming back into the room. "Joe Smiles—remember who he was before he died and probably didn't go to Heaven?"

"Smiling Joe Smiles—of course I do."

"Senator Smiles, and his widow must be richer than mud. If she could stand being married to that old robber she must be fairly tough."

"Oh, I hope not; I'm going to try to pay her a call this evening—it's only a little after nine."

"Rushing things, ain't you?" Schenck looked at him curiously.

"I have no time at all." Gamadge swallowed the last of his whisky.

"Well, to-morrow I'll try to find somebody that knows one of Belden's partners; that's the best I can do."

"I want to know what Belden's like."

"You'll get me kicked out of my job yet. I'll have to think up some story."

"Wouldn't impose on you, but the matter's urgent."

"Really urgent?"

"Er—probably life and death."

Schenck whistled again. Gamadge went on: "While I'm calling on Mrs. Smiles, Clara will give you an outline of the case. Did Harold transcribe my notes, Clara?"

"Yes, he did." Clara, poring over the board, had not heard the conversation. She now exclaimed: "I see it!"

"Then take back that knight's move," said Schenck, "and we'll go on from there."

Gamadge went into the hall, looked into the open telephone book, and dialled. The chess players frankly listened.

"This Mrs. Smiles' apartment? Henry Gamadge speaking. I should like to speak to Miss Cecilia Warren; tell her, if you please, that I'm acting for Mrs. James Greer."

He blinked at his wife and Schenck, and said: "Manservant. English." Presently he spoke into the mouthpiece again:

"Oh, Mrs. Smiles? I'm very sorry indeed to disturb you, but I—of course. Naturally you wish to protect Miss Warren from annoyance; I dare say she's had a great deal. . . . No, I'm not a newspaper man. I really am doing some business for Mrs. Greer; you could call her up. . . . Oh, thanks very much. I'll be with you in half an hour."

He came away from the telephone smoothing the back of his head and screwing up his eyes. "Nice old thing she seems to be, but officious. Wants to have a finger in whatever's going on. Sounds as if she were fat. She evidently knows who Mrs. Greer is, all right. I have a feeling that if I'm to get the best results I'd better change into evening clothes. Hope they'll give me confidence. Well, I'm off. You may never see me again—I have a notion that if I upset Miss Warren, Mrs. Smiles may kill me."

"Are you going to upset her?" asked Clara.

"I upset Mr. Benton Locke. He finished by springing to his feet, clenching his fists, and making the kind of face you see on a totem pole. That's more or less the kind of face he has anyway. He's a trifle primitive."

"Excuse me." Schenck raised a hand, and Gamadge paused in the doorway. "Who *is* Mrs. Greer, if I may ask?"

"Mrs. Greer is Mrs. Curtis Gregson." Gamadge fled before Schenck's clamour, and hurried to his room. There he changed into dinner clothes, and took from its box a new bowler hat of rakish and knowing cut which Harold had pronounced too young for him. He put it on, looked with satisfaction in the mirror, and went downstairs. As he quietly passed the library door, he was amused to see that Schenck sat absorbed while Clara recounted to him the story of Mrs. Gregson.

Gamadge's walk was somewhat ungainly, but it got him from one place to another with considerable speed. He covered the few blocks to Mrs. Smiles' apartment in a few minutes; and then, standing with his hands in his overcoat pockets and his bowler tilted to the back of his head, surveyed the front of an ornate and elderly building—elderly, at least, for New York. Columned portals framed the entrance on the side street, and a stone balcony, jutting out above it, lent a massive dignity to the façade.

He found, when he went into the high and gloomy hall, that tenants coped with their own visitors; there was no switchboard. No doubt tenants owned their flats. An elevator, run in a leisurely fashion by an ancient operator, took him to the fifth floor.

The manservant who had answered Mrs. Smiles' telephone ushered him into a lobby, took his coat and hat from him, and announced him at the door of a huge, two-storied living-room. But huge as it was, Mrs. Smiles was not lost in it; no space could have absorbed her. She was a vast, short woman, with little eyes in an immense face, and a small, humorous mouth. She sat in a Jacobean arm-chair, her antiquated black silks and laces flowing about her, and held out a short, bare, shapeless arm on which a gold bracelet two inches wide looked like a handcuff.

Gamadge hastened across twenty feet of rug to shake hands.

"Sit down, Mr. Gamadge. Cecilia will be with us in a minute—she is dressing to go out." Mrs. Smiles had a wheezing treble voice, which sounded emotional.

She loves all creation, thought Gamadge. He sat down in another Jacobean chair, and found a tray at his elbow laden with repoussé silver and cut glass.

"Old-fashioned, sir, or highball?" asked the manservant. Gamadge agreed to a highball, and it was mixed for him; after which the butler or major-domo glided from the room.

"I wouldn't have you think," said Mrs. Smiles, "that I wish to intrude upon my dear Cecilia's private affairs; but I try to stand between her and the world. You know her history?"

"I only know what the public knows, Mrs. Smiles."

Mrs. Smiles' great face sagged into lines of pity. "Such a beautiful girl, and so unfortunate. Do you know how I met her, Mr. Gamadge? Did Mrs. Gregson tell you about it?"

"Not a word."

"I read about her in the papers during the trial, and I saw her pictures. They said she was an orphan, with no money, and no relative but Mrs. Gregson. I wondered what would happen to her if the trial went wrong. Some friends of my husband's have a little influence, and they got me into the courthouse on the days when she gave her evidence and was cross-examined."

"They must have had plenty of influence, Mrs. Smiles."

"My husband was very good to his friends, and some of them think for some reason that they ought to be grateful to *me*. You have no idea what that trial was like, Mr. Gamadge, or what the town was like. I can't describe it."

"I've read descriptions."

"Nothing could do it justice; it was frightful. I thought I should be crushed to death, but I didn't care. I was not actuated by curiosity, Mr. Gamadge; my great interest is humanity."

"Could there be a more commendable one?"

"When I am privileged to give in charity, I go personally to look into the cases. I go to prisons and hospitals. It was in the same spirit that I went to that trial. That lovely girl, Mr. Gamadge, and what character she has! That lawyer—Mrs. Gregson's lawyer; I suppose he thought he was doing his duty by his client, but his methods were outrageous. He didn't frighten Cecilia; she sat there like a statue.

"I got in touch with the prosecuting attorney, who had been a young friend of my husband's. He managed an introduction for me, and Cecilia and I took to each other on the instant. It's all a pattern, Mr. Gamadge; Cecilia and I were part of the design, and we were woven together from that moment."

Gamadge's face assumed the polite but slightly dazed expression that it always took on when symbolism became too much for him.

"Cecilia says she won't marry until people have forgotten," continued Mrs. Smiles. "But will they ever forget? And meanwhile Paul Belden is waiting for her. I really don't know how I shall get on without her when she does marry, but if I could make it possible I should do so to-morrow. Smoke, please."

The highball, his second within the hour, was beginning to permeate Gamadge's system with a warm glow. It had been even stronger than the first. The room was hot, and Mrs. Smiles' monotonous treble had a somnolent effect on him. She began not to seem quite real; a gigantic good fairy, capable at any moment of disappearing into a cloud. He lighted a cigarette. "Kind of you," he said. He meant her request that he should smoke, but she understood him otherwise.

"Not at all. Mr. Belden has had reverses, and is not at all well off, but he is charming, and Cecilia has loved him almost from their childhood. Unfortunately, I can do very little for anyone. My husband left money, Mr. Gamadge, as you may know; but I only have my portion of his estate during my lifetime. I save as much as I can," she told him with some pathos, "but there are many calls upon me. When I die the principal will go to the Senator's children by his first wife, and to the college he founded."

Gamadge mistily thought of Smiles College, the strings attached to its endowment, and the dreadful efforts of faculty and trustees to sever them. He murmured something.

"But while I live," said Mrs. Smiles, "Cecilia will have a home."

Gamadge wondered whether he might not be able to amass considerable information about Mr. Paul Belden there and then; information which Schenck would never learn from Belden's partners. Mrs. Smiles was very loquacious, and her gossip highly personal. But at this moment a young woman came through the room from the lobby, and advanced straight upon them. She passed him, to bend over his hostess. He got to his feet, feeling invisible.

"How is the ache in your shoulder, dear Mrs. Smiles?" she asked.

"Much better." Mrs. Smiles patted her hand. "Here is Mr. Gamadge, Celia, and I only hope his business is as agreeable as he is."

Miss Warren acknowledged Gamadge's bow with a nod.

"I only hope your poor cousin is in no trouble." Mrs. Smiles put her hands on the arms of her chair, and began to rock herself backwards and forwards; no doubt as a preliminary to getting upon her feet. She said: "I'll leave you."

Miss Warren gently restrained her. "Don't think of it." Her voice was low and clear, and Gamadge was sure that it had been carefully cultivated since its owner left Omega, N.Y.

"But his business with you seems to be private."

"We'll go into the writing-room."

"But dear, he's settled here with his drink."

"I've quite finished." Gamadge had been seizing these few moments to study the girl who, according to Benton Locke, had lost her humanity. She was tall and very slim, with densely black hair arranged high on her head, and sharp-cut features in a narrow face. Her eyes seemed to be a very dark grey; her eyebrows, he thought, had once been straight and thick. Now they curved upward, two thin lines. He thought that her natural complexion was pale, but her make-up was vivid. She wore big, multi-coloured ear-rings, and a costume, apple-green and spangled, which looked— except for the spangles and the length of skirt—like a tailored suit.

"Well, go along then." Mrs. Smiles patted the spangled coat sleeve with a proprietary air. "Of course I like it, Celia," she declared, "I knew I should. And that hairdresser knows how to get the right effect. Just like the girl in the shop."

"I'm glad it's a success." Miss Warren laughed down at her employer.

Mrs. Smiles took her in, from the curls of her topknot to the lacquer on her fingernails that matched the paint on her lips. She said: "It's just right. Did the slippers come?"

Miss Warren put out a foot in what looked like a fragment of green-and-gold net.

"The girl's her hobby," thought Gamadge.

Miss Warren led the way for him across the room, and through an archway in the northwest corner of it. As they entered a little oblong space which communicated with the hall by an arched door, she turned and looked him full in the face. "I never heard Vina speak of you," she said.

"Mr. Colby introduced me this afternoon."

The writing-room was pretty yet sombre; with dark-gold Japanese paper on its walls, and three pieces of black-and-gold furniture; a desk and two chairs. Miss Warren lighted a lamp on the desk, and sat down on one of the chairs. She sat very straight. Gamadge, facing her, was glad that he had brought his cigarette along with him; he was sure that Miss Warren would never invite him to smoke, or to make himself in any other way at home.

She looked at him, the bluish light of the desk lamp bringing out her masklike decoration of eye shadow, mascara, and rouge. Gamadge attacked brusquely:

"Your cousin, Mrs. Curtis Gregson, told me this afternoon that in the last few months there have been four attempts on her life."

Miss Warren continued to look silently at him, but Gamadge thought she had ceased to see him; she was engaged in fierce inner consultation. He waited until she spoke.

"Are you a detective?" she asked.

"Me? No."

"Are you connected with the police?"

"Certainly not. I sometimes investigate cases when I'm asked to do so by people I like. Colby asked me to investigate this one."

"Vina has never mentioned these attempts to me."

"But Mrs. Stoner has done so. Did she call you up this afternoon? You knew who I was, I could see that."

"Of course Minnie called me up."

"Did she tell you about the anonymous letters, too?"

"Yes."

"I advised Mrs. Gregson to consult the police, you know. She refused to do so."

"I don't blame her."

"But practically all that *I* can do for her is to ask questions. I have seen Mr. Locke, and to-morrow I shall drive up to Burford and talk to Mrs. Stoner."

She asked quickly: "Are they going back there?"

"Mrs. Stoner didn't call you up and tell you that she's going? Mrs. Gregson is going to disappear for a while—by my advice."

After a moment Miss Warren said: "I suppose that's wise."

"Yes, the matter seems urgent; too urgent for a delicate approach. Can you illuminate the darkness in any way, Miss Warren? As I explained to Mr. Locke, I have a free hand; I shall treat what you say as confidential, unless I am forced to use it to prevent a crime."

"I have no information to give you, and I can assure you that Minnie Stoner has none. We are both completely bewildered by the story."

"You can recall nothing significant, which may have escaped you at the time, about that mackerel with the poison in it?"

"I never thought of poison. It's perfectly horrible and perfectly incredible—all of it." She turned her head away from him.

"Yet there was arsenic in that fruit cake. Tell me, Miss Warren: is there any possibility of Mrs. Stoner's not being in her right mind? She seemed a trifle vague and wild to me."

"Of course she's in her right mind. If she's vague and wild, she has every reason to be." Cecilia Warren turned her head back to stare at him. "Don't put this on her. It's ridiculous. She has no motive."

"In a case like this, the field widens to include friends of the parties directly interested."

Cecilia Warren suddenly looked as though she had run into something in the dark. Gamadge went on: "The same can be said for the Gregson case three years ago; but evidence was not forthcoming to justify other arrests, and murder trials are a great expense to the State."

There was a long pause. Then she said, again looking beyond him: "I always believed that it was suicide."

"Well, I grant you that motive for suicide is often obscure, too obscure to be understood in a court of justice. Motives shade off into one another until they're hardly what the average person recognizes as a motive at all."

"Yes, and men disappear, and nobody ever knows why they ran away."

"They do indeed. Now Mr. Locke favours the accident theory."

"Accident?" Miss Warren looked as if she would have liked to develop the theory herself, if she had ever considered it.

"You must get him to tell you about it; it sounds quite plausible, as plausible as suicide."

She gazed at him in silence.

"What I must do first," said Gamadge, looking about him, and then disposing of his cigarette end in a black glass ashtray, "is to get this business last August as straight as I can. It's not easy to get things straight after three months, but I must do my best. You went up there on a train that arrives at Burford at seven twenty-two?"

Miss Warren seemed to seek information from the gold walls. She said at last: "Oh, yes. I remember that I couldn't take a train before six. Mrs. Smiles had come in from a trip to the country, just for overnight. She was going to Long Island. I had to see her off before I went up to Burford."

"When did she go?"

"About half-past three, I think."

"Nobody saw *you* off?"

"No."

"The servants here knew when you left the apartment?"

"There were no servants here; it was closed for the summer. I got Mrs. Smiles' room ready for her the night before, and we went out to dinner at a restaurant. I got her breakfast for her in the morning."

"Did you come back here after you had put Mrs. Smiles on her train?"

"She never takes trains. I put her into her car, and saw that she had her luggage. Then I took my own bag down to the station."

"Nearly three hours to kill on an August afternoon in New York. How did you manage the process, Miss Warren?"

"I don't remember."

"Surely you must. Did you shop, or call up a friend?"

"I think I called a friend up, but he was out of town."

"Mr. Belden, perhaps?"

She looked at him, coldly. "Yes."

"Really, I should think you would have gone up to the country on an earlier train."

"You're trying to——" there was sudden horror in her glance. "You think I went up there earlier, and put that stuff on the step."

"Say that I'm trying to help you prove you didn't. Why *didn't* you take an earlier train? I'm only asking."

"I had errands. I remember now."

"Mr. Belden: was he away on holiday, or only for that afternoon?"

"Just for the day. His work takes him out of town a great deal."

"Did they tell you where he had gone?"

Miss Warren said with dry composure: "There was nobody in the office but the girl at the telephone, and she didn't know. It was a Friday."

"I thought that Mr. Belden might have gone off for the week-end."

"Perhaps he had. I don't really remember. I thought it was only for the afternoon, but I may have forgotten."

"He didn't tell you at some later time where he had been?"

"I never asked him. I am up at Mrs. Smiles' place in the Adirondacks most of the summer, myself."

"When you reach Burford, Miss Warren, and get out at the station, are the cabs in full view?"

"Nothing's in full view from that side; nothing but trees. The ticket office is across the track, and the cabs park behind it."

"You climb stairs to cross?"

"Yes." Miss Warren's mouth curved down at the corners in an expression of contempt. "And I don't think the conductor is acquainted with me; I don't go up there often. Nobody knows what train I went up on."

"You don't get up there often, nor does Mr. Locke. He says that he goes because Mrs. Gregson has remembered him in her will."

"I hope you won't tell Cousin Vina that."

"I may not need to tell her that. On Saturday morning, when Mrs. Gregson was made so ill by eating mackerel, you were all 'in and out of the kitchen' before she came down; so Locke tells me."

"I don't remember; we usually do go in and out of the kitchen. I don't know how whatever it was got into the mackerel. I know Vina came down last."

"Do you have time off in the afternoons, Miss Warren?"

"I go out whenever Mrs. Smiles can spare me—except on Tuesdays."

"Where do you go on Tuesdays?"

"To a concert; to hear chamber music."

"On Tuesday last, at about five o'clock, you were at this concert?"

"Yes. It's a series."

"Mrs. Smiles doesn't go?"

"No, she doesn't care for that kind of music," said Miss Warren gravely.

"How about your evenings? You are going out tonight; did you go out a week ago Wednesday night, do you remember?"

Miss Warren turned to the desk, and looked at an engagement pad bound in black-and-gold leather. She said: "I seem to have been dancing."

"With Mr. Belden?"

"With Mr. Belden."

"At a private house?"

"No, a night club."

"Thank you very much." Gamadge uncrossed his knees, but she gave no sign of meaning to rise. She asked: "Did Benton Locke answer all these questions as meekly as I have answered them?"

"You've been very patient. I didn't ask him the questions I've asked you. Mr. Locke has no elevator man and no doorman, and there is no way of checking up on his incomings and his outgoings." He rose, and so did she. "You don't look like your cousin Mrs. Gregson," he said.

"I look like—the other side of the family."

"You were born in Omega?"

"I left it when I was quite young, to go to school."

"And never went back?"

"I went back, of course."

"When were you there last, Miss Warren? When your father died?"

She looked at him with that cold contempt. "No; he died suddenly, and I was working hard."

"Might I ask you what he died of?"

"Heart disease."

"One moment more: I have advised Mrs. Gregson to clarify the situation so far as she herself is concerned by making a new will."

There was a whiteness around the bright red of her lips. "A new will?"

"She is reluctant, but I advise it strongly. It's a step that should protect others besides herself, Miss Warren."

Cecilia Warren walked quietly out of the little room, Gamadge in her wake. A caller had arrived in their absence; a tall, big loose-limbed young man with red hair and a broad smile. His dinner coat was so ancient that it had shrunk, through many cleanings, away from his wrists; there was a limpness about his black tie, and his tremendous shoes had a cracked look. He rose from his seat beside Mrs. Smiles and strode across the rug to put his hands on the girl's shoulders. They looked huge there.

"Gorgeous," he said. "And what have you done to your hair?" *His* speech had not undergone cultivation; the *r*'s rolled out richly.

"Mrs. Smiles wanted me to try something new. This is Mr. Gamadge," she said stiffly.

Gamadge and Belden shook hands. Mrs. Smiles inquired tremulously: "Doesn't she look lovely, Paul?"

"But I don't know her. The way these girls get themselves up, Mr. Gamadge!"

"I told you he'd hate it." Cecilia Warren had a look, as she watched her fiancé, that Gamadge had not seen on her face before. "I'll go up and take it all off, Paul; the dress too, if you like."

"This one is fine, but I always like the red one best."

"All right, if Mrs. Smiles doesn't mind." She bent over the squat figure in the big chair. "Do you, Mrs. Smiles?"

"You do just what he says; but you look so smart like this!"

"I'll wear it the next time *we* go out together."

Mrs. Smiles cackled gently. "Don't you like girls to look smart, Mr. Gamadge?"

"The smarter the better. My wife can't look too smart to suit me," said Gamadge, who would have suffered tortures if Clara had lacquered her nails.

"I should have loved to be smart when I was her age."

Miss Warren went off smiling, but she was still walking stiffly. Gamadge said: "I'm just going. Delighted to have met you, Mr. Belden."

"Oh, you mustn't!" implored Mrs. Smiles. "Do wait and visit with us until Celia comes back."

"Nothing I'd like better, but it must only be for a few minutes." Gamadge and Belden sat down, and Belden, officiating at the silver tray, poured a stiff drink. "This how you like it, Mr. Gamadge?" he asked.

Gamadge said that that was how he liked it. Belden poured one for himself. Mrs. Smiles, already accommodated with a stiff one of her own, nodded gaily at them both.

"I hope your business with Cecilia wasn't too difficult and troublesome," she said. "I hope Mrs. Gregson is all right."

"Perhaps she'll be all right now." Gamadge swallowed whisky. Belden remarked that he wished Celia didn't have to have anything to do with the Gregson woman.

"Now, Paul dear! Don't wish to interfere with the pattern," begged Mrs. Smiles. "That's so bad for the spirit."

Belden, winking openly at Gamadge, a demonstration which caused Mrs. Smiles to shake her finger at him, said: "Some patterns would be a good deal the better for a good long bath in a vat of dye."

"Now, Paul! Celia has been taken care of, and Mrs. Gregson has been taken care of too. Didn't you think Celia a lovely creature, Mr. Gamadge—spiritually, I mean?"

"If I'm allowed to be impertinent," said Gamadge, "I should like to say that I think it very strange the Gregsons didn't give her a full education and a chance to develop her faculties. She has had good fortune"—he bowed to Mrs. Smiles—"but she might possibly have completed her life pattern as a typist and stenographer. It's ludicrous."

Belden said: "Too be quite fair, Mrs. G. had no money; and a good many people wouldn't think Gregson had any moral reason to spend his on his wife's cousin. But I agree with you, it was a crime to put her into a business college. She only needed a chance—she could have got anywhere. Look what she's done with herself as it is! You ought to have seen her back in Omega when she was eleven or twelve—skinny, freckled, and a voice like a buzz saw."

They all laughed, but Gamadge did not feel like laughing; this last drink was depressing him. He said: "What did she do about it?"

"Her father sent her to a first-class boarding-school, and kept her there till his money gave out. Thank God she hasn't tried to remodel me, though." He drained his glass.

"Be sure you take her to the Cloud Club," Mrs. Smiles adjured him. "I have an account there, you know."

Belden leaned forward to crush her hand in his great knuckly one. Gamadge said: "I really must go."

The major-domo got his hat and coat for him from a little room under a winding stair; Cecilia Warren came down the stair as he left—handsome in her red dress, and very pale. They exchanged no farewells.

Not long afterwards Gamadge lurched into his library, hands rammed into the pockets of his overcoat and his hat over his eyes. Clara, reclining on the chesterfield, was at work with paper and pencil. She looked to him fresh and young in her long, dark-blue dress and her sandals.

"Mr. Schenck told me just how to start at the library to-morrow," she said.

"Forget about to-morrow. Clara——" Gamadge gritted his teeth.

"Yes, what?"

"How would you like to go out dancing somewhere?"

"To-night?"

"Now."

She leapt from the chesterfield, and flung herself into his arms.

VIII

Rest Cure

When Gamadge rose next morning his natural amiability was in a state of total eclipse. He decided, as he swallowed his coffee, that five hours' sleep were not enough for a man of thirty-five with something on his mind. He showed no interest when Theodore told him that Clara and Harold had gone out, and that Harold had been carrying Gamadge's best bag.

"Tell Mrs. Gamadge I'll be back for dinner." Gamadge hurried to the garage in a neighbouring street, got out his fine new four-seater, and presented himself at the iron gateway in the wall at something less than half-past nine. Mrs. Gregson was waiting for him, a dressing-case and a suitcase on the step beside her. He stowed her luggage away, and settled her in front.

"Mrs. Stoner gone?" he asked, as they drove off.

"Yes, she went early." Mrs. Gregson showed a certain animation this morning, but it was the dubious animation of one who is trying an experiment. "I'm very nervous about this trip, Mr. Gamadge. I haven't been among strangers for so long."

"You won't have to see any of them till you get used to the place."

"It was awfully good of you to arrange it all for me. I didn't half thank you, yesterday."

"I was glad to get Tully and Lukes a customer so late in the season."

The first half of the forty-five mile drive made Gamadge thankful for the first time that Clara had wanted a radio in the new car. Mrs. Gregson evidently liked music, and could tolerate even bad music; she amused herself by fiddling with the knobs until they were in open country, where bright yellow and faded red leaves still hung on the oaks and maples. Then she sat looking out of the window and prattling easily of life in Omega.

"Oh, it was very quiet there," she told Gamadge. "But it's not just a village. It's a nice town, with old families."

"I suppose yours has been there since the early days."

"Yes, a hundred years."

"Have the Warrens been there a hundred years?"

"Oh, no. Mr. Warren settled there after he married my aunt, Nellie Voories. He was from Utica. He was a very brilliant man, but he wasn't steady; he was irresponsible. He fell in love with some girl in his office in Utica, and then Aunt Nellie had a dreadful time. We always thought she died of it; more than twenty years ago, that was."

"After she died, what did Warren do about the girl in his office?"

"I don't know what happened; she left, or something, and Uncle Cecil took to drink. But he didn't do it in Omega; he used to go off."

"Dear me." Gamadge bore to the right, and Mrs. Gregson asked: "Aren't you going up by the route, past Burford?"

"No, I take this back-country road when I come up; it's very pretty."

"He used to go off for days," continued Mrs. Gregson, "and he would come back a perfect wreck. At last he shut himself up in the Omega house, with just a hired man to look out for him. Before that he used to bring the queerest people home, and of course Cecilia couldn't stay there. She didn't even come home from school in the holidays. She stayed at the school, or she came and stayed with us. That was before my mother and father died. They were killed in that awful train wreck—the Limited from Buffalo. Do you remember it?"

"Dimly. How tragic!"

"Yes, it was. I was married and in Bellfield by that time. Uncle Cecil had spent all his money, and so Cecilia came to Bellfield for good. She insisted on going to a business college— she has so much will power, she always does what she makes up her mind to do."

"And Mr. Warren drank himself to death?"

"No, he finally developed heart trouble, and he died of it in the hospital—in Utica."

"Perhaps it would be better for Miss Warren if she had taken after the Voories side of the family?"

"Oh, have you seen her?"

"Last night."

"I think all that about her father affected her. She was a solitary kind of child, and after she'd been to school a while—at Coverly, you know——"

"Coverly!"

"Yes, it cost a fortune. She did very well there, and she was prominent in the dramatic club, and we thought it rather spoiled her for Omega. And for Bellfield," added Mrs. Gregson, with a rueful look. "She had her own friends out of town and she used to go and stay with them overnight. She had her own life. Mr. Gregson didn't like Celia, and he didn't like Paul Belden; but I did. Do you know, it's the queerest thing, Mr. Gamadge, but girls and women have always fallen in love with Paul Belden. Little girls fell in love with him when he was only twelve or thirteen years old. And he was the homeliest boy, and such a bad boy, too!"

"Did he improve as he grew up?"

"No, he was very dissipated, and he didn't have a good reputation in Omega at all—or in Amsterdam, either. He came of very nice people, too. We used to ask Celia how she could stand being one of the flock—Paul Belden's flock, you know. She never seemed to care. He fascinated her, and I never could understand it; but I couldn't help liking him, he's so funny."

"He exudes vitality and confidence."

"Oh, did you meet him, too?"

"Yes. Is he hard up?"

"I don't really know."

"Why don't they marry, if he's not?"

"Celia thinks——" Mrs. Gregson fell silent. Gamadge did not press the question, and they talked about the war in Europe until they had swooped downhill to Cold Brook village. Gamadge followed the next road to climb out of it again; this meandered through thinly settled countryside for two miles and more, and at last reached a low white house. There was a circular driveway in front of it, but Gamadge turned the car into a lane. It ran past the house and the garage, past outbuildings, and into the country beyond.

He stopped just before they reached the garage, which

was on the left of the road. Mrs. Gregson stood beside the car while he got out her luggage, looking with interest at what could be seen of Five Acre Farm above a low garden wall.

"Mrs. Tully thought you might like to come in by the garden entrance," he said. "She knows you don't want to meet people yet. You won't see them now—they're having their elevenses."

"Their what?"

"They sustain themselves in the middle of the morning with milk and what not. You can have yours in your room, if you want it."

"I feel quite hungry."

"Good for you; you'll eat like a trooper here." They went through a green door in the wall and entered a large enclosure, with a faded garden merging into an orchard, which in turn merged into a forest of evergreens and oaks.

"How pretty," said Mrs. Gregson.

"It is, in summer."

They went along a bricked walk, and mounted two steps of a bricked terrace. Doors ran the length of it along the back of the house.

"Some patients," explained Gamadge "seem to want fresh air and not much else. These rooms are for them and at this time of the year they're mostly unoccupied."

"Nobody's shut up here?" Mrs. Gregson seemed agreeably impressed by Five Acres.

"Oh, no; if people want to go they walk out—all except the ones that are really ill or disabled, and have nurses."

"I've never seen a sanatorium. I was rather dreading it."

"I wish I'd explained before what this one's like."

"You did; I just didn't quite understand."

She looked quite happy as they went into a pleasant hallway and up a flight of stairs. A fat woman in a white uniform waited for them, her sharp blue eyes twinkling at them merrily. She had waved yellow hair and pink cheeks, but there was nothing doll-like about her.

"Right on the dot, guy," she said, after smiling brilliantly at Mrs. Gregson.

"Cut out the slang in front of this lady." Gamadge deposited the bags on the floor of the upper hall. "Mrs. Greer, this is Mrs. Tully; you may not believe me, but you'll like her."

Mrs. Tully shook hands. "Come right along to your room and get settled," she said. "Lucy Lukes is busy with the egg-nogs."

"Don't you call them thai, it's blasphemy." Gamadge reassumed his burdens, and carried them into a room at the end of the corridor, on the north-east corner. "Egg-and-milk shakes, Mrs. Greer, and personally I never touch them; they're bad for my liver."

It may have been as well that Mrs. Gregson, looking with some pleasure about her corner room, did not see the vulgar dig in the ribs which Mrs. Tully administered to Gamadge with a strong elbow. Gamadge put the suitcase on the luggage rack and the small bag on a table, and also glanced about him admiringly.

"You and Lucy never gave me anything like this," he said.

"It's the next to the best one we have; Mr. Pole always takes the other corner one. Now, Mis' Greer," said Mrs. Tully, "I want you to feel that you can be as independent and private here as if you were in a hotel. You'll get plain food, though, and there are no movies this side of Cold Brook, and we only have two house cars. Here's your bathroom."

Mrs. Gregson looked into the bathroom, said it was lovely, and crossed to the east window. "What a nice view!" she exclaimed. "I love this kind of rolling country. And the north window looks over the garden."

"Yes. The roofs of the outside terrace rooms are under you."

Mrs. Gregson looked down at the roofs, a long flat ledge. She said: "I should think they'd be cold."

"You won't be. There's your fireplace, if you should feel like a fire when the wind gets up. When you want anything just holler, you know; we don't have bells, because nervous patients ring them just for the fun of it, and we don't exactly encourage them to get us out of bed in the middle of the night; but Miss Lukes and I are right around the corner. Do you want your meals up here for a while?"

"Yes, I'd like to have them here."

"You might take your stroll in the garden and up the lane after an early lunch; all the other guests are resting then. When you want to rest, just hang out your sign—there it is." Mrs. Tully pointed to a neat cardboard sign which said: "Do

Not Disturb." She explained: "Hang it on your doorknob, and nobody'll walk through it, not even Lucy Lukes or me." She added sharply, as Mrs. Gregson remained at the north window, looking down: "You're not nervous about that roof, are you?"

"No, not really." Mrs. Gregson turned back into the room.

"You can lock that window, if you are; but you don't need to. There's only one young fellow"—she winked surreptitiously at Gamadge—"nice fellow, name of Thompson, going to be on the terrace, and the house is full of people, and Mr. Pole says he never sleeps a wink, and we're right around the corner."

"Of course."

"There's your own private telephone, direct wire, you can't be overheard in the booth. If you want a radio you can have one, only for gracious sakes play it low; there's one old lady here can't make out what you're saying if you tell her it's a nice day, but she can hear a radio through six walls and a passage. If you get lonesome, Lucy or I will take your walk with you."

"I shan't be lonely." Mrs. Gregson faintly smiled.

"You don't want to see the doctor? He's here now, comes every day."

"No, thanks; there's nothing the matter with me."

"You certainly look fine."

But when Gamadge had shaken hands with Mrs. Gregson and bade her farewell, promising to keep in touch with her by telephone; and when he and Mrs. Tully were in the passage, with the room door closed behind them, Tully faced him, frowning.

"What's the matter with her?"

"Just needs a rest cure."

"She hasn't a nerve in her body. That woman's seen trouble."

"You bet she has."

A dark, stocky girl, also in white, came up the stairs. Gamadge respected her highly. He shook hands.

"Go help the new patient unpack, Lucy," said the other partner. "I don't know what you'll think of her, but I'd say she was a good strong woman worn down. She don't know how to laugh. I don't like not knowing who she is, Gamadge."

"She's been in the papers, and she's hiding from publicity. I told you all that."

"Under that style she's nothing but folks. What got her in this state?"

"She was a member of one of the best families in a small town, and she got in the papers; doesn't that tell you anything?"

"She needn't be afraid anybody'll recognize her here," said Miss Lukes, who was not talkative. "I don't think any of them ever looks at a newspaper, even when they're at home—any of them but Mrs. Billings, and she's one of these saints. She wouldn't gossip about the devil himself."

"I don't like this Mrs. Greer, as you call her, being alone all the time," said Mrs. Tully. "She looks to me as if she's been frightened."

"She's here for privacy. Don't you rent her a car and let her go driving herself around the country, though; make her let Harold or one of the men on the place drive her. Say it's a rule."

"What is this?" Mrs. Tully was indignant. "We don't take mental cases, even if the doctors are always trying to slip 'em over on us."

"If Mr. Gamadge sends her, that's enough," said Miss Lukes. "I'm glad Harold's coming; he always fixes the lights and the kitchen taps first thing."

"If he does, that proves he likes you. He knows who Mrs. Greer is," said Gamadge, "and he'll look out for her."

"It sounds like monkey business to me." Mrs. Tully scowled. "I won't have anything going on here that's likely to upset the patients."

"Mrs. Greer won't upset them. She doesn't know who Harold is, or why he's here, and I don't want her to. It would make her nervous, and I want her to feel safe." But he had a guilty look, which Mrs. Tully instantly recognized for what it was. She said: "None of your detective stuff here, Gamadge. This isn't Bellevue."

Lucy Lukes shook her partner's arm. "You let Mr. Gamadge fix this his own way," she insisted. "And just remember what that room rents for. If you feel like turning down ninety a week in late November, I don't."

"Neither do I, but——"

"And Harold's paying thirty-five for one of the cubbyholes. Are you crazy?"

Gamadge was biting his forefinger. He said: "I had to put her somewhere. I know it's a good deal to ask—taking somebody in under a false name."

"You leave her here and forget it," said Miss Lukes. "We wouldn't be here ourselves if you hadn't put up capital."

Gamadge patted her shoulder, and went downstairs. He passed through a large sunroom or lounge, observed by two old ladies and an old gentleman, and went out on the front porch. He sat down on the steps in the sun, smoked, and waited.

Harold drove up in a station cab at a quarter past twelve. He ignored Gamadge, carried his bag and suitcase across the porch, rang the bell, was admitted, and disappeared. In a few minutes he came out and sauntered over to sit beside his employer.

"Mrs. Gregson is above you in the north-east corner," said Gamadge, speaking low.

"So Lukes told me. They gave me the room just under her. I'll freeze to death; did you know those cells have no windows? Only the Dutch door."

"That's enough, I should think."

"I should, too. Do you know what the nights up here are going to be like?"

"Sleep in the daytime. Nobody could get in here then without a permit; but I want her looked after at night, when windows go up."

Harold's voice suddenly changed as a man strode up the drive. He said: "Seems a nice place. Did you just get here, Mr.—er—?"

The newcomer, a distracted-looking individual in a cap and a leather coat, paused in front of them. He said: "Nice? It's a tomb. Twilight comes down on these forsaken hills like a pall."

Gamadge looked mildly up at him.

"One escapes from those wrecks and ruins of humanity in the lounge," continued the man, "one goes up to bed and lies there and listens to the crickets and the tree frogs. One begins to think of one's sins, and to wonder if there may not be a hereafter in spite of all."

"Keep up your courage," said Gamadge.

"I came up here to write. My doctor said I should be

able to write here. I can't write, I can't sleep until dawn, and then come the roosters."

"I rather like the roosters."

"They drive me to frenzy."

"You can't be well."

"Perfectly well, if I could have quiet. How long are *you* up for?"

"I'm not staying. How long are you up for, sir?" inquired Gamadge politely of Harold.

"Not long," said Harold. "You can bet on that."

"Can you sleep?" asked the distraught man.

"No; I roam around."

"They don't let you."

"They do me; I have a deck stateroom."

"Pay me a call after hours, via my south window; we might have a game of something."

"See what I can do. Where are you?"

"South-east corner." He went in, and Harold observed glumly: "He ought to spell me."

"I don't trust these insomniacs," objected Gamadge. "They sleep a lot more than they think they do."

An old lady came out of the house, pretended to admire the view, and after a moment shyly addressed Gamadge. He rose.

"So you really are Mr. Gamadge; I knew you the moment I saw you through the window." She was delighted.

"How nice to see you again. You're Mrs. Billings." Gamadge shook hands.

"You play such a nice game of bridge, and you were so nice to play with." Mrs. Billings glanced politely at Harold. "I wonder if that gentleman plays."

Gamadge said: "I'll find out." He turned to Harold and asked: "May we know your name, sir? Mine is Gamadge. My friend, Mrs. Billings, and I would like to know if you play bridge."

Harold got up off the step. "My name's Thompson, and I'm sorry to say that I don't play bridge at all."

This was not true, and the falsehood bid fair to do Harold no good; for Mrs. Billings said eagerly: "We might teach you."

"I'm not sure if I'm going to stay."

"Oh, dear. I did hope for a permanent fourth. The maid

tells me that a new patient has come, a Mrs. Greer, but that she's taking a complete rest cure. I did so hope that we could get up a nice table in the evenings; they are so long, and Mr. Pole often doesn't wish to play. Would you—would you like to join us for a rubber just until lunch, Mr. Gamadge?" Mrs. Billings' old face gazed up at him wistfully. Gamadge said: "Of course. I'll be delighted to."

"I'm afraid we only play for a fortieth."

"Quite enough."

Mrs. Billings, glowing with pleasure, went into the house. Gamadge followed her; Harold, grinning, pursued him with an admonition not to forget Blackwood, and went round to the back, where a chauffeur-handyman rushed out of the garage to ask him something about a new camera. They retired to the chauffeur-handyman's rooms over the garage.

Gamadge played bridge until after one, when the luncheon gong released him. His partner had been Mrs. Billings, and his opponents old Mr. Bitterfield and the distraught Mr. Pole. Mr. Bitterfield still played a sound game of auction in the Work tradition; Mr. Pole's tendency was to respond with Blackwood to his partner's first bid; and Mrs. Billings, a gentle and timid player, never raised her partner at all. She explained the omission whenever it occurred by saying: "If I do, you'll jump away up."

They were still struggling with the first rubber when the gong sounded. Gamadge's suggestion that the winners of the first game should be paid, with the usual bonus, satisfied everybody. Mr. Bitterfield and Mr. Pole had held all the cards, and were the victors; Mrs. Billings only wanted to play, and did not care who won.

They all went into the dining-room and sat down to eat a well-cooked and delicious plain meal; Gamadge delightedly watching Harold, at a corner table, reluctantly absorbing the kind of food he took least interest in. After lunch Gamadge smoked a cigarette, conversed with Mr. Bitterfield on the subject of blood pressure, and at last wandered up to the second floor. On seeing a lunch tray, well cleared, outside Mrs. Gregson's room, and the "Do Not Disturb" sign on her door, he wandered down again and out to Harold's quarters on the terrace. He was dropping with sleep.

Harold was exchanging his coat for a sweater, and suggested that Gamadge take a nap. Gamadge looked longingly at the pile of extra blankets on the cot. "Hanged if I don't," he said. "I can get to Burford in half an hour from here."

"Going to that place—Pine Lots?"

"Yes; I'll stop there. It's on my way home."

"I still don't see why all the fuss over Mrs. Gregson. Nobody but Mr. Colby knows she's here."

Gamadge did not reply, but proceeded silently to take off his coat and shoes.

"I'm going back to the garage," said Harold. "That feller wants some help developing his pictures."

"Ask him if he'll condescend to take time out and fill up my car, will you?"

Harold nodded and left. Gamadge rolled himself up in blankets, and lay down. He fell asleep almost as his head touched the pillow, sinking consciously and deliciously into kind darkness.

He woke slowly, and lay for a minute looking out through the upper half of the Dutch door at a mellow sky and a far-off line of hills. Autumn scents came to him on a chill breeze. He consulted his watch, and was gratified to find that he had had nearly two hours of oblivion; it was well past four.

He assumed shoes and coat, feeling some amusement, as he combed his hair at Harold's mirror, to think that this was the first time he had ever used the tortoise-shell comb in his wedding outfit. Strolling afterwards along the back of the house on his way to the side lane, he was still further amused to hear loud snores proceeding from the window of Mr. Pole.

He found his car turned and waiting, climbed in, and drove away; catching as he did so a glimpse of Harold, looking very dirty, at the upper window of the garage. Harold grinned and waved. Gamadge left Five Acre Farm, and drove towards Cold Brook down the steepish, winding road.

IX

The Stump Lot

Gamadge, on the lookout for the branch to Pine Lots, slowed as he approached a likely-looking road on his right. A bus passed him labelled *Danbury*, and he heard the faint whistle of a train; the railway must be over the hill to the west.

A two-seater came down the by-road, going fast; Gamadge, waiting for it to make the turn, had a clear view of the driver's profile; but he would hardly have recognized Mr. Paul Belden if that gentleman had not cast a momentary look at him as he flashed by. Perhaps he also recognized Gamadge, but he gave no sign of doing so—his hard, set, almost ferocious expression did not alter. It was so nearly a grimace that in the uncertain daylight it made Belden look more like a gargoyle than a man.

Gamadge watched the car streak southwards; then he entered the by-road, and drove along between stubble fields in which a few pumpkins still glowed among the stacks of corn. Stony pastures followed, and to the north a deep belt of pines. The land rose steeply in front of him and to the south. He passed a small, shabby farm on his left, set back among maples at some distance from the road.

The farmer came round his house, a bucket in each hand, and glanced over his shoulder at the woods rising steeply to the south-west. A dog was barking somewhere in that region. He set his pails down as Gamadge stopped his car, and came to the road along a dirt path.

"Am I right for Pine Lots?" asked Gamadge.

"You be."

"You're Mr. Hotchkiss?"

"That's right."

"Mrs. Stoner get back to-day?"

"Yes, come up this mornin'."

"Mrs. Greer says you take good care of them."

"Try to; they're nice ladies."

The angry barking continued. Hotchkiss said: "That's my pup. Guess he found a woodchuck; hope it ain't a skunk." He whistled piercingly, and a spotted dog with hound's ears came running down the cleared hillside. He ran up, and his master admonished him: "You ferget them animals and come in and eat your supper."

"Well, good evening," said Gamadge."

"Good evenin'."

Gamadge drove on, over a ridge, past a stump lot on the left, past a tongue of pine trees which came down to the road. He stopped at sight of a white house. It had a yard planted with old trees; from where he sat Gamadge could not see the side door. He got out of the car, and skirted the pines until he was in sight of the garage in the rear. He had seen the curtained upper windows and the side entrance, and now he was looking at a latticed kitchen porch. He strolled to the garage; it contained no car, but a well-kept sedan stood in front of it.

A burst of wild barking somewhere above and behind him made him turn; he frowned, as it changed to a long, rising wail. The Hotchkiss dog had come back. Gamadge crossed the yard again, pushed through the belt of pines, and came out on the stump lot. Dusk was beginning to take the colour from its russets and yellows, but the light was still clear enough; as he climbed, choosing footholds on the slippery grass, the spotted dog rushed down to meet him. It leapt up to paw him, its tongue hanging out.

"All right, old boy; what's the matter?"

The dog wagged its tail, dashed away, and stopped to look back at Gamadge. As Gamadge came on it bounded off again, leaping the stumps and the low bushes. Gamadge toiled after it, avoiding loose stones. The dog waited for him beside a fallen log, or what looked like one; but Gamadge, coming up to it, stood rigid. It was not a log, although its coat was the colour of one.

The dog stood motionless beside it, looking at Gamadge, and Gamadge, bending slightly forward, stood agaze. Then he advanced, still staring at the body and at the shattered back of its head. There was some blood on the collar of its brown overcoat. A felt hat lay where it had fallen as Locke went down. What could be seen of his face was like pale-grey marble. His hands were covered by grey driving-gloves.

After a moment Gamadge bent to flex a cold wrist; it was not rigid. He turned, went over to a broad stump, and sat down. The dog came to shiver against his legs.

Gamadge put a hand on its long head. "You're a good boy," he murmured. "Keep quiet, now, and stay here." He sat looking at the body in furious concentration; it was several minutes before he could make up his mind to act. At last he got up, his expression not only grim but desolate. He had never felt so alone in his life; far away was Harold, and out of the question; far away was Schenck, and out of the question too. He couldn't bear to think of Clara.

He got a silk handkerchief out of his overcoat pocket, and went over to Locke's body; he wrapped the handkerchief carefully round Locke's head and neck, and fastened it. Then he picked up the felt hat, folded it, and stuffed it in his pocket. A search to right and left and a little behind the body rewarded him with a gleam of metal; he picked up and pocketed a shell.

After studying the position of the corpse, which lay uphill, he got its arms round his neck, braced himself, struggled upright, and had it on his back. He went down the slope obliquely, and laid his burden down by the roadside, in the shelter of the pines. The dog trotted confidently at his heels, followed him to his car, and got into it at a word. Gamadge turned it, and drove it back to the spot where the body waited.

He got out, and stood for some time looking up and down the road. He could hear nothing; stillness had fallen on the countryside, and the Gregson house had seemed at his last glimpse of it to be still unlighted. He opened the back of the car and got out a rug. The silk handkerchief which he had knotted round Locke's head showed no stain; he got Locke into the back of the car, put the rug over him, and slid under the wheel. Hotchkiss' dog made room for him, whining gently.

At the Hotchkiss farm he stopped; the farmer was not in sight. He opened the car door. "Home, old man," he said, "your part of the job's over." The dog jumped out and trotted up the path.

Gamadge drove to the highway, and turned south towards Burford. Tempting roads branched off into what looked like deep country, but he resisted them, his jaw set. The railway curved in—he could see shining tracks under a light beyond a field, and presently sheds, and the station. Burford village was almost deserted at this hour of twilight, few cars were parked at the kerbs, and he was thankful to see none at the filling-station. He drove on past a lighted drugstore, a dreary little hotel, scattered houses, a church. He was out of Burford, into a zone of darkness and arching trees.

He thought he would never find the sort of by-road he needed, but two and a half miles down, there it was—a lightless track rising to the skyline. Gamadge turned left and drove upward, between banks topped by fences. He stopped in front of a big tree, and with some difficulty turned the car; his actions were slowed by fear of some hitch or accident. Then he got out and opened the back door.

He was just in time—the body was stiffening. He got it out, and behind the tree; laid it face downwards as he had found it, and took the handkerchief from its head. He dropped the hat a couple of feet away. His last glimpse of Locke's dead face had been strangely comforting; it was quite unmarred— the bullet was still in Locke's skull; and the primitive features looked serene.

He heard himself gasp as the sound of an engine came to him from up the road. He jumped into his car, and was at the turn into the highway long before whatever rattling old vehicle it was caught up with him. In fact, the driver of it never saw his car; nor would anyone trace him by tyre marks—a "black" road, as well as a lonely one, was what he had searched so long for.

He went at a moderate speed through Burford, afraid to call attention to this second trip through the village; beyond it he accelerated, and shot round the turn to Pine Lots almost as recklessly as Belden had done. His journey past the Hotchkiss farm called forth no more than a perfunctory bark from the dog. He drew up at the Gregson house just after half-past six.

The lower floor was lighted, and there was a light on the porch. Gamadge mounted three stone steps to the lawn, and followed a gravel path, bordered by flowerbeds in need of weeding. He climbed two more stone steps, and rang a bell beside a green front door.

Mrs. Stoner, a purple knitted coat round her shoulders, answered the bell. She stood gazing at him.

"You remember me, Mrs. Stoner?"

But she had not seen him look as he was looking now. She said tremulously: "You're Mr. Gamadge."

"Yes. May I telephone?"

She stood aside, and pointed to a telephone on a table. The hall was narrow, and lighted by an oil lamp hanging from the low ceiling; facing Gamadge was an enclosed stairway, the door of which was closed with a latch.

"I'm calling Mrs. Gregson," he said, "and I'm afraid the call is private." She backed towards a room on the right, and he went on: "Somebody dumped some more evidence on her—practically on her doorstep; I couldn't have kept *it* out of the papers."

"Some more..." Her voice died. Then she asked: "Isn't she safe there—where you took her?"

"I'll find out."

He took up the telephone receiver, and she went into the room on the right, and shut the door. He gave the Five Acres number in a low voice, and when he had it asked for Mr. Thompson.

Harold's voice, when it came, was peevish: "Can't you leave us in peace for three hours?"

"Peaceful, are you? How's our friend?"

"Fine. She had her sleep, went for a stroll, and when she came back she asked for a radio. I installed Miss Lukes' little portable for her, and we had quite a talk. Mr. Colby's coming up to see her to-morrow."

"How did you find that out? I do hope you haven't been listening at keyholes, Mr. Thompson?"

"The memorandum's right here this minute, under my eye. 'Message for Mrs. James Greer. Mr. Colby is driving up to-morrow afternoon.'"

Gamadge frowned. He said after a moment: "I suppose he'll take her out in his car."

"Want me to go in the rumble?" Harold was jocose.

"No. Stick to your job, though. Good-bye."

He hung up, and went over to the closed door. At his rap Mrs. Stoner opened it.

"Mrs. Gregson is all right," he said. "I'm sorry to have missed the conference this afternoon. Did Benton Locke get to it?"

She stood in the middle of the long, low room, gazing at him helplessly. It was a room that suited her; with its plain furniture, its windows curtained in white muslin, its old, loud-ticking clock, it might have been made for Mrs. Stoner.

"He never came," she said.

"Too bad. Most disappointing for Miss Warren and Mr. Belden. Mr. Belden left here before five o'clock. How about Miss Warren?"

Mrs. Stoner was dumb, and the clock ticked.

"Or hasn't she gone yet? You know, if I were you I'd lend her Mrs. Gregson's car to get home in. I should think Belden would have driven her back to New York, but I dare say they know what they're doing. They must have been very anxious to hear what Locke was going to say; important, it must have been to bring a busy man like that all the way up here."

"He only wanted to discuss the situation with us."

"No, I think it must have been more than that. I think Mr. Locke was full of information. I think Mr. Locke was on the warpath."

Mrs. Stoner said with pale dignity: "Celia and Benny know nothing of what has happened, Mr. Gamadge. They wouldn't do anything wrong."

"At least Benton Locke isn't actuated by regard for Mrs. Gregson. He doesn't care a button for her. All he's afraid of is losing that money she was going to leave him—he practically told me so."

"He needs it dreadfully. I do hope Vina won't—they both need it dreadfully."

"They don't protect you as you protect them."

"I don't need protection, Mr. Gamadge."

"You need it very much. You're the one who had the best opportunities to make attempts on Mrs. Gregson's life. The facts speak for themselves, and now there are additional facts."

Mrs. Stoner said in a quavering voice: "The mackerel was perfectly fresh; I bought it myself. I don't know what can have got into it. I don't think anybody put poison in it."

"Well, how about the gas oven, and the fruit cake?"

Mrs. Stoner looked distracted. "I can't think!"

"You must see who's the logical suspect in all these matters, Mrs. Stoner."

"But I found the poison in the cake!"

"People might say that you had merely been trying to frighten the life out of Mrs. Gregson."

"But why should I? Why should I, Mr. Gamadge? I don't want to frighten Vina; I stay with her because she's so lonely and has had such a dreadful time. I have my annuity."

"People might think the annuity wasn't enough for you, Mrs. Stoner. They might say you hoped to cut Miss Warren and Mr. Locke out of that will, and get the whole thing for yourself."

Mrs. Stoner took a step backwards. There was silence, and the clock ticked.

"You really ought to tell me," said Gamadge, "what Benton Locke was coming here to say."

There was a creaking noise in the hall. Gamadge looked over his shoulder to see the door of the enclosed stairway open, and Cecilia Warren step down the lowest stair. She was neat and fashionable in a tweed suit and a toque, and there was a handsome piece of fur about her shoulders. She came into the room rather quickly. Gamadge met the furious look in her eyes with a smile.

"That last was too much for you, was it, Miss Warren?" he asked. "I rather thought it would be; if you were still here, you know."

She said: "It's the most contemptible thing I ever heard of in my life. Trying to frighten Mrs. Stoner into giving Benny Locke and me away! She has nothing to tell."

"I wish she had; I only wish she had, and would tell it. Locke was greatly worried about her when I saw him, and I'm greatly worried too. I'd rather frighten her, Miss Warren, than sacrifice her in this miserable intrigue."

"You send her up here to be alone, and then you come to bully her. Disgusting."

"Why didn't Mr. Belden stay here and protect you both from me?"

"Because Benny didn't get here, and Paul had to get back to town."

"Did you come with Mr. Belden, may I ask, or by train?"

"I shan't tell you how I came. I shall answer no more of your questions."

"It's really most important."

Mrs. Stoner said; "She came by train, Mr. Gamadge. Celia, Mr. Gamadge is only trying to help Vina."

Miss Warren looked at the other woman with something resembling wild exasperation. Gamadge spoke mildly: "Just trying to prevent a ghastly crime; another ghastly crime. Why do you object?"

Miss Warren's anger froze into something more formidable. Mrs. Stoner quavered: "Another! You—you don't mean *Curtis Gregson*?" She looked ready to sink to the ground. Gamadge went and got a chair, lowered her into it, and then straightened himself to look down at her.

"Are you nervous here, Mrs. Stoner," he asked, "all alone?"

"No. You said I was to come." She seemed confused.

"I didn't quite realize—how isolated you are. Would you rather go back to New York to your boarding-house? I could take you."

"I like it here. I love the country. Mr. Hotchkiss is on the party line."

"Could you manage without a car for a while?"

"Mr. Hotchkiss has a Ford I can use when Vina has hers out."

"Are you willing to lend Mrs. Gregson's car to Miss Warren for a few days?"

"Oh, yes."

"I'll get it back to you, if she can't."

Mrs. Stoner seemed incapable of questioning him, incapable of thought. She sat supine, her hands clasped loosely together; but Cecilia Warren, whose frozen look had gone, spoke sharply: "I'm going by train."

"Well, I wouldn't."

"Why not?"

She faced him, and there was something in his glance that daunted her. He said: "You ought to be obliged to me for the suggestion. People in country ticket offices notice well-dressed ladies who buy tickets at this hour of the evening. Take the car. It may be foolish of me, but I should like to know that it was garaged in New York to-night."

"Are you going to trail me—or try to?"

"I'm going down behind you. Why should you try to lose me?"

Miss Warren went over, bent down, and kissed Mrs. Stoner's cheek. Then she left the room, and hurried along a rear passage. Gamadge departed by the front door, and waited in his car until she drove round the house and into the road.

He followed her easily, hoping as they went through Burford that no idle person had been collecting car numbers that day; and wishing that some inner urge did not impel her to drive so fast. He had no wish to be arrested in her company. She could have lost him at several intersections in New York, but made no attempt to do so. She garaged the car between Lexington and Third Avenue, on the street that contained Mrs. Smiles' apartment house. Gamadge did not wait for her to come out of the garage; he drove home.

X

News On the Hour

At a quarter to ten that night Gamadge lay on the chesterfield sofa in his library, coffee beside him on a little table, and a concert coming to him over the radio. He had had a late but satisfying meal. Athalie the cook had come upstairs to forgive him for missing his dinner; and Martin the cat lay across his mid-section, fast asleep.

Clara sat opposite him, arranging her notes. She said: "You're too tired to bother with what Mr. Schenck and I found out to-day."

"I'm in good condition. I had a two-hour nap at Five Acres: while others worked, I slept."

"Just the same, you look awful."

"Thank you, my darling."

"I mean so awfully tired. How did Mrs. Gregson like Five Acres?"

"Very much indeed. Harold installed a radio for her, and I have no doubt that she's listening to this symphony now. I wish we could."

"Wouldn't you rather listen than hear this stuff?"

"I must hear the stuff. No, don't turn it off; I like a musical background, if the music's good."

"Did you get to Pine Lots?"

"I did."

"What's Mrs. Stoner like?"

"Reduced gentility personified, with high standards of behaviour. I don't know how high her moral standards are, but I think that she could always manage to reconcile them to propriety."

"People say that if your manners are really good, your morals are good too."

96

"I love to think so. Mrs. Stoner is at present being crushed between the upper millstone of one loyalty and the lower millstone of another. Well, what have you there for me?"

Clara chose a typed page. She said: "Mr. Schenck went and saw a Mr. Ormiston, an artist—"

"No!" Gamadge laughed. "Schenck's a wonder."

"—and Mr. Ormiston gave him an introduction to one of Mr. Belden's firm. What's Mr. Belden like, Henry?"

"He has curious charm, terrific vitality, and the sensibility of a rocking horse. He's magnetic, coarse-grained, and companionable. Hasn't a nerve in his make-up. I should think he would have made a good surgeon; don't know how he came to impinge upon the arts."

"His father was an architect."

"Ah, I see."

"He went to Cornell, and talked himself out of two suspensions. He got into awful scrapes. He's supposed to have brains."

"Oh, he has."

"He can work when he likes. He got into financial trouble about ten years ago—"

"Who didn't?"

"—and he and the firm nearly went out of business. But he has no private means, to speak of, and he's very hard up still. He lives anyhow, Mr. Schenck says, and spends every cent he has on boats and racing."

"What about his morals? Or did Schenck put them into an enclosure for my private eye?"

"Of course not. Here they are; Mr. Schenck says: 'Tell Gamadge that he's always very much sought after, and always found. But nothing interferes with his engagement to Miss Cecilia Warren, which seems to be of long standing. She seems to be part of the guy's life. There was a sort of a breach of promise suit pending five years ago, but he talked himself out of that. His partners are fond of him.'"

"Is this Lothario ever going to marry his first love, does Schenck gather?"

"She wouldn't even announce the engagement—or at least it didn't get announced—until after the Gregson trial."

"When she acquired prospects—financial prospects."

"But she won't marry him because she thinks some people think she killed Mr. Gregson."

"Romantic of her. Too romantic. Sounds more like a stall on the part of the unromantic Mr. Belden, but you never can tell."

"I think he sounds very romantic, all these affairs, and still being faithful to Cecilia Warren."

"Faithful in his fashion."

"I'd rather have somebody faithful to me in that fashion than not faithful at all."

"You don't know what you'd rather."

"Yes, I do." Clara put aside Schenck's notes, and took up her own. "Cecilia Warren's father married Mrs. Gregson's aunt, Miss Voories. He died ten years ago——"

"Of heart trouble; complicated, I believe, by drink."

"She went to Coverly School when she was thirteen. She left Omega for good when she was sixteen, and came to live with the Gregsons. She went to a business school, and Mr. Belden got her a job in his office as a stenographer and typist."

"And she was so busy there that she never even went back to Omega when her father died. He was in a hospital in Utica for some unspecified length of time, but she didn't go to see him in Utica, either. The defence made great play of that; I must say that Applegate's rhetoric always did give me a horrible pain, but he had something there."

"Didn't Miss Warren ever explain why she never went back to Omega?"

"She says her father died suddenly; but he was in hospital for a while. However—we are not Applegate, and we needn't take a lofty moral attitude in the matter until we know more about it."

"We don't know much about Mrs. Stoner, either. She and Mr. Gregson's mother went to the same school near Bellfield. When her husband died she was going to some kind of poorhouse, because she didn't even have enough money to get into a home."

"Most depressing."

"You can imagine how glad she was when Mr. Gregson took her in."

"Perhaps the Gregsons were glad to get an unpaid lady-help; I imagine that Mrs. Stoner earned her keep." He added, lazily stroking Martin's ears, "What did Mr. Stoner die of?"

"I don't know, Henry."

"Never mind."

"Mr. and Mrs. Gregson were married in 1919. By that time old Mrs. Gregson was dead. Old Mr. Gregson died in 1928."

"What of?"

"I don't know." Clara frowned as she looked at him.

"Too bad."

"Henry, are you thinking of that morphia? Because the newspaper says that there wasn't any morphia in the Gregson history."

"Certainly there was none involved in Mr. and Mrs. Voories' deaths. They died in an accident."

"Vina Voories was an only child. She has no relations but Miss Warren, and Mr. Gregson left no relation but an old man named Parrott, who's in a sanatorium—before, he lived in San Francisco. Now he's in a sanatorium, for good."

"For good, is he?"

"He has something incurable and stays in bed. Mr. Schenck telephoned out there to some friend of his, and found out all about Mr. Parrott. He thought you wouldn't mind paying the charges."

"We really must do something for Schenck."

"I think he likes to come to dinner."

"Ask him for to-morrow night; ask him regularly. He ought to have a standing invitation. Did you get anything about Miss Arline Prady?"

"Just that she's a native of Bellfield, and the girl Benton Locke took out the night Mr. Gregson died. Her father was the druggist, and she worked in the store. Benton Locke met her at a charity fair, and they got to be friends through their dancing."

Gamadge said, his eyes half-closed: "A druggist. Does that fact interest you?"

Clara looked quickly at him. "But Henry! A druggist wouldn't keep old, old tubes of morphia in stock."

"Perhaps he wouldn't."

"And Benton Locke had no motive for killing Mr. Gregson, and you said Cecilia Warren's testimony cleared him and Mrs. Stoner."

"If her story was true, it cleared them; but something else clears them of actually administering the morphia—clears them more effectively than uncorroborated statements by Cecilia Warren; Gregson may have laughed in the night; he might have laughed if Mrs. Gregson had been with him, if Miss Warren had been with him, or even—conceivably—if he had been alone. But if Locke or Mrs. Stoner had walked in on him and invited him to take another dose of bicarbonate of soda, I think he would have sworn."

"Well." Clara, studying his enigmatic features, put her notes together. "That's all."

"Not quite all. We have discussed the principals in the Gregson murder case, but we have not discussed all the principals in the case that Mrs. Gregson has now asked me to investigate."

"Who else is there?"

"Colby's an interested party."

"Mr. Colby! He's only in it because he's Mrs. Gregson's friend."

"If I were trying the case I should feel bound to ask myself whether that was the fact, or whether he had not on the contrary been *Mr.* Gregson's friend."

Clara was quite horrified. "But he hardly knew Mr. Gregson!"

"So he says."

"Henry!"

"What if Colby really knew Gregson very well, and liked him very much? They had years and years of those trips on the Commuters' Special to Bellfield, and ever so many golf meetings. What if Colby had constituted himself the Avenger?"

"You're making fun of me."

"Not at all. It's part of the general inquiry. I shouldn't be at all justified in leaving it out of consideration."

Clara asked, gazing at him: "Is this what detecting means?"

"This and worse."

"I never heard anything so wild. Mr. Colby isn't like that."

"When people get a fixed idea nobody knows what they're like."

"But he couldn't possibly—what about the cellar stairs

and the mackerel? He couldn't have done either of those things."

"Why not? Colby knew Pine Lots very well; he rents it for the owner. Do you suppose he isn't acquainted with its cellar stairs, and its kitchen, and its side door? He may know Mrs. Gregson's hours and her ways; we have no idea how often he's been there."

"If you think Mr. Colby's type could have written those letters and done all those things—"

"He certainly had keys to that apartment of hers here in New York, and I'm sure he knew that she liked fruit cake. Nobody could cultivate a person like Mrs. Gregson for three years——"

"Cultivate! If ever there was a nice, simple person in the world, it's Mr. Colby."

"I must study the case from all angles; if I don't, somebody else may—somebody much less humane than I am."

Clara looked as if she thought that Gamadge in his present mood was not particularly humane; but just then the concert ceased. A voice announced: "News on the hour," and proceeded to talk urgently.

"Shall I turn it off?" asked Clara. "No, don't move; you'll disturb Martin."

Gamadge said: "He's getting too hot and heavy for me. Take him off."

Clara lifted the large orange cat, who hung limply and at incredible length from her encircling hands; he pretended to be unable to set foot on the floor, so Clara established him in a chair. Suddenly she noticed Gamadge's head turn on its cushion, and the fixity of his eyes.

". . . Westchester County, two and a half miles south of Burford," said the announcer. "The young man has been identified as Benton Locke, a promising young dancer in the Diehl ballet. Raymond Jeffers, a farmer, who discovered the body while on his way home at ten o'clock this evening, says he does not think it was there when he came through about half-past six this evening, but that he may have missed seeing it, as it was behind a large tree. Locke had been shot in the back of the skull, just above the base of it; no pistol was found. The young man's wallet and wrist watch had not been taken. Police are checking up on car bandits, who may have stolen his car, killed him, and made a getaway when they heard Jeffers' approach.

"Now the weather. To-morrow——"

"Turn it off," said Gamadge.

Clara did so. Then she came over and sat on the end of the chesterfield. "Henry, what does it mean?"

"Well, I don't think it means car bandits."

"They'll stop looking for car bandits to-morrow, won't they, when they remember who he is? They'll remember the Gregson case."

"You bet they will."

"Why, you must have driven past the very road he was found on; or did you come home by the back route?"

"I didn't have time to take the back route home."

The telephone rang, a long peal. Clara shook her head at Gamadge, who had begun to rise, went into the hall, and brought the instrument into the library on its thirteen-foot wire. Gamadge balanced it on his chest.

"Mr. Gamadge?" It was a high voice, muted.

"Yes." He motioned to Clara, and she bent to the receiver.

"This is——"

"Just as well not to mention names. Those walls up there are none too thick."

"Mr. Gamadge!" It was a cry. "I was listening to the radio——"

"Yes; gently! So was I."

"Oh, poor Benny!"

"Yes; careful."

"I've done him a dreadful injustice. I must have."

"Well, we don't know."

"Perhaps he was just trying to find out!"

"Perhaps."

"Why should he have been on that road? Why was he there?"

"Better there than farther up, don't you think?"

"But if he was on his way to Minnie, why did he turn off? And what's happened to his car? I wish you were here."

"You're all right."

"But they'll connect him—connect him——"

"Not with Mrs. Greer. They may never find out a thing about the present situation, you know. We may never have to tell them a word of it, and I don't suppose the other parties will."

"I'm terribly frightened. Terribly." Clara heard the shiver in the distant voice.

"He's been completely cut off from the old life and the other place; he's been dancing all over the lot. Night clubs, everywhere. They'll look for something in his later background."

"If only they don't find me! If only I shan't have to be in the papers again!"

"There may be a mention, a picture or two; you won't see them."

"It's so nice here. I hope I shan't have to go. I wish you'd let me call up Minnie Stoner—she'll be distracted."

"If you want safety, don't lay a trail of telephone calls."

"I was rather sorry Mr. Colby decided to drive up to-morrow."

"So was I, but I think he'll be careful."

"I feel so safe in this place; they lock it up after ten, and nobody can even get out without getting a key from Mrs. Tully or Miss Lukes."

"Yes; I used to crawl out of the window when I wanted a moonlight stroll with a fair patient."

Mrs. Gregson laughed, faintly and briefly. She asked: "When shall I see you?"

"I'll communicate when I have something to tell you."

"Good-bye."

"Good-bye."

Clara took the telephone from him. She said: "Her voice sounded so *numb*."

"Yes; it was a fearful shock to her, but she has nerve. She can take it."

"I don't know how she can live through it all. Henry——" Clara stood, clasping the telephone, her eyes searching his. "Do you think you'll ever find out? About Benton Locke, and everything?"

"I'll find out if I can. I'll find out," said Gamadge between his teeth, "if it's the last thing I do."

The telephone went off in a tremendous jingle, startling Clara very much. Gamadge took it from her.

"Yes?" he asked. "Oh, Colby."

"Great heavens, old man." Colby's voice shook. "Have you been listening to the radio?"

"Yes. Great concert, wasn't it?"

"Concert!"

"We all seem to have been taking it in."

"Did you hear the news afterwards—about that fellow?"

"I did."

"Great heavens, what does it mean?"

"Well, Colby, to tell you the truth I'd rather not discuss it at all over the telephone. If you don't mind——"

"I understand all that; I had to call you and ask if you'd heard."

"Naturally."

"Have you any line on this thing, Gamadge?"

"Early days to ask that."

"Have you told our friend in the country about B.L.?"

"She just called me."

"How is she?"

"All right so far. I'd much rather not talk about any of it on the telephone, Colby."

"Great heavens, though; I've been out looking at properties all day, and as soon as I get home——"

"I know. Very upsetting. Take a drink, and let me do the same and get to bed. I'm tired myself."

Colby rang off, muttering. Gamadge turned to Clara with a smile. "It's really very unfortunate from the investigator's point of view," he said. "The gentlemen in the case have jobs that take them all over creation all day long, and you can't check up on them. They look at properties, and they look at landscapes. What is one to do about it?"

XI

Gamadge Irregulars

When Gamadge—as seldom happened—reached the small hours of a morning after a bad night, he turned off the switch of his bedside telephone; he did so at four a.m. on the day following his momentous decision in the stump lot, and at five a.m. he fell into a dreamless sleep.

No member of his household had ever dared on any previous occasion to knock at his door if his telephone did not answer; but on this same morning, at ten o'clock, Theodore not only knocked; he afterwards put an apologetic face into the room.

"What the devil," murmured Gamadge.

"Beg pardon for disturbin' you, sir, it's police."

"Tell them to come back later."

"It's Lieutenant Durfee. Mis' Gamadge is entertainin' him in the liberry."

"Oh. Well, bring my breakfast here. I'll see him when I'm dressed."

Not long afterwards he sauntered into the library, where Clara was eagerly explaining something to a lean man in a blue suit.

"This whole book is a forgery, Lieutenant Durfee," she was saying, "and so is the author's signature and the date on the flyleaf. Here it is, see? *Your oblig'd John Pipkin*."

"Why should the feller forge a whole book? Why didn't he buy this *Poems of John Pipkin*, and forge the signature into it?"

"Because there's only one other *Poems of John Pipkin*, and that's in the British Museum—unless they've moved it on account of the war. And that copy has no signature on the flyleaf."

"The feller expected to make a lot of money out of this, then?" Durfee studied the thin green book with interest.

"Oh, no; even the real one—the British Museum one— isn't worth much. Nobody cares about Pipkin, his poems aren't good."

"I don't catch it; why all the misery, then?"

"Because the man who forged this, or had it done, only collected unique books, and a Pipkin with a signature would have been unique."

"But what's the fun of owning a thing that isn't real?"

"Why, he could show it to all his friends."

Gamadge came forward. "How's that for a motive to give a jury, Durfee?" he asked.

Durfee turned a thin, lined, reddish face toward him, and

got up. He said: "I see you're bringing your wife up right, Mr. Gamadge."

"She's just started on the handwritings; Pipkin's, for instance. The Pipkin *i* is what gives the show away."

"Can you do anything with printed writing?" Durfee accepted a cigar.

"Certainly, but it's not easy to get other specimens of it for comparison." Gamadge lighted Durfee's cigar, and his own.

"I have a crank letter I want to show you some time—if necessary; I can't show it to you yet. You know how these things crop up when a sensational murder case gets into the papers."

"Is there a sensational case in the papers?"

"This murder case up in Westchester County, below Burford. Feller named Locke, Benton Locke. That's what I came about; I understand that you called on him at his rooming-house night before last."

Clara replaced John Pipkin on a shelf. She remained with her back to the room, fingering the other books in the row. Gamadge said: "Oh, yes. I suppose Miss Prady gave you my name."

"That's right, Miss Arline Prady." Durfee was studying Gamadge with some degree of exasperation. "You didn't think we'd be interested?"

"My dear good man! Of course I was going to call you. I only heard that he'd been shot last night, over the radio; I've been in bed ever since. I don't know who shot him, or why; and I certainly wasn't the last virtuous person who saw him alive."

Clara said, turning away from the bookcase: "Will you excuse me if I go? I have some errands." She shook hands with Durfee. "I'll bring your carbon paper home with me, Henry."

"Thank you, my darling."

She flitted from the room. Durfee, looking after her, said: "I was going to suggest finishing our conversation in your office or down-town. I didn't want to remind Mrs. Gamadge of the fact that people you pay calls on quite often die by violence shortly afterwards."

"Quite often is good. Twice isn't quite often."

"It's quite often from the police point of view."

"I busted that case for you. Perhaps you didn't want to remind Clara of the fact that if it hadn't been for me you people would have arrested her as accessory to murder."

"You can't blame me for wondering if your baleful influence hadn't been at work again; you call on this feller, and the next day he gets killed."

"Lots of people I've called on are still alive and well."

"You think I ought to look at it as a coincidence?"

"Look at it as cause and effect, if you want to be so foolish; but however you look at it, you can look at it sitting down. And smoking a cigar."

Durfee sat down behind the big table. He said: "It's quite an interesting tie-up."

"What is?"

"The Locke case and the Gregson murder case."

"You found a tie-up, did you?"

"We didn't realize until this morning that he was that Benton Locke."

"What's the tie-up?"

"I might ask you that. I will ask you why you went to see him Tuesday night."

"Private business."

"Now don't get obstinate; you'll be called when they hold the inquest, you know. They've adjourned it, but when they hold it you'll be invited."

"I'll be there."

"And you won't be able to plead private business there."

"By that time the business will probably not be private. Can't you lay off me for a few days? You know very well that I don't obstruct justice."

"Not very long; not till two or three people get killed, anyhow."

"Really, Durfee! I call that too bad of you. I was astounded by Locke's death—astounded."

"Do you know what I think?" Durfee squinted up at him. "By what I know of you, I think you put some idea in his head, and he acted on it, and got shot as a result."

"If I knew who shot him, or why he got shot, I'd pass the information along to you—instantly."

Durfee smoked in silence for half a minute. Then he said: "The hitch comes with the word 'knew.' I'd like your opinions; I don't require a statement under oath, or something all ready to present to a jury."

"If you know me as well as all that"—Gamadge smiled at his guest without rancour—"you know that I won't go around spilling a lot of nonsense. I'm not fond of handing out half-baked notions to the police."

"They'd like to be the judge of what's important and what isn't. How do you suppose I can lay off you, as you suggest, if the whole department, and the D.A., and the newspapers know that you were calling on Locke night before last?"

"You can manage it, all right. Tell them I'm worth waiting for," said Gamadge airily. He went on, ignoring Durfee's scowl: "How long had he been dead when they found him?"

"Six to eight hours, but nobody saw him on that road until ten. The farmer that did find him came past on his way to Burford more than two hours earlier and didn't see him at all."

"That's possible; perhaps the farmer's headlights weren't on when he made the first trip."

"They weren't, and it's easier to see what's behind that tree when you're coming from Burford than when you're going there."

"You keep saying Burford; why Burford? As I get it, the road's quite far down the highway from Burford."

"Manner of speaking; Burford's the nearest town. Why," asked Durfee, plaintively, "should he have gone up that road? It leads out into the country, no town for miles."

"Or why should he have been coming *down* that road, you know." Gamadge asked after a pause: "No sign of his car?"

"No. It's a second-hand Ford convertible coupé, and he kept it in a garage near his rooming-house."

"No sign of the pistol, I suppose?"

"No; nor of the shell. But Locke was killed with a .38 automatic; we have the bullet, and that's all we have." Durfee's expression was so odd that Gamadge looked curiously at him. He went on: "They tell me that there ain't any underworld characters in his kind of dancing game. They tell me it's all full of angels."

"Well—of course he'd been dancing for years in night clubs and resorts."

"I'm not much interested in that angle, to be frank with you. I'm interested in the tie-up with the Gregson case."

"Who wouldn't be?"

"Just the kind of case you'd enjoy digging into, too. That Warren girl——" Durfee looked thoughtful. "I always had an idea she knew more about it than ever came out at the trial." His hand wandered towards his breast pocket, and came away empty. "I wish you'd tell me about your business with Locke," he said irritably.

"Eventually I will."

"Eventually." Durfee looked contemptuous. "I want information to-day." He said after a moment: "Whatever became of Mrs. Gregson, I wonder—and that housekeeper of hers? They vanished right off the map."

"So they did."

"Miss Warren's with a Mrs. Smiles. We had this crank letter this morning; posted in Burford yesterday afternoon at three o'clock; and that's 'why Burford,' by the way."

"Oh—really?"

"The letter's too crazy to act on without due caution. We can't upset people and get their influential friends and their laywers in our hair on the strength of an anonymous letter, and a crazy one at that."

"Can't you?" Gamadge showed amusement.

"Not without an O.K. from the big shots. The D.A. will be back in town late to-night; I'll get hold of him, no matter what time it is. There were bushels of these crank letters after the Gregson trial, and they were none of 'em worth the ink on 'em."

"Is this a reminder of them?"

"Yes. One of those original cranks may have remembered Locke's connection with the Gregson case, and started up again. The commissioner won't let me talk to you about the thing till I've seen the D.A."

"The crank must be trying to involve somebody of vast importance."

"Indirectly." Durfee rose. "There'd be the dickens and all to pay if we made a mistake, I can tell you that." He faced Gamadge, and his expression was sombre. "Look here; after you left Locke that night he made two calls—dial calls; they can't be traced. He didn't get any between the time he saw you and the time he left, and we don't know when he did leave yesterday—Miss Prady was out, and can't tell us; but the house telephone is in the lower hall, and it's pretty certain he got no message. It's a fair inference that he made those two calls on account of what you said to him. Now I know you have sense, and I know you get results; but I'd advise you to give me what information you have—here and now."

"I have no information that would do you any good, Durfee; if I have any at any future time you'll get it—immediately."

"You can't fool with this. This is going to tear the Gregson case wide open again."

"Let me venture to give you a layman's inconsiderable crumb of advice: *you* can't fool with it. Do you remember what sometimes happens to people who tear old murder cases wide open again?"

Durfee walked out of the room, and pushed the button of the automatic elevator. He said, without turning his head: "If it wasn't for that poor unfortunate little wife of yours..."

Gamadge looked solemn enough as he escorted Detective-Lieutenant Durfee down to the front door.

The telephone was ringing when he returned to the library. Harold's voice, intensely calm, greeted him over the wire:

"I just saw the papers."

"You have the advantage of me; I haven't seen them yet."

"You mean to tell me you don't know what happened yesterday just off the route below Burford?"

"I don't mean to tell you that. After all, several people were bound to call me up."

"Did *she* call you up?"

"Last night—she got it on the radio, which is more than you seem to have done."

"She's shut up in her room, probably half-crazy worrying."

"No; shocked, but not crazy. Keep awake from now on."

"You bet I will."

Harold had no sooner rung off than Gamadge was recalled to the telephone. He said "Hello" rather crossly.

"Is this Mr. Gamadge speaking?" The voice on the wire was tremulous. Gamadge said: "Yes, here I am, Mrs. Stoner."

"Mr. Gamadge, Hotchkiss brought my paper."

"Oh. Yes."

"I couldn't believe my eyes. Poor, poor Benny."

Gamadge waited until sobs no longer came to him from far away. Then he said: "Yes. Too bad."

"That's why he never came! Oh, who could have done such a thing?"

"Not a crank this time."

"No. It must have been a bandit!"

"Well—I think not."

"I can't stay here. I'm coming to New York. Mr. Hotchkiss will drive me to the noon train."

"That's sensible of you."

"Have you told Vina Gregson?"

"Yes, she knows."

"I hate not knowing where she is. Couldn't you tell me, Mr. Gamadge? She'll want to talk to somebody. She'll be so frightened. She'll be so shocked."

"I'd rather not have anyone know her whereabouts just now. She's being looked after better than you are, Mrs. Stoner."

"She's among strangers."

"Don't worry about her. May I have your city address?"

Mrs. Stoner gave him a street and number in the east Fifties, and then seemed to fade away from her end of the telephone. After listening for some moments to an empty kind of buzzing, Gamadge put his end on its cradle and went into the library. He found Clara sorting mail. She asked: "How did you manage about Lieutenant Durfee? I had to go, I couldn't stand it."

"Durfee feels very sorry for you. I think he'll let me alone for a day or so—not longer. He gave me a good deal more information than I gave him. What's that thing?"

The thing which had called forth Gamadge's exclamation of fastidious disgust was a large, square, scented envelope, mauve in hue, with a purple line round its pointed flap. Clara turned it over; it was practically covered with immense and almost illegible handwriting, and was addressed to her. She opened it, and took out a sheet of notepaper, monogrammed and bordered in mauve and purple. She read aloud in a surprised voice:

> "*Dear, dear Mrs. Gamadge,*
>
> "*Please forgive my informality, but I have had the pleasure of meeting your charming husband, and he will tell you who I am. I wonder whether you will both humour an old woman, and dine with me at half-past seven to-night.*
>
> "*The party will be in a sense a business conference. Poor Benton Locke's tragic death has shocked me very much, and quite shattered my friend and secretary Cecilia Warren, who had known him for years. I am asking her fiancé, Paul Belden, and Benton Locke's fiancée, a little Miss Prady. I am also asking a Mr. Colby, Mrs. Gregson's friend.*
>
> "*We must all put our heads together, and try to make something of this dreadful affair. It occurred to me that no one is more capable of doing so than your clever husband, about whom I have been making inquiries, and who seems to be a truly distinguished person.*
>
> "*Cecilia joins me in hoping that you will both make a great effort to come. Yours most sincerely, Rosette Smiles.*"
>
> Thursday.

Clara stared at Gamadge.

He said: "It's a wake."

"Why is she asking us, and all those people?"

"Well, she's evidently the sort of festive old thing that lives for company. I dare say she snatches at any excuse for a doings."

"A doings! I simply can't understand it. Shall we go?"

Gamadge wandered over to the sofa and sat down. He said: "We'll go, and we'll take Schenck."

"Take Mr. Schenck! Why?"

"We need him."

"But we can't. It's a dinner—we can't bring a strange man."

"It's a business conference. Mrs. Smiles likes strange

men—she'll be delighted to have him, all the more because he'll make eight for dinner."

"What excuse can we possibly give?"

"Call him up and see if he'll come."

"He's already promised to dine with us."

"Then what could be more simple?"

Clara called up Mrs. Smiles. "Yes, we'd love to come," Gamadge heard her say, "but the trouble is that we've already asked a friend to dine with us—a Mr. Schenck. . . . Oh, thank you so much, I'm sure he will. He's very nice. . . . Oh, most discreet—he's an insurance investigator. . . . Seven-thirty, then. . . . Good-bye."

She came back to say that Mrs. Smiles sounded very nice and kind, but rather silly.

"She's silly in a way, but I think she's very shrewd too. I believe that she and her cronies have the entire police department buffaloed, homicide squad and all."

"How in the world did you know that?"

"Never mind. Call up Schenck, will you, and tell him to wear a white tie." He added: "Tell him to stop for us at seven-fifteen."

Clara did so; Gamadge heard her struggling against Schenck's no doubt passionate demands for further information. At last she said: "Yes, Mr. Belden and Mr. Colby and Miss Prady and us. No, *not* Mr. Locke—somebody killed him. . . . I said killed him. . . . Yesterday; don't you read the papers? That's what the party is about, Mrs. Smiles wants Henry to tell her who did it. . . . I'm glad you can come, and I don't know any more about it than you do, and please excuse me—I must go. Good-bye."

She came back and sat down beside him. "Mr. Schenck is simply raging to know more about Benton Locke."

"He'll know more about him before he's through. Look here, Clara." Gamadge, sitting forward on the sofa with his hands hanging between his knees, turned his head to look at her sideways. "This is a very bad case."

"I was afraid it was."

"It's so bad that I'm going to ask you to do something I wouldn't dream of suggesting, if I weren't afraid somebody's life was in danger."

"Of course I'll do anything."

"I believe you would; but this is delicate, exacting, even

perhaps dangerous; and it's extremely unpleasant. The trouble is, I have no time."

Clara, returning his harassed look, said nothing.

"The Smiles apartment is a duplex," he went on. "The drawing-room, or living-room, is two stories high, and the second-floor bedrooms are evidently along the front, and are approached by a little winding staircase to the right of the front door as you go in. They're above the dining-room and kitchens. To the left of the front door there's a little cloakroom and washroom for male guests.

"Mrs. Smiles hasn't, I should say, a large staff of servants; in that apartment she wouldn't need more than a butler, a cook, a housemaid, and a kitchenmaid. She seems to have no personal maid—Miss Warren waits on her. With a dinner for eight on hand, I don't believe there'll be a maid upstairs when you go up to take off your things."

Clara listened in wonder.

"If there is, we'll have to try to work out something—after dinner, perhaps. As it is, we'll get there a little late; we'll hope that Miss Prady will have left her wraps and gone downstairs. You must find out which Miss Warren's room is."

"How can I?"

"You can't fail to. At most, there can't possibly be more than four bedrooms, with the necessary baths—not in an apartment of that size. The big one, with a big double bed in it and all kinds of lace counterpanes and fixings, will belong to Mrs. Smiles. There may be another luxurious but sombre one—Smiles' dressing-room, if he ever lived there. I don't have to tell you what spare, or guest, rooms are like; and the remaining one, with belongings in it, will be Miss Warren's. You'll probably be directed to the spare room; you must immediately find Miss Warren's, and search it thoroughly."

"Search it!"

"Not all at once, you know; begin when you leave your wraps, before dinner—you'll have a few minutes. Your second chance will be after dinner, when you'll gracefully absent yourself to powder your nose. The third chance will come when we all go home."

"But what am I to search for?"

"A thirty-eight calibre automatic pistol."

Clara's mouth fell open.

"It's biggish, heavy, and a thing that can be felt before

it's seen. It ought not to be hard to find, unless she's locked it up—and I don't think she'd do that."

Clara made an effort to speak. At last she said: "I shan't know where to look."

"Just decide where *you'd* hide it; not too deep, you know—you might need it again."

"In the lowest drawer of my dresser."

"Look in all those drawers first—it won't take you a minute. Where next?"

"On the top shelf of the closet."

"That's too bad; it means you may have to stand on a chair. Well, do your best; unless——" He looked at her dejected face: "Unless you'd rather not. Say the word, and I'll give up the whole idea."

"Of course I'll do it."

"Schenck and I will be in the offing, you know; we won't let anybody catch you at it unless they mow us down first. I'll be on the stair, and Schenck in the drawing-room doorway. We'll whistle for danger. Is there anything special that you'd like us to whistle?"

Clara would not smile. "If anything goes wrong they'll put us out of the house, and call the police."

"Probably. I told you it was a nasty job."

"I won't find it. She's locked it up or thrown it away. She'd never keep it!"

"I say it's there."

"What shall I do with it if I find it?"

"Well, for God's sake, be sure that the safety catch is on. I've shown you where the safety catch is on an automatic."

"Yes, I know where it is."

"See that it's on, and then—let's see. You'll have to carry some sort of wrap."

"I'll wear a little coat that matches my pink dress."

"Wrap it up in the coat, and bring it down to me. I'll take it, coat and all."

Clara suddenly began to smile. She said: "Mr. Schenck will be furious."

"I don't know. He may actually enjoy it. We must look at it as if it were a parlour game, Clara; just a parlour game."

"Mrs. Smiles won't think it's a parlour game."

"I bet she adores them. Perhaps she'll make us bob for apples."

"How did you ever get the idea that there was a gun in Cecilia Warren's room, Henry?"

"Logic, pure logic, partly based on a tip from Durfee which he didn't know he gave me. The moral of it is, never write letters, Clara; not even anonymous letters in block print."

"Oh—has there been *another* one?"

"You bet there has."

XII

Parlour Games

Mr. Schenck arrived at a quarter past seven to find the Gamadges ready for him. Clara was radiant in a pink dress and a little fur-trimmed pink jacket. Schenck himself was as usual up to the minute, in tails so long that they made Gamadge's look docked; but Gamadge's had come from Savile Row some years before.

Schenck glowered at him while he explained the strategy of the evening.

"Going to drag your wife into it, are you?"

"I'm dying to look for a pistol," said Clara.

"Like fun you are. When they catch you at it, I suppose this guy will explain that you're a kleptomaniac."

"I won't get caught if you whistle."

"Whistle! I may have to break somebody's leg. This is some party you've got me invited to."

Gamadge, holding Clara's fur coat for her, said: "I don't deny it's tough. If it wasn't tough, I shouldn't have asked either of you to pitch in."

Schenck looked sharply at the blunt, amiable visage of his friend. He said: "I suppose Locke's murderer will be right on hand. *He'll* have that thirty-eight calibre automatic pistol, with all the rest of the bullets in it. We'll probably all get shot except you."

"I'm glad you have the situation well in view. It's more than I have."

Clara said: "Lieutenant Durfee told him something, Mr. Schenck."

"Inadvertently," said Gamadge. He adjusted a silk hat, gazing with admiration at Schenck's glittering new one, and they all went out and got into the Gamadge car.

At Mrs. Smiles' door the major-domo respectfully asked Mrs. Gamadge to go upstairs—first door on the left, madam. Clara, without a glance at her escorts, climbed to the second floor and disappeared from view. Schenck and Gamadge were ushered into the little cloakroom on the left. They disposed of their outer garments in something like thirty seconds and came back into the hall, where the major-domo was waiting to announce them. Gamadge leaned nonchalantly against the newel post of the winding stairway, and Schenck stood poised just outside the drawing-room door.

Clara descended, wearing the jacket; she shook her head. Gamadge patted her on the shoulder, and they went into the big room.

"Mr. and Mrs. Gamadge, Mr. Schenck," said the major-domo.

Five persons looked up from their places round the fire; they seemed a mile away. Mrs. Smiles, impressive in petunia-coloured velvet, extended a hand and nodded eagerly. Her chins billowed above a dog collar of pearls with diamond slides, and there were two diamond stars in her hair. Miss Warren, who looked well-bred and pale in the brick-red dress, stood beside Belden. He towered above her, his back to the doorway; his broad smile, as he looked over his shoulder at the late-comers, was full of amusement.

Miss Prady sat on a low chair beside Mrs. Smiles. She made an odd, forlorn picture in a yellow dress which had outlived much dancing, some of it no doubt in public. There was an elaborate yellow ornament in her hair, which had been curled tightly for the occasion. She looked ill at ease and unhappy; Colby, who seemed to have been trying to talk to her, appeared no less so. His square red face brightened when he saw Gamadge. He advanced a step, and then hesitated.

"Now this is really nice of you!" Mrs. Smiles made no apology for remaining in her arm-chair; she took Clara's hand in both of hers, a giant clam enfolding a minnow. "I have only to look at you to know what you're like, Mrs. Gamadge. I hope you'll always be my friend."

"Oh, thank you, Mrs. Smiles."

"Let me introduce Miss Prady and Miss Warren. This is Mr. Belden; and of course you know Mr. Colby."

"And this is Mr. Schenck, Mrs. Smiles."

Mrs. Smiles beamed upon Schenck, who was equal to the occasion: "My company had the pleasure of handling some of your husband's insurance."

"How interesting. Did you know my dear husband, Mr. Schenck?"

"I'm sorry to say I hadn't the pleasure." He longed to add that he was perhaps the only private investigator in the city who had not at some time or another had a shot at investigating the great bandit Smiles.

When all the introductions had been made and Gamadge stood on the edge of the group drinking his cocktail, Colby edged up to him.

"My God, Gamadge," he muttered, "what is all this about Locke getting killed?"

"Don't ask me."

"But I do ask you."

"Ask away."

"I mean, he must have been headed for—for one of two places."

"Don't tell the police so. We must keep a certain party out of it, as I suppose I needn't remind you."

"She's half out of her mind! She thinks it must be the beginning of a massacre, and who knows if she's wrong or not?"

"Who knows?"

"I hardly like to leave her up there."

"It would be very difficult to get at her without her permission."

"But suppose it was someone she trusted."

Gamadge looked at him. "Do you imagine her to be a complete fool? But she trusts you, Colby. How did the drive come off?"

"She wouldn't go. I don't think she does trust me now— me or anybody; not entirely. I don't blame her."

"She doesn't blame me, I hope, for allowing Benton Locke to get himself killed?"

"No, no, of coure not."

Belden came up to them, at the top of his form; he tilted the remainder of a cocktail into his large mouth, and followed it with a little sausage rolled in bacon. "I've been telling Miss Prady," he said. "Benton Locke would have liked the idea of this party. He hated cant, and he loved the dramatic and the picturesque. Real artist, that boy was."

"So he seemed to me," agreed Gamadge.

"He would have liked Mrs. Smiles' notion of funeral baked meats." Belden seized another little skewered sausage from the passing tray. He put it into his mouth, and laid the skewer on his cocktail plate. "He would have liked to see Miss Prady mourning him in yellow net and a bunch of artificial flowers."

"Miss Warren," said Gamage, "mourns him in red."

"I hope she'll mourn me in red. No reason why she should mourn him at all."

Gamadge's eyes rested on the slim red figure, and moved to Cecilia Warren's impassive face. He said: "She is affected by the event."

"Very sensitive girl."

Dinner was announced; Mrs. Smiles laboured to her feet. They all moved into the dining-room, Gamadge beside his hostess. She said: "We'll have our dinner in peace, and you men will have your coffee with us afterwards; then we can talk about poor Mr. Locke."

"Much the best plan."

The long, low dining-room, panelled with brocades that had been made three centuries before in Venice, was lighted by candles in carved Italian sconces. A bed of crimson roses ran down the middle of the table, which was covered by a lace cloth. Mrs. Smiles evidently liked her little dinners to resemble little banquets. She placed Gamadge on her right and Colby on her left; Miss Warren sat at the foot of the table, with Belden and Schenck at her left and right. Miss Prady was between Gamadge and Belden, Clara between Colby and Schenck.

"People must eat," Mrs. Smiles told Gamadge, "and they can't eat while they're thinking. Poor Miss Prady—she's very thin."

"And nervous." Miss Prady was fumbling at her white evening bag, which had lost many of its beads.

"She is so anxious to hear what we all think about Benton Locke's sad passing."

Gamadge did not care for euphemisms, but he realized that Mrs. Smiles used them naturally; she was incapable of using stark words. She used many others, however, and engrossed Gamadge during two courses with a description of something she called the Pattern of Life. Gamadge learned that it taught Acceptance, and spent a good deal of time persuading Mrs. Smiles to admit that the theory had not been formed to embrace insect pests, colds in the head, or burglars. Murder seemed to be on the border-line. Woolly on the edges as the system appeared to be, he thought it not a bad one for the widow of a scoundrel to live by.

"The thing is," she informed him, "to interfere only when interference seems definitely indicated by the Weaver."

Game arrived on gold plates, and Gamadge was at last allowed to turn to Miss Prady. She had had champagne, and looked feverish.

"Where do you dance, Miss Prady?" he asked.

"I'm just learning. I won a competition, and the Ballet is giving me lessons free."

"You must have what it takes to get ahead like that."

"Benny got me into the competition." Her face grew tragic.

"He was a good friend."

Miss Prady's eyes turned to Mrs. Smiles. "*I* don't accept things like that," she said. "Like people killing people."

"Nor do I. We must humour our hostess."

"That policeman, or whatever he was, wanted to know who Benny had been quarrelling with; I couldn't tell him anything; I don't know Benny's friends, except some dancers— I hardly know anybody in New York."

"Had you been engaged to him long, Miss Prady?"

"It wasn't announced," she said, with what Gamadge thought infinite pathos.

"I'm going to find out who did for him—if I can. Will you back me?"

She looked at him, doubtful and moody. "I didn't think you were on his side."

"I am, though."

"I didn't think anybody was." She glanced round the gleaming table, and Gamadge followed her glance. Colby was talking busily to Clara about the eighth hole on the Bellfield golf course, and the means he took to conquer it. Schenck was asking Miss Warren if she had seen *Kick Off*. Belden sat listening to them, in a state of latent jollity; but his eyes also were wandering. Cecilia Warren might have been half-drugged; she listened and answered, turning her head slightly from one man to the other, as if in a dream.

When the ices came, Gamadge returned to Mrs. Smiles and the Pattern of Life. Luckily for his reason, the end of the dinner came quickly; Mrs. Smiles ceased to murmur with closed eyes, "Accept, accept," and permitted him to help her out of her chair.

"Now we're all going into the other room," she said, with more gaiety than seemed quite appropriate to the occasion, "and I warn you that I have a surprise for you."

They streamed through the dining-room doors; Clara, with some embarrassment, flitted away; Gamadge took his coffee cup into the lobby, where he studied a worm-eaten and precious tapestry; and Schenck planted himself solidly in the middle of the drawing-room, half-way between the entrance and the hearth. He gazed about him, over walls and ceiling, until Belden came up and assisted him in his survey with a semi-jocular dissertation on Jacobean Gothic, as applied to living-rooms in apartment houses. Schenck's eye returned, ever and anon, to Miss Prady; but she made no move to follow Clara, and Gamadge hoped that Schenck would not be forced into physical encounter with her.

Minutes dragged while coffee and liqueurs were passed from guest to guest. Gamadge felt perspiration destroying his collar, and he would not meet Schenck's increasingly truculent stare. At last he could bear it no longer. He went to the foot of the little staircase and whistled. "Clara," he called, "what's keeping you?"

"Coming." She appeared in the doorway above, and began to descend. Her jacket was over her arm.

"In the closet," she murmured, as she reached him. "On the top shelf, under a summer hat."

He took the jacket from her, grasping the hard and bulky object through its covering of satin and fur. They went into the drawing-room and joined the others round the fire. Clara said apologetically to Cecilia Warren: "I just needed a safety pin."

"My dear child, why didn't you ring?" Mrs. Smiles was apologetic too. "But sit down beside your husband, now; there's a nice little table for you both, and there's your coffee and your cognac waiting. I don't know whether you take cognac; if not, you can have whatever else you like."

Clara downed the cognac, as Gamadge afterwards told her, like a bar fly. He sat beside her, the jacket lying on the settee between them, and toyed with his own brandy in a gentlemanly manner. The company had formed a rough semicircle in front of the fireplace.

"Blatchford," said Mrs. Smiles, "you may clear away, and if I want anything I shall ring."

There was silence until the major-domo departed with his tray, and closed the dining-room doors behind him.

"Now," said Mrs. Smiles. She glanced about her complacently. "My idea was to compare notes on this sad event—poor Benny Locke's passing—and submit our results to the proper authorities. I only wish that poor Mrs. Gregson were here with us to-night, but she still shrinks from new faces. Miss Prady welcomes our little investigation; she says she won't let it upset her. She says she'll be brave."

Miss Prady, on her low chair beside Mrs. Smiles, had begun to react unfavourably to her cocktails, her champagne, and her cognac. Her mouth drooped. She looked very sullen, and her fingers played with the white bag.

"Have you all cigars and cigarettes?" asked Mrs. Smiles. "Aren't you smoking, Mr. Colby?"

At the sound of his name Colby started violently, and smiled. He got out his cigarette case.

"You won't have one of these? Well, then; we seem to be all ready. Of course everyday people like ourselves can't pretend to know how to approach dreadful affairs like this; we are not trained to marshal facts and to weigh evidence. Are those the correct phrases?"

She looked about her. Paul Belden took his cigar out of his mouth to answer her: "You're doing fine, ma'am, but where are you heading for?" Cecilia Warren, beside him, sat motionless; her hands folded in her lap, her eyes cast down. Gamadge thought: This is driving the girl mad; but she couldn't stop the old lady from doing it.

"Why, Paul," answered Mrs. Smiles, "that's the surprise! We all know by this time that Mr. Gamadge is a document expert whose hobby is criminology, and that he investigates cases for his friends; but he's solved three celebrated cases himself, and he's consulted by the police! They think the world of him!"

Mrs. Smiles' announcement fell flat; nobody responded to it, but she did not seem to observe their apathy; she went on, jubilant:

"So this is to be a little court of inquiry. Mr. Gamadge, who knows just what to do, will question us all, and we must tell him everything we know. Then he can take the results to the police. It will be so interesting to watch his methods."

Gamadge sat back on his settee, smoking, and looking at his hostess with a smile. He felt no annoyance at being asked to perform; he realized that this was indeed no more than a parlour game to Mrs. Smiles, and that she meant to flatter him by making him the master of ceremonies.

"Well," he said easily, "I see no objection to talking things over; but it's impossible for me to proceed as you suggest; impossible for more than one reason."

"Oh, but why?" Mrs. Smiles looked ready to shed tears of disappointment.

"I'm not connected with the police, I'm a mere amateur; I never present them with anything unless I'm sure they'll know what to do with it. I shouldn't dream of offering them hints and conjectures."

"But evidence? You'd not withhold evidence of a crime, Mr. Gamadge—if you came across it in the course of an investigation?"

"I shouldn't offer the police anything less than proof which would stand up in a court of law. They must act on their information, you know, whether it gets innocent people into trouble or not. And then these hints and guesses get into the newspapers, you know, and that's convenient for the guilty and wretched for the innocent. Police procedure and legal procedure must run their appointed course, or we should have no law and no justice at all; but a private individual can use his own judgment."

"You don't seem very sound on your duty as a citizen, I must say." Belden surveyed him humorously.

"Well, I really am; all I mean is that I don't go dashing to the police with the wrong things."

"Then we must all take a vow," said Mrs. Smiles comfortably, "not to repeat anything that goes on here to-night."

"That might help," agreed Gamadge, "in getting us over my second difficulty. Any investigation of this kind, Mrs. Smiles, no matter who conducts it or how it's conducted, is bound to hurt people's feelings, shock them, distress them, and make them furious. Nobody likes impertinent questions, and nobody answers them. The inquiry would turn out to be painful and futile."

"Shall we risk it?" Mrs. Smiles turned her face from guest to guest. "Shall we allow Mr. Gamadge to do his worst?"

Nobody spoke, to assent or to protest; until Miss Prady suddenly astonished everybody by saying in a loud and angry tone: "I say go ahead."

Mrs. Smiles turned to gaze at her in surprise.

"I say go ahead and ask questions," repeated Miss Prady, "and put them in the papers. I want to know who killed Benny Locke."

"Any objections?" Gamadge questioned each set and mask-like face in the semi-circle. When he came to Colby's, the latter said brusquely: "Watch your step, Gamadge."

"I'll try to be discreet."

He became suddenly very business-like; pulled the little table up in front of him and Clara, found a gold pencil in his waistcoat pocket, and asked for paper. "I must take notes, you know," he said. "That's part of the game."

Mrs. Smiles opened her mesh bag, and produced therefrom a little pad with gold corners. She handed it to him, chuckling.

"Thanks very much. Now: we must have closed doors. This is in camera, you know, and it's highly important that we shouldn't be overheard or seen."

Belden went to the dining-room doors, opened them, and looked between them. He said: "They've cleared away, the place is dark." He closed the doors again, fastened them, and went to the hall. He moved chairs from in front of the big glass doors, and closed them, too.

"There's a door from the writing-room into the lobby," said Mrs. Smiles. Belden went into the writing-room, and came back to report that he had locked that one.

"Now for it." Gamadge fixed Mrs. Smiles with a bland look. "I'm to give a demonstration of my methods, the more sensational the better. Is that what you want, Mrs. Smiles?"

"That's just what we want!"

"Something a little more spectacular than trying to dig a lot of probably useless information out of a lot of people who don't want to part with it. Well, I can oblige you; I have an exhibit." He lifted Clara's pink satin coat, unrolled it, and laid the automatic pistol on the pale, shining surface of the table. Against that background it looked very big, very black, and curiously formless.

There was not a sound in the room; Clara had a glimpse of Colby's staring blue eyes, of Cecilia Warren's bloodless, parted lips.

"I have every reason to believe," continued Gamadge, "that this is the gun that killed Benton Locke. It's a .38 Colt, and my wife happened on it while she was looking for that safety pin in Miss Warren's bedroom."

Miss Prady was leaning forward, her face, under its mass of curls, strongly reminiscent of a Medusa's head. She pointed at the gun, and shrieked: "That's Benny's pistol! It's the one he always carried in his car!"

XIII

In Camera

"Well, Miss Prady." Gamadge's expression as he looked at her was almost affectionate. "We seem to be making progress, we really do; but how can you tell that this is Mr. Locke's pistol?"

Miss Prady cast an intense look at him, and then back at the incongruous object lying on the satinwood table. She rose, and advanced slowly towards it; her hand was nearly upon it when Gamadge put out his own.

"I wouldn't touch it, if I were you," he said. "Probably

there are no fingerprints on it except my wife's; still, I wouldn't touch it."

Belden had also got to his feet; there was even now a smile on his lips, but otherwise his face had taken on a resemblance to the gargoyle mask which Gamadge had caught a glimpse of the day before. He asked, his eyes on Gamadge: "Shall I turn these people out for you, Mrs. Smiles?"

Mrs. Smiles was also gazing at her guest of honour, with very much the expression of one who has been stroking a catlike animal and suddenly discovers it to be a cheetah. She made no reply.

Gamadge shook his head at Belden. "Mrs. Smiles doesn't want you to do that," he said. "She's very much obliged to us for finding the thing in time."

"Time?" Belden's smile was threatening.

"Before the police found it. Please sit down, Mr. Belden; we must not waste minutes indulging in recrimination; the law may possibly be on its way already."

Belden slowly sank back upon his chair. Gamadge asked again: "How do you know this is Locke's pistol, Miss Prady?"

"It's just like his."

"I think it probably *is* his. If you'll resume your seat, we'll continue the investigation."

Miss Prady backed until her reverse progress was stopped by the edge of her chair. She sat down on it, her eyes still fixed on the gun. Gamadge took out his handkerchief, wound it round his fingers, and examined that weapon thoroughly.

"One cartridge gone from the clip," he said. "Did Mr. Locke have a licence to carry this, I wonder?"

"No, he never bothered. It was his father's," said Miss Prady.

"It wasn't heard from during the Gregson trial, three years ago."

"Benny hid it under some dirt in the tool shed."

Miss Warren turned her head stiffly, and looked at Miss Prady. She looked away again, resuming the quiet pose, that was yet so full of tension, which she had maintained throughout the evening. She might lack humanity, thought Gamadge, but she did not lack courage.

"He hid it in the tool shed when Gregson died?" Seeing affirmation in Miss Prady's face, he went on: "Because he didn't want it confiscated; I see. Quite natural. Well, it's now become an even more compromising piece of property. What shall we do with it?"

Miss Prady said hoarsely: "*Let* the police find it! Tell them where it was!"

"I'm afraid that wouldn't do at all." Gamadge smiled at her in a conspiratorial manner. "Wouldn't do at all."

"Why not? Why not?"

"Well, the police have to look at a thing of this kind from all points of view. It's their job, you know, and they're not fools at it by any means. They'll assume first, of course, that Miss Warren hid the pistol in her room; in which case Mrs. Smiles and Mr. Belden may be involved as possible confederates."

Mrs. Smiles got a little handkerchief out of her mesh bag and applied it with gentle and agitated pats to her forehead, her cheeks, and her mouth.

"But their secondary assumption will be as follows:" continued Gamadge. "That somebody planted it there. Now, who could have planted it there? Why," and his eyes wandered from guest to guest, "every single person in this room except Schenck and me. Mr. Schenck had no opportunity to go up to the second floor, nor did I; neither before dinner nor at any time. As for my wife, why should *she* plant it merely to unearth it again? Perhaps I should also except my friend Colby, though. Did Blatchford announce you when you came, Colby?"

Colby's red face seemed to swell. "What is all this? Why shouldn't he have announced me?"

"I don't know. Did he?"

Belden suddenly broke into raucous laughter. "He didn't. After he let Colby in, Blatchford came into this room; Mrs. Smiles called him. Colby joined us here after a short interval—unannounced."

"Why the—why should I plant a gun on Miss Warren? I don't even know where her room is." Colby was fuming.

"Any room would do. I'm not accusing anybody of anything, I'm simply trying to explain to Miss Prady why we mustn't be too impulsive in the matter of this gun. I know where it was, she knows where it was; there is no deception."

Belden asked in a rallying tone: "And how did you know where it was, if I may inquire?"

"I didn't know; I guessed."

Mrs. Smiles at last found her voice. She demanded shrilly: "Why didn't you tell me in private, then? You should have told me in private."

"That wouldn't have done at all, Mrs. Smiles. You needed independent witnesses, and that's what Schenck and I are; *we* can't be accused of favouritism or conspiracy."

"I needed witnesses to prove that that thing was in Cecilia's room?" Mrs. Smiles squeaked in her indignation.

"You did indeed. But we have no time; at any moment we may have unwelcome visitors. They may not arrive until morning, I hope very much that they won't; but on the other hand, they may arrive to-night. Somebody has tipped them off. I couldn't for the life of me imagine what other piece of evidence existed which might interest them, so I assumed Locke's pistol."

Cecilia Warren stirred in her chair. Mrs. Smiles looked dumbly at Gamadge. Belden half-rose.

"I'll get it out of here," he said. Gamadge was on his feet and between him and the table before he could take a step.

"Oh, Lord, Belden, don't *you* touch it!" He spoke irritably. "We must keep the record clear from now on; don't you see that? The servants and the apartment house staff must be able to swear that to the best of their knowledge none of us left early—nobody left earlier than anybody else; and all of you must be able to swear that you don't know where it is." He looked down at the pistol, exasperated. "It's the dickens of a thing to hide, too; it won't come to pieces and go down a drain, it mustn't be picked up in the street, and as for concealing it on the premises, that's impossible; you've no idea how a trained man searches a place. If it's in the apartment they'll find it."

Mrs. Smiles' double chin suddenly quivered. "Mr. Gamadge," she asked, "what shall we do?"

"Nothing. Can somebody oblige me with a ball of string?"

Cecilia Warren rose and went to a marquetry cabinet. She returned with a ball of thin green twine, suitable for tying up Christmas packages. She handed it to Gamadge without meeting his eyes.

"Couldn't be better," he said cheerfully. "Now, if you'll excuse me for a minute or two—I suppose I shan't run into Blatchford in the hall?"

Mrs. Smiles shook her head. "They're all out at the back. He won't come now unless I ring."

"Good. Miss Prady, I hold myself responsible for this pistol." He picked it up in the handkerchief and stood before her, holding it out for her inspection. "Can you trust me to produce it again, when and if its appearance seems necessary?"

She looked about her, and back at him. "They're all scared to death of you, so I guess I needn't be."

"You guess correctly." He slid the wrapped pistol into a tail pocket, crossed the room, and opened the lobby doors. He went into the lobby, climbed the winding staircase, and chose the middle door of a row in the upper hall. He entered a large, luxurious bedroom, lighted by a dim pink lamp on a night table; the table stood beside a vast painted bed, canopied, and raised on a shallow platform—authentic Louis Seize. There were two tall windows, draped with brocade curtains.

Gamadge parted the curtains of the right-hand window, lifted the sash, and leaned out. Four stories below him he saw the dark well of the stone balcony, and its row of little trees in big pots. No one was walking along this quiet street, there was no traffic, and his was the only car parked at the kerb near the awning.

Scowling at the light on the Park Avenue corner, he fastened the free end of the green twine to the trigger guard of the pistol; then he leaned out and lowered the pistol gently down. When it had sunk out of sight into the darkness of the balcony he emptied his pockets of loose change, and picked out the nickels and pennies; these he rolled tightly in his handkerchief, and then stuffed the roll into the middle of the ball of string. He leaned far out again, holding his breath; the ball also fell straight into the darkness within the balcony railing. He withdrew his head and shoulders, closed the window, and readjusted the curtains.

When he returned to the drawing-room he found the party scattered. Mrs. Smiles alone had remained in her chair; she had got a bit of lace and a steel crochet needle out of her bag, and was working on it. Cecilia Warren stood alone at the other end of the hearth, an elbow on the mantelpiece. Miss Prady was wandering in and out of the writing-room, and Belden, at the grand piano in a corner, was picking out bits of *The Three-Cornered Hat*; his great hands spread powerfully over the keyboard. Schenck had found a pack of cards, and was showing Clara a trick; Colby stood watching them—his face expressed deep dissatisfaction. He stopped Gamadge, to say: "Look here—I want an explanation."

"We must have no secrets from the rest of the party; that was understood." Gamadge proceeded across the room, went to Mrs. Smiles, and lifted his empty hands. He said: "I don't think they'll find it."

Mrs. Smiles looked up at him, grave and wary. "Why not, young man? Why shouldn't they?"

"Because they don't trust the source of their information enough to make them feel they can tear the building to pieces. I don't like to break up the party, Mrs. Smiles, but I really think it would be best for all of us to go—together."

As Clara rose, Belden got up from the piano bench. He slouched over to her. "I think perhaps I owe you an apology, Mrs. Gamadge," he said.

"I don't blame you for being angry."

"It's obvious the man wouldn't have made you look for the thing without good reason. I'm apologizing to your wife, Gamadge; let me do the same by you and your friend."

Gamadge said: "No apology is required. I suggest that we all go down in the elevator together; we must avoid the faintest suggestion of conspiracy." His eyes wandered to Miss Prady.

Belden said: "I'm staying—all night, if necessary. You don't think I'm going to leave those two women to deal with cops? If"—his smile widened—"there really are going to be cops."

"If they're alone there'll be no trouble with the cops," said Gamadge. "If you're here, there may be. A couple of men will probably arrive, armed with a warrant; they'll civilly ask permission to search, they'll find nothing, and they'll go away. If you hang about trying to give them orders they'll stay longer, and they'll ask more questions; and it will seem very queer to them to find a dinner guest still on the premises."

Mrs. Smiles looked up from her lacework. "You'd better go, Paul."

Cecilia Warren rang, Blatchford appeared, and Clara and Miss Prady went upstairs. Gamadge joined Miss Warren at the door.

"Have you the key to the Gregson car?" he asked.

"Yes."

"May I borrow it?"

She went into the writing-room, and came back with the key. As she handed it to him, Gamadge looked steadily down into her pale face. "If you have a duplicate," he said, "don't use it."

She said: "I don't know what you mean. I don't know what any of this means."

"Don't you?"

Her eyes fell. She was about to turn away, but he said again: "Don't take that car out, Miss Warren."

She moved away as if she had not heard him.

Six persons crowded into the elevator, and the night-man thought it was rather a quiet going-home party. Of course Mr. Belden cracked a few jokes with a red-headed man whom the night-man had never seen before; he had never seen any of them before except Mr. Belden. He thought it was a funny kind of a mixture, but trust old lady Smiles to round up all sorts.

Colby's last attempt to buttonhole Gamadge was foiled on the kerb. Gamadge had offered Miss Prady a lift, and was getting her into the back of the car with Clara; Schenck awaited him on the front seat.

"Gamadge," insisted Colby, "you owe me some sort of an explanation, and I want it to-night. You can't expect me to let things go like this, without asking a question."

"Not now, old man, if you don't mind." Gamadge got into the driver's seat. "Miss Prady's gone to pieces; I must take her home."

Miss Prady, in fact was in floods of tears, and Clara had taken her hand. Colby drew back, embarrassed. "Well—the first thing in the morning, then."

Gamadge made no reply, but started the car.

"It must have been awful for you, Miss Prady, simply awful," said Clara. "I don't wonder you're upset."

"I hate that Belden," sobbed Miss Prady. "He was laughing and sneering because I tried to be cheerful and not spoil the dinner party."

"You were splendid," said Clara.

"That Belden seemed to think I was a joke."

"It's just his manner."

"He'd better not joke about that pistol."

"I think he was dreadfully frightened when he saw it."

"I nearly fainted. Was it really in Miss Warren's room?"

"Yes." Clara looked troubled. "I hated doing that, Miss Prady, it was awful; but my husband wanted me to, and he wouldn't have asked me to do it if it hadn't been necessary."

"I thought you were fine. They were all scared half to death." Miss Prady dried her tears. "I wish Benny could have seen them. That Warren girl—she was actually scared stiff, and it's the first time I realized what that meant. I've often said it, but I never saw it happen before. Stiff. She could hardly walk. I wish Benny had been there."

"Well, but, Miss Prady; if he'd been there none of it would have happened."

"You know what I mean."

A red light stopped the car. Gamadge said, over his shoulder: "You think they're all in it, Miss Prady."

"I don't suppose that Mr. Colby is in it. That Belden looks so cruel."

"He was certainly very nervous—perhaps for the first time in his life."

Schenck remarked: "He wasn't any more nervous than I was. You're enough to make a rhinoceros nervous. What was that gunplay for, anyhow? You didn't get a thing out of it that I could see."

"I got a lot out of it; I got what I wanted out of it."

"I think it was wonderful," said Miss Prady.

"He's a wonderful feller," said Schenck, "but this time I don't care for his technique."

"Did you ever hear a saying about desperate remedies?" inquired Gamadge, driving on. "And have you ever been to the city of Utica?"

"Utica? Of course I have. I've been everywhere."

"Can you tell me anything about the night trains going there?"

Schenck turned his head to fix Gamadge with a startled eye. "You're going to Utica?"

"To Omega. I have to go to Utica first, I'm afraid."

"There's a train from the Grand Central to Utica at about midnight. It gets there around eight a.m." Schenck still gazed at Gamadge's profile. After a moment he asked: "You're going up there *to-night*?"

"If I can catch the train."

Gamadge drew up in front of the rooming-house, but did not allow Schenck to get out of the car. He himself assisted

Miss Prady to the pavement, and accompanied her up the steps and into the vestibule. They conversed in low tones while she got out her key. Schenck leaned over the back of his seat.

"What's he going to Utica for?" he asked.

"I didn't know he even thought of going. It's all so strange."

"You married a strange character."

"Yes, but since Tuesday he hasn't been a bit like himself. What's the matter with him? Talk about Mr. Belden being nervous! Henry's so nervous he's half-sick."

"I must admit I've never known him to go on this way before. I can't make any sense of it."

The front door of the rooming-house closed behind Miss Prady, and Gamadge came back to the car. When they reached the Gamadge house Schenck was about to open his door; Gamadge again restrained him.

"Did you think we'd dump you?" he asked. "After the pal you've been to-night?"

"I thought you were in a hurry to go to Utica."

"So I am. Will you drive yourself home, and call up our garage, and get a man to put the car away?"

"I'll drive to the garage, you maniac. I know where it is."

"That's asking too much."

"Is it?" laughed Schenck.

"Well, I must dash."

"Call them up; that train may go a minute or so before midnight. In any case, you have plenty of time."

Schenck watched the Gamadges into their house, shook his head, and drove away. Gamadge rushed upstairs, followed by Clara. He began to change into day clothes, shouting directions to his wife while she packed a bag for him.

"Just for overnight, you know, but don't forget my razor blades. Call the station, will you, darling?... 11.59, is it? I'll make it, easy. How much money have you in the house? I want all of it, and all mine. Look in my desk."

"When will you be back? To-morrow?" Clara scurried from one errand to another.

"I'll telephone. Expect me when you see me."

"You said overnight."

"I hope that's all it will be."

Clara jammed a toilet-case into the bag. "Will the police

ask us all questions?" she inquired. "Everybody who was at the party this evening?"

"Don't know why they should be interested in the party."

"Eight people, including me, know about my finding that pistol! Eight is an awful lot of people to keep a secret."

"Eight hundred can keep a secret if each one of them is determined to keep it."

"Will Miss Prady keep it?"

"Yes, she will."

"Your bag's ready, Henry."

"And I have nineteen minutes." He picked up the bag, and they went downstairs. Gamadge put on his coat and hat, and then seized his wife in his arms. She said: "I wish I knew how I could find you to-morrow."

"I don't want you to know. If Durfee should call up, tell him you have no idea. Tell him I'm doing his job for him. I'll never forget what a sport you were to-night, Clara. I wouldn't have asked you to do it, but I was in a jam, and I had no time."

"It's all right."

"Never again."

Gamadge picked up his bag and ran. He caught the South Shore Express with a minute to spare.

XIV

Omega

At eight o'clock on the following morning—Friday, November 28th—Gamadge found the city of Utica bathed in sunshine. He found a restaurant, had a comfortable breakfast, and then went to a garage and hired a car. He reached the uninteresting little town of Omega at half-past nine.

He inquired his way to a brick-faced building on Main Street, and climbed a flight of uncarpeted stairs to the second, and top, floor; there was a sign directing him to the office of the Omega *Times*. He found the editor and proprietor, a sweater over his shirt sleeves, reading a copy of his own newspaper at a desk in front of the window. A stove burned redly in one corner.

"Good morning," said Gamadge. "My name's Henry Gamadge; I came up from New York last night to call on you, if you're the editor of the *Times*."

"That's who I am, name's Davis." Mr. Davis pushed back his spectacles and took in the well-dressed caller, who would have looked even better dressed if he had held himself properly. As it was, he stood with one shoulder slightly higher than the other; and he had the stoop that comes from poring over papers.

"I wanted a little information about some of your Omega residents—or ex-residents; and I thought that this was the place to apply—if you'll be kind enough to give me a few minutes of your time. Er—is the paper a daily, Mr. Davis?"

"We come out regular once a week. Sit down, Mr. Gamadge." Davis waved a freckled and ink-stained hand towards a chair.

"Thanks very much." But Gamadge chose a corner of a pine table. He slid his coat from his shoulders, and laid his hat beside him. Davis stroked his chin, which needed a shave.

"You a newspaper man yourself?" he asked.

"No, I examine documents; handwriting, that sort of thing. But I do a little writing on the side. I've published several books on forged writings and so on. If you want credentials I'll be only too delighted to foot the bill for a long-distance call to my publishers in New York."

Davis said: "You looking up evidence about forged writings in Omega?" He really said "Omegy"; the upstate terminal *y*-sound fell pleasantly on Gamadge's ears; Gamadge had spent the summers of his childhood near Cooperstown.

"No, I'm interested in an old murder case."

Davis said: "We only had one of those."

"I know."

"It's been written up about a hundred times."

"You'd be surprised how popular a certain kind of write-up would still be; a new slant, you know, Mr. Davis. New point of view, new treatment of the background."

"We had fellers up here from New York, Albany, Philadelphy; we had a man from Boston."

"Naturally—looking up stuff about Mrs. Gregson; looking up the Voories background. That was before the trial, Mr. Davis, wasn't it? They were concentrating on Mrs. Gregson, weren't they?"

Davis said nothing; he regarded Gamadge steadily.

"But I thought of doing something about the other people in the case; new material there, Mr. Davis."

Davis said nothing.

"For instance: Miss Warren emerged as an interesting personality—almost as interesting as Mrs. Gregson herself."

Davis said ironically that she certainly did.

"But her background didn't emerge. By the time Gregson died she really had none; she'd been away from Omega for years, her mother had died twenty-odd years before, her father seven."

"That's so."

"There's a human interest angle to it. I understand that the father sent her to a good school, and that she was a promising kind of girl; then she goes down to Bellfield, Connecticut, to live with her rich relations——"

"Gregson wasn't supposed to be more than well-to-do."

"But he really was a little better than well-to-do, after all. Miss Warren was put into a business school, and became a typist and stenographer. If the Gregsons couldn't do better for her than that, why should she have left Omega at all? She could have got a job in Utica, I suppose; lived at home, and helped her father. Even if he'd lost all his money——"

"Spent it," said Davis. "He had just enough left to keep himself, and pay the man that looked after him."

"He must have spent a lot of it on her. But she never came back here, not even when he was dying; not even when he died."

Davis chewed a red moustache. Then he said: "I understood he went to pieces after his wife died, and never came together again."

"How? Drink?"

"Not in Omega, he didn't drink; that's something the folks in a place like this can check up on, no matter how secluded a man lives. The Warren house is off by itself, but in a dry town people know whether a man has a boot-legger or not."

"What was the matter with him, that he couldn't have his daughter at home? I understood it was drink."

"Nobody around town knew exactly what was the matter with him. His mind went towards the last, and then his heart gave out. He was in the best hospital in Utica for a couple of months before he died."

"What did your obituary notice say?"

"Heart trouble was what Dr. Lamb gave us. I didn't hear there were any complications."

"Except that he'd gone out of his head."

"That was the general impression around town; but the house is pretty far out, as I said, and no close neighbours. The Warrens never mixed much with us Omegans; Warren's practice was in Uticy."

"This Dr. Lamb—is he still in practice here?"

"Right on Elm Street." Davis squinted up at Gamadge. "I wouldn't exactly care to send you to him about this. I wouldn't care to be quoted on it."

"You haven't told me anything I couldn't get from anybody; you've just been kind enough to save me some steps," said Gamadge, looking much surprised.

"The way the trial went, I wouldn't care to turn any kind of a spotlight on Cecilia Warren. *She* didn't get acquitted of murdering Gregson."

"Don't you go putting ideas into my head!" Gamadge smiled at him as if amused.

"I'll try not to." Davis was evidently puzzled. He continued to look up at Gamadge with his head on one side.

"Would it be against your principles to tell me something about the man Miss Warren intends to marry?"

"Who's that?"

"Mr. Paul Belden, of Amsterdam."

"Going to marry him, is she?"

"So I believe."

"I don't know anything about her, haven't known anything for years, except what I read when the papers ran the murder and the trial."

"You Omegans were agreed on murder, were you?"

"Most of us thought it must be murder. I never even saw this Paul Belden, but I understood that he was quite a cut-up here and in Amsterdam. With the girls, you know. There was quite some talk about a girl like Cecilia Warren going with him. You can imagine that people raked up all kinds of old stories when the papers began to run the case." He added: "I wouldn't care to be quoted on it."

Gamadge's smile was quizzical. "But if new light were ever thrown on the Gregson case I suppose your paper wouldn't absolutely refuse to print the facts?"

"We absolutely print anything, except libel."

"I shouldn't care to dabble in libel myself. I don't know what's worrying you so much, Mr. Davis. The Gregson case is still news."

"If some city snooper dug around and found out that Warren was crazy," said Davis, with sufficient good nature to rob his words of offence, "people might wonder if the girl wasn't loony herself; loony enough to kill Gregson without motive. It always sounded kind of loony to me—that story about hearing Gregson laugh."

"I should think that that *would* have come out—Warren being crazy."

"People had it that he used to run around at night—run wild. But most of the talking about him came later, as I said—after the trial had got a good start. People were good and mad about that evidence—Gregson laughing, you know. The Voories family was always well liked here."

"Better than the Warren family?"

"Cecilia Warren was a stiff kind of girl, they tell me; little too good for Omega."

Gamadge slid off his corner of the table, and pulled on his coat. He said: "I can't say how much obliged I am to you for giving me so much of your time. I wish I could express my gratitude in some way. Do you smoke cigars, Mr. Davis?"

"Too many." Davis rose.

"That's something for me to remember." Gamadge shook hands with him across the scarred desk.

He did not think that Mr. Davis would carry his scrupulousness so far as to telephone and warn Dr. Lamb, but he lost no time in getting himself to Elm Street. A brass sign beside the front door of a neat, pumpkin-coloured frame house encouraged him to stop the hired car.

The middle-aged woman in the checked apron who answered his ring said that the doctor was on his rounds, and wouldn't be in the office till noon. Gamadge left word that he would be back at that hour, and drove to a drugstore. He entered its telephone booth and called Five Acres.

Harold informed him that the patient was fine. "She got over the news about Locke; she eats and sleeps and takes walks."

"Stick right with her from now on."

"How often do you think you have to tell me that?"

"I mean *right* with her. Unless you're sure she's safe in her room, string along; keep awake at night."

"How long am I to go without sleep?"

"Till to-morrow. I'll be back by then; I'm in Omega, N.Y."

"For gosh sakes!"

"Nice town, reminds me of Fourth of July parades and raffles for the benefit of the church carpet."

"Mr. Colby called up this morning."

"Damn. Why can't he let her alone?"

"She wasn't in."

"Put her telephone out of order."

"What?"

"Bust her telephone."

"Tully——"

"Never mind Tully."

"She'll use the booth down here."

"No, she won't. If he comes up, tell Tully to tell him Mrs. Greer can't be disturbed. I won't have him upsetting her," shouted Gamadge.

"The message was that he couldn't come up, but that he'd try to make it during the week-end."

Gamadge muttered something, and rang off.

He got back into the car, and drove himself on a tour of inspection through the village of Omega, admiring first the old Voories homestead among its now all but leafless maples; it was occupied, so a passing native told him, by people from Rochester named Brant. He then travelled out to the edge of town, and contemplated a desolate white house with a pillared porch; it was so far back from the road, so screened by evergreens, that only one dark window stared at him through the branches like a malevolent eye. A sign on the picket fence said that the property was for sale.

Ten years had broken one of the pillars, and had turned

the sloping lawn into a wilderness. Gamadge's inner eye
projected an odd and disquieting picture upon that background—a moving picture of a man in a floating red bathrobe
flitting among the firs, pursued by a questionable shape in
white; which turned out to be a male nurse or orderly. Why
his imagination should clothe Warren in red, or give him a
flying red belt with tassels, Gamadge did not know.

He turned the car, and drove slowly back to Dr. Lamb's.
The doctor was in this time, and would see him; Gamadge
was ushered into a combination sitting-room and office, very
snug, where a man of sixty-something with a grey beard sat in
a Morris chair and read a medical journal. At Gamadge's
entrance he got up, looking pleased and inquisitive.

"I saw by your card that you've come all the way from
New York, Mr. Gamadge," he said, shaking hands with the
visitor.

"Yes. I hope I'm not delaying your patients, Doctor, or
your lunch?"

"Not at all." Lamb's eyes roved from Gamadge's head to
his feet, and back to his face again. "As for lunch, I hope
you'll join us for it. My wife would be pleased."

"Awfully good of you, but I hope to catch the early
afternoon train from Utica."

"Well, sit down and let's see what I can do for you. I
don't suppose you're here for a diagnosis?" He smiled. "I
understand that there are some competent men down your
way."

Gamadge admitted that he had not come for a diagnosis.
He sat down in the comfortable chair designated by his host,
but he himself felt far from comfortable. He said: "I do
research work on manuscripts, documents, old books. I've
written some things, for the most part on literary forgeries. I
mention them because they and my job have somehow led
me into the field of criminological investigation. I'm an
amateur, but I have worked with the police."

Lamb's cheerful face had altered. He said slowly: "That
must be interesting."

"It's interesting enough, but in the course of research I
find myself occasionally forced to ask embarrassing questions
of total strangers."

"We doctors are forced to ask embarrassing questions in

the course of research." Lamb, now definitely uneasy, maintained a smile.

"I hoped you would be willing to help me in getting to the truth of a matter of some importance. Let me beg you to believe that my motives in asking you for your assistance are high; mixed, you know, as human motives are so apt to be; but on the whole, high."

Lamb's smile had faded.

"I may say," continued Gamadge, "that I shall not publish the results of my investigation unless I should be absolutely forced, in the interests of common justice, to do so; I don't think I shall be. I need facts, Doctor, and I need them quickly. The only person who can give them to me without delay is yourself."

Lamb said: "I don't know what you can possibly want of me in the way of facts."

"I'll put my business in the form of a statement, which we can discuss later. Cecil Warren, when he died, had been a morphia addict for more than twenty years. He died in a Utica hospital of heart trouble, whether induced or aggravated by morphia does not matter to me; and the hospital records can and, if necessary, will be produced to show what his condition was when he went there. I don't want to waste time over the procedure involved in the production of hospital records; and the last thing I want is to go to the police. I intend to keep this whole investigation private—if I can.

"Morphia was the reason why Cecil Warren sent his daughter away from him and kept her away. Whether or not he knew that he was dying, he wouldn't even have her sent for by the hospital. He had chosen, once and for all, between her and his drug, and he stuck heroically to his choice—he gave her up."

The Morris chair creaked as Lamb's strong hands grasped the arms of it. He said nothing.

"The tube of morphia which was produced at the Gregson trial," continued Gamadge, "was more than twenty years old. You of course knew, Doctor, where it had come from."

"Knew? Knew?" Lamb glared at him.

"Had you really any doubts?"

"If you suppose that I, as a physician, would have been justified in coming forward with guesswork——"

"Well; Mrs. Gregson was on trial for her life."

"I knew they'd never convict!" Lamb pounded the arms of his chair. "They had only to look at Vina Gregson."

"You should see her now."

Lamb frowned heavily. He said: "I suppose you're going to try to reopen the Gregson case; I suppose you're out to ruin that girl." He laughed. "Do you know that when tubes of morphia were knocking about in the Warren house she wasn't seven years old?"

"We don't know how long that particular tube had been in the Warren house. She didn't leave home for good until she was sixteen or seventeen. What would you have done, Doctor, if Mrs. Gregson had been convicted?"

"Don't remind me of the possibility." Lamb threw himself back in his chair. "I have nightmares about it yet."

"I don't wonder."

"If I'd come forward at that trial and talked about that tube of morphia, there'd have been a miscarriage of justice."

"I don't know Miss Warren."

"Handsome girl; brilliant girl; and her father was one of the most brilliant men I ever knew in my life. His wife and I had him cured three times—or thought we had. She died of it at last. And when he really began to go under for good, the house wasn't a fit place for a girl to live in. Cecilia Warren's childhood was a tragedy. For years, no outsider knew that anything was the matter with Warren; and then he was supposed to be drinking, or out of his head. Nobody ever guessed drugs, and only about six people ever knew he took morphia. Three of them are at the hospital—one doctor and two nurses."

"You kept the secret very well."

"I promised his wife I'd keep it. We didn't keep it well enough," said Lamb morosely, "if you got hold of it. That poor girl—she made friends with a young fellow named Belden; talky, irresponsible kind of lad from out of town. He made a tomboy of her, kept her away from the kind of friends she ought to have had. Of course it came to nothing."

"They're now engaged to be married."

"I'm sorry to hear it. Well, I've given you a notion of what she grew up with; I take my hat off to the way she pitched in and went to work afterwards."

"Very strong character."

"Why was I to suppose she'd have any of that morphia in her possession after all that time?"

"She might have found the tube among her mother's effects. I dare say Mrs. Warren had a supply, if she was helping you with her husband's cure; I dare say he hid his own supply in all sorts of places."

"All over the house. Look here—I've always argued that Gregson's death wasn't murder. If that tube was among Cecilia's traps—if she really did keep it—he found it, and took an overdose. Accidentally or not, who can say?"

Gamadge met Lamb's almost pleading look with a smile. "Well, Doctor, you know what juries are."

"I know I wasn't prepared to trust one of 'em with Cecilia Warren's life."

"That celebrated tube of morphia must have weighed heavily on you, during these last three years."

"I thought I intimated as much." Lamb spoke with exasperation.

"More heavily than you have intimated. Do you know, I think you could have identified it, Doctor; I think you could identify it still."

Lamb's face looked greyish in the sunlight. He said: "Nonsense."

Gamadge faced him gravely. "I said I wouldn't use this information about the morphia unless I absolutely had to use it. Now I'll say more. I needed it, and I need your positive identification of that tube of morphia, to establish a working theory of this case. I give you my word that I won't go to the police with it, and I'll never publish a word of it in any form. You'll never hear of it, you'll never be involved, and all you will have done is to help me right a wrong and perhaps prevent a crime."

They exchanged a long look. Gamadge added gently: "And that tube of morphia needn't trouble your dreams any more."

Lamb silently interrogated the blunt features and the clear gaze of his remarkable guest. Then he said: "Warren got a batch of tubes from some medical quack or mal-practitioner. The serial numbers had been torn off the labels to protect the man who was selling them. I always thought it was some scoundrel of a doctor."

"I imagined so." Gamadge rose, and stood looking down into Lamb's woeful face. "Set your mind at rest."

"There's more to my side of it than you know about. If I could explain, you might exonerate me in the matter."

"I think I do know your side of it."

"That's more than I can believe."

"Do you take me for a fool?"

They exchanged another long look. The doctor rose, and slowly put out his hand; Gamadge took it. "In your position," he said, "hanged if I know what I should have done myself."

He drove back to Utica, turned in the car, and had some lunch. By the time he had bought a paper-covered book and a magazine the south-bound express came in; he boarded it with the presumption that as usual he would have no trouble in killing time. But the five-hour trip strained his mental resources beyond their capacity. He sat turning the case over in his mind until he found to his horror that he was getting a nervous headache; this he remedied with a cup of almost boiling tea in the club car, and a period of grim inactivity with the shade pulled down behind him and his eyes closed. When he could stand no more of it, he tried the book, tried the magazine, tried a crossword puzzle—in vain. He got a pack of cards from the porter, but his game—a last stand against nervous irritation—was interrupted by a little grey-faced man in the next chair, who wanted to talk about woollens and war. It seemed that he had conscientious objections to manufacturing army blankets.

Gamadge couldn't tackle it. "A moral problem's a personal thing," he said. "I don't feel competent to offer an opinion."

"But this is an economic problem, too. I have a family."

"Can't help it, it's a thing you must settle for yourself," said Gamadge, refraining from the observation that it would probably soon be taken out of the little man's hands and settled for him.

"Would you sacrifice *your* family to an ideal?"

"Can't say off-hand. Would you sacrifice yours to a mixed indignation?"

"A . . . ?"

"That's what I did, last night."

The little man stared. Gamadge went into the dim and swaying vestibule; he remained there, feeling stuffy and confused, until the train crawled into the tunnel at exactly seven twenty-five p.m.

XV

Gamadge Refuses a Drink

A succession of porters escorted Gamadge and his bag into the lobby of the Hotel Biltmore, and a page-boy led him to the desk. He engaged two rooms and a bath, explained that his friend might or might not arrive by a late train, and was taken up in the elevator. Once in his room, he made as careful a toilet as the contents of his bag allowed; he then dined in the grill.

Afterwards he took a cab to his garage. He seemed rather anxious about the weather, and consulted the taxi driver. "I don't think it's going to rain," he said.

"I don't, too."

Gamadge transferred himself to his own car, and drove up-town. He stopped several doors east of the Smiles apartment, got out, and walked slowly along towards the columned doorway, his head in the air; he was contemplating the balcony which jutted out, not so far above him, from the second floor. It tantalized him almost beyond endurance, but he hadn't the courage to attempt operations by means of a step-ladder and the house porter.

He went in, strolled to the elevator, and asked for the second floor. When he reached it he walked confidently to the left and rang a bell. A well-turned-out maid answered it.

Gamadge produced a card. "I'm awfully sorry," he said, "but I'm in a silly predicament, and I should be very much obliged if you'd give my card to the lady or the gentleman of the house. Perhaps they'd see me for a minute."

The maid was not in her first youth, and looked capable of dealing promptly with strangers who were not expected and did not state their business. She looked at Gamadge, made no gesture towards accepting the card, and said she didn't think anybody was at home.

"I'm sorry for that. Perhaps you'll see whether they are or not. You can leave me out in the hall, you know."

"Would you mind saying what your business is?" Gamadge plainly baffled her.

"I lost something on their balcony."

The maid gave it up, shut Gamadge out into the hall, and then opened the door again to take his card from him. Gamadge waited for some time. At last she reappeared, said that he was to come in, and led him to a long and high drawing-room. She waited in the doorway.

Gamadge's eyes turned first to the big glass windows, reinforced by wrought-iron arabesques and huge locks and handles, which gave on the street. They looked capable of withstanding the assaults of a maddened proletariat. When he glanced away from them he met the protruding stare of a little man in dinner clothes, carefully manicured and massaged, who stood beside a table with one hand on a telephone. A tray on the table contained two cups of coffee, a silver pot, a silver sugar bowl, a little glass-and-silver decanter, and two small glasses.

"I do most sincerely beg your pardon for intruding on you like this." Gamadge stood discreetly just within the door. "And I solemnly assure you that I am not a stick-up man."

The small gentleman in dinner clothes smiled, took his hand away from the telephone, and said: "Evidently not. You can go, Mabel."

The maid backed slowly into the hall; a faint whisper of sound told Gamadge that she had departed. He said: "I don't blame you for taking precautions. Might I know to whom I'm indebted for this extreme courtesy?"

"Well—my name's Bulliter."

"Mr. Bulliter, I'm in the stupidest quandary you ever heard of, but please don't look horrified—I don't want to borrow money of you."

Mr. Bulliter ceased to look horrified; he looked mystified instead.

"As you see," said Gamadge, "I live not far away. I was on my way home, just now, and I may tell you that I'm in a devil of a hurry to get there; but I have a most unfortunate habit of throwing things up in the air and then catching them."

Mr. Bulliter considered this, his prominent eyes blank as those of a crab.

"Like a fool," said Gamadge, "I threw my cigarette case—family thing, old as the hills—I threw it up into the air in my idiotic way, just as I passed under your balcony; and this time I didn't catch it. It fell among the flower pots."

Mr. Bulliter's relief at having at last made some sense out of Gamadge was so great that he released his breath audibly. He even laughed.

"You can imagine," continued Gamadge, "what a fool I feel. I absolutely couldn't bring myself to explain to the maid!"

Mr. Bulliter said: "Tee hee. Don't blame you."

"Or to the people downstairs," said Gamadge. "I simply came up to throw myself on your mercy. I should have waited until to-morrow, or telephoned, or something; but it looks like rain."

Mr. Bulliter glanced at the long glass door, and back at Gamadge. He was entertained. "You really must let me tell my wife," he said. "Agnes, my dear."

Mrs. Bulliter came in from an adjoining parlour. She was taller than her husband, but her handsome dress compressed a figure as opulent as his own.

"Mr. Gamadge, my dear," said Bulliter.

Mrs. Bulliter, smiling and curious, asked how he did, and Gamadge asked how she did. Mr. Bulliter explained Gamadge's antics with his cigarette case, and their sequel; Mrs. Bulliter laughed very much.

"I can't tell you how I feel about this," said Gamadge plaintively. "I've interrupted your coffee."

"Have some, and have a drink," said Bulliter, his hand on a bell.

"Absolutely not, thank you all the same. I'm in the dickens of a hurry to get home. If you'll just let me go out on your balcony," said Gamadge, "I'll find it in no time." His skin crawled at Bulliter's expected and dreaded reply:

"Very dirty out there, I'm sure. Let me call the house-man."

"Or Mabel," said Mrs. Bulliter.

"No, really, I shouldn't think of it. I know just where the thing fell." Gamadge's hand tightened on the brim of his hat.

"Well, at least you've kept your coat on." Mr. Bulliter suddenly started forward. "Good heavens, are we all dreaming? Let me have your hat, and take your coat off, do. Agnes, my dear, in the excitement Mabel never took Mr. Gamadge's coat and hat."

Mrs. Bulliter looked absolutely lost. She said: "I never heard of such a thing."

Gamadge laid down the hat on a table. He said: "I'll just keep the coat, if you don't mind. Now confess, Mrs. Bulliter; you were standing out there in the other room with your lips glued to the house telephone."

Mrs. Bulliter laughed gleefully, and said no. "I wasn't a bit frightened, because Mabel told us there was only one of you."

"Well, there'll be none of me in two minutes." Gamadge sidled in the direction of the balcony doors. Mr. Bulliter reached them first, and began to struggle with a stiff handle. Gamadge assisted him, and the heavy door swung inwards. Gamadge stepped with alacrity over the sill and down into a stone trough. He said: "Do step away, it's pretty cold."

Mr. Bulliter stepped away, but not far. Lamplight poured out over dusty shrubs in earthen pots, and Gamadge, squeezing himself between them and the wall of the building, could only hope that he made an effectual screen for his own activities. These consisted in feeling wildly among prickly branches and along a stone floor. He thought he would never find the things; but at last his hand closed on the pistol, and he ran his fingers along the cord attached to it, and seized the ball of string. He rewound it hastily, and pushed it into one pocket, and the gun into another. He got hold of his cigarette case, turned, and stepped back into the room.

"Found it!" He held it up in triumph, while Mr. Bulliter pushed the door shut. "Just where I thought it was." Relief flooded him, cooling as a fan; he realized that he had been bathed in the sweat of terror.

The Bulliters politely studied his battered old silver case; it had originally been a snuff-box, and eighteenth-century fingers had tapped away much of the fine chasing from the lid of it. Gamadge would almost as soon have parted with his house, but neither of the Bulliters showed enthusiasm over the relic.

"Very nice." Mr. Bulliter got out his own dull-gold affair, and Mrs. Bulliter extracted an onyx and platinum trinket from her bag. These, they civilly didn't say, *were* cigarette cases. Gamadge admired them from all angles; he felt a sudden hideous temptation to produce the object which was pulling his right-hand coat pocket out of shape, and ask the Bulliters to admire *that*. He could not help wondering what on earth would then happen to the Bulliters' pink faces.

The mad fancy died even as it was born. Mrs. Bulliter said: "I do wish you'd change your mind and have a cup of coffee with us, and some kümmel."

"You're awfully good, I mustn't stay." He picked up his hat.

"At least let us explain why we were a little nervous when you came," said Bulliter. "The police were in the house this morning."

"No; were they?"

"I thought you might be a plain-clothes man," continued Bulliter. "That was my second thought, you know—before I saw you."

"What were police doing here?"

"Oh, not *here*; the elevator man said they were up in Mrs. Smiles' apartment," said Mrs. Bulliter. "I don't know whether you know who she is—Mrs. Joseph Smiles?"

Bulliter winked at Gamadge. "Old Smiling Joe's widow. In the old days none of us would have been much surprised to hear that the police had visited old Joe."

"I should have been surprised," said Gamadge, "very much surprised. From what I hear, the police never had the slightest chance of catching up with him. But why should they call on his widow?"

"Perhaps he left her that oil stock nobody could ever find," tittered Mr. Bulliter.

"Perhaps burglars got some of those enormous diamonds she wears," said his wife.

Gamadge said, "Perhaps," shook hands, and told the Bulliters once more how sorry he was to have disturbed them, and how grateful he was. A smiling Mabel let him out of the apartment, and he went down in the elevator with his hat pulled rather low, and his hand on the gun in his pocket.

He got into his car, drove round the block, and headed south.

XVI

A Door Is Found

Every night, after the last patient had gone up to bed, Mrs. Tully or Miss Lukes went round below-stairs, put up chains and shot bolts, locked doors with her special key, and retired, confident that Five Acres was secure without and within. Harold could have told her that it was not; he had found a window in the new east wing—a pantry window—which could be operated on with a pen-knife. He used it to make his own late entrance for his private tour of inspection, and departed afterwards by the same way. He was impelled to this course of conduct not only by a scientifically thorough turn of mind, but by a heavy sense of responsibility; this was the first time that Gamadge had left a matter of real importance entirely in his hands.

But strangers would not know about the lock on the pantry window; moreover, the east wing, which contained the dining-room, the kitchen, pantries, storerooms, and a laundry, was on his end of the house. He could take care of it, and of the roof that sheltered the outside cubicles, and that ran under Mrs. Gregson's window and along the back of the place. The front upper windows were all locked at night; they belonged to empty bedrooms, a sun parlour, a little infirmary, and the doctor's office. Harold was obliged to hope that the occupied bedrooms could not be entered at night with impunity.

On Friday, at about half-past eleven, he left the house by the pantry window, snapped the bolt, and retired to his terrace room. He left the door wide open, rolled himself in blankets, and lay down on his cot. It was early for possible marauders, but soon he would make another patrol of the grounds. He wished that he were back in his room at the top of Gamadges' house in New York, with noises in the street outside; there were noises here, plenty of them, but they were veiled and ambiguous. He had investigated several of them the night before—rustlings and scrabblings, sounds like footsteps on the terrace, a creak and a thumping near the garage. They might have been caused by wind in the shrubbery, squirrels, bats, cats; they might have been his imagination; but at least no human being had produced them.

The night was very dark; there had been a leaden sky since dusk. He couldn't see the line of hills to the north-east, he couldn't see much of anything, now that the patients' lights were out. Darkness like this seemed to make night noises even more vague and numerous, but for a while he heard nothing at all. Then there was a faint, a very faint sound not far beyond his open doorway; it might be coming from just round the corner of the house. It sounded like footsteps on grass, but Harold took no stock in it. However, he got up, pushed his feet into rubber-soled shoes, and buttoned his sweater. When he reached the terrace he looked up; Mrs. Gregson's north window was closed and dark.

He was actually at the angle of the house wall, had actually peeped round it, before he heard the voice. It was only a whisper, but he caught the words: "... won't go without seeing you. Can't I come up?"

A figure, curiously hunched, stood ten paces away from him; under Mrs. Gregson's east window, looking up. It was hatless, but something shrouded its head and obscured the shape of it. To a being so shadowy among shadows, so absorbed, Harold felt invisible; but he withdrew until—clinging against brickwork—he was just able to see round the corner.

Mrs. Gregson was at her open window. She leaned out to murmur: "I tell you you can't get in. I'll come down."

The figure moved back, melting into the dark of the shrubbery. Mrs. Gregson came out of the window backwards, found a foothold on the coping beneath, lowered herself to the sill of the lower window—it belonged to the lounge—and jumped to the ground. A sweater was round her shoulders, fastened at the neck, and her handbag was on her arm.

"Darned fool woman," thought Harold angrily. But she seemed not to have lost all her common sense; she remained where she was. The figure came out from among bushes, and stopped too. "I brought your car," it said. "We can sit in it."

It moved off, towards the front of the house, and Mrs. Gregson followed. There were at least four yards between them; Harold, as he stalked them along the wall, knew suddenly what the leading figure reminded him of. He had seen a coyote in the zoo, and he remembered the way it had cringed along, afraid yet menacing, ready for defence or safe attack.

It went straight past the house, diagonally across the lawn, and to the highway; glancing up once at the dark front windows, and then plodding on, its head down, as if it were on a trail. Mrs. Gregson kept steadily on behind; a determined look about her, too; determined and cautious. "She thinks she can handle it," thought Harold. "She wouldn't like it if she thought Mr. Thompson was following her around, all ready to jump into her business."

The little procession went down the highway, a black tunnel under its interlacing tree branches; not so black, though, as the pocket of darkness that seemed to open on the right. The women turned into it. Harold, muttering, put on speed; a car stood within the lane, its rear towards him, its lights off. He was up behind it as Mrs. Gregson got into the right-hand front seat, and had gained the running-board below the left-hand window as the other closed that door and slid under the wheel.

He craned up; the strange woman was bending forward, her profile a dim enigma; Mrs. Gregson sat back, watching her, her face set and stern. It was in a kind of incredulous stupor that he saw Mrs. Gregson's left arm come up, and saw the knife in her hand.

He heard himself shout as he plunged. He would have received the long blade in his arm if another hand had not come from the dark rear of the car to grasp her wrist. For a second he had a glimpse of her face as the lights came on—an unforgettable and frozen mask; then, as Gamadge's appeared behind it, he ceased to look at Mrs. Gregson.

"For goodness' sake," said Gamadge, "drop the thing."

The knife fell from her fingers. Harold caught it—a kitchen knife, sharp and pointed. He stared at it, stared at Gamadge, and turned to look at the other woman; she lay forward over the wheel, and he wondered vaguely whether she had fainted.

"All right, Miss Prady," said Gamadge. "Harold, see if Miss Prady's all right, I shouldn't blame her if she'd collapsed."

Miss Prady raised herself, to say in a gasping voice: "It's just that I was too scared."

"Slide out of the car and get in here with me."

Harold opened the door for her, and helped her to the road. Her face, framed by the silk scarf she wore round her head, looked greenish in the car lights. Her shoulders were still hunched as if against an expected blow.

"I was afraid every minute that she'd do something." Miss Prady's breathing was still uncertain as she climbed into the back of the car.

"You were a magnificent sport. But you knew she wouldn't try anything till she had you in the car; and if I hadn't seen my friend here come out after you I'd have stuck by you myself. As it was, I ran round the house and cut across lots to get here ahead of you. Harold, will you get in there under the wheel?"

Harold got into the seat beside Mrs. Gregson. She had not moved in any way since she released her weapon; she sat with fixed eyes, hardly seeming to draw breath. Gamadge held her wrist lightly. He said: "Miss Prady and I are here to make a deal with you, Mrs. Gregson."

She might not have heard him; Gamadge went on:

"It's good of Miss Prady, you know, since you killed her best friend; but she's obliged to me for clearing up the situation. It's good of me, too; if you'll forgive me for taking a personal view of the matter. You made a catspaw of my friend Colby, you tried to make one of me, and you did in fact make an awful fool of me on Wednesday when you walked away from Five Acres—before I'd even finished my lunch—and met Benton Locke, perhaps here in this very lane. I'm sure you got a good deal of amusement out of it; and if the case had been less serious, and Miss Warren's danger from you less great, your own sublime ignorance of the fact that I had already begun my campaign against you would have diverted *me*."

Mrs. Gregson's imprisoned wrist moved a little; then it was still again.

"I knew almost from the first," continued Gamadge, "that there had been no attempts against your life, and that you had written yourself that anonymous letter. I knew it

when you refused to change your will. A woman in terror of
her life would have changed it, if only as a temporary
measure; but you couldn't; you had to retain your suspect,
and to do that you had to keep her supplied with a motive.
Money could have been Miss Warren's only reason for trying
to kill you; you hoped to convince the world that it had been
her motive for killing Gregson.

"Which brings us to your motive; and it had become, as
I saw when I first met you, an obsession—a fixed idea. I
warned you against it, I begged you to take the money you
had killed your husband for and let these people alone. But
you were in a blind alley, or—let us say—the house without
the door. You would find the door, or smash down the walls.
Do you know, I was fool enough to pity you. Much as I hate a
poisoner, I confess that I pitied you.

"You didn't want pity, except as it furthered your cause.
All you wanted was to be cleared of Gregson's murder, once
and for all; to go out into the only world you cared about,
well-off and respectable; to live the only kind of life you
understood. But there was only one way to bring about that
consummation—you had to make a case against someone
else. Well, I've done my best to protect the victim; I've had
several tries at it; I even put you up here, fondly hoping that
you would be unable to plant evidence against her while you
were guarded night and day at Five Acres. You won the first
round of the battle; the others were to me. But I had to
persuade you to an indiscretion—before witnesses. Miss Prady
was good enough to help me, and so you see us here
to-night."

Mrs. Gregson spoke for the first time: "I thought *they*
had moved Benny."

"Never mind who moved him. The point that interests
me is this: safety from the law means nothing to you, isn't
worth a dime; but you may still, for all I know, be safe from
the law. I don't know what I can prove against you—I don't
know what a judge and jury would make of Miss Prady's foray
to-night; perhaps they would believe that you were merely
trying to defend yourself against blackmail and intimidation.
But I have been to Omega, Mrs. Gregson, and I have seen
Dr. Lamb."

She turned her head and looked at him. Gamadge went
on:

"He wouldn't bring that evidence against you at your trial; he wouldn't be the means of sending you to your death by telling how you had had opportunity to possess yourself of a tube of morphia with one corner torn off the label of it. Miss Warren has been terrorized by that tube of morphia, because she thinks it involves her, and *she* has never been acquitted of Gregson's death; that's why she regretted the impulse that made her tell how Gregson laughed. She withheld evidence, and her motive is forgivable; more so than Locke's, who withheld it because he knew that if you were to be convicted the Gregson money would all go to a Mr. Parrott in California.

"But Miss Warren didn't understand you; she never understood the depth and the power of that fixed idea of yours. You would never have mentioned that tube of morphia to a living soul, because it's the link that connects you with Gregson's murder. If people knew of it they would never believe that you are an innocent woman. They'd never believe it if they heard my story—the story of these last days.

"So we now arrive at the point I have been building up to, that it is quite useless for you to go on with your quest; and I repeat that Miss Prady and I are ready to make a deal. What have you done with Locke's car?"

Mrs. Gregson frowned. Then she said, her lips hardly moving: "I don't understand. What deal?"

"If you'll show us where you hid his car—you must have put it somewhere in this vicinity, but you couldn't let it be found near you—if you'll show me where it is, we'll all get out of this one; we'll leave you to drive on."

"On?"

"Wherever you want to go. We'll give you a long start—we'll give you till dawn. Nobody but ourselves knows when you attacked Miss Prady; we'll say you got away from us. You have plenty of money in that bag, I suppose? Your car's full of petrol and oil; there's a felt hat and a tweed coat back here, and a pair of gloves in one of the car pockets. You'll be quite comfortable. I don't see why you shouldn't get clean away, leave the car, and lose yourself. What do you think of the scheme?"

Mrs. Gregson sat silent, frowning. At last she said: "Drive straight along this lane."

Gamadge released her wrist, and she turned to face forward.

Harold started the car, and drove it up a narrow, steadily rising road. There were at first rolling fields to right and left, then the deep darkness of woods. They emerged again, always climbing. When they had gone a mile from the highway Mrs. Gregson said: "Stop here."

They were on the ridge of a hill. In front of them the headlights cut into emptiness, hemmed in by the shapes of trees. On either side of the road, beyond white railings, there seemed to be nothing.

Gamadge opened the car door and got out. He said, from the rail: "It looks a mile deep."

"There's a dry stream below the trees down there," said Mrs. Gregson, "but you can't see it, even in the daytime. I sent the car down at the end of the railing; I didn't want to leave a broken place."

"Well, we'll take your word for it that it's there."

"In the daytime you'll see the marks where it went over."

Gamadge had walked to the end of the railing. He struck a match, and after a moment said: "I can see them now. Thanks. All out, please."

As Harold left the car, Mrs. Gregson moved under the wheel. He remembered the firmness with which she grasped it, the indifference in her face as she looked ahead. Miss Prady got out, and began to walk away; all of a sudden she was crying violently.

"Oh, look here!" Gamadge came up beside her. "You've been magnificent; don't give way now. Harold, take her other arm—we'll get her away from this."

Miss Prady, between her sobs, said: "I didn't know what it was like, catching them."

"Yes. No fun in it."

They went along through darkness. Harold, looking over his shoulder, muttered: "Why don't she drive on?" And then: "Look out—she's turning; she'll be on top of us."

He pulled Miss Prady to the side of the road; but Gamadge stood in the middle of it, hands in pockets, facing the car. It backed across the lane, the throbbing of its engine a threatening roar. Suddenly, as if shot from an enormous gun, it leapt forward, through the railing, out and down.

They heard the muted crash of tree branches, a louder, ripping sound, and then nothing.

Miss Prady had clutched Gamadge's arm. She shrieked: "Why? Why?"

"She had to get out," said Gamadge. "That was the only door that was open. We must hurry a little, if you feel up to it; I must get to a telephone."

XVII

Driving Out of It

"How're you going to telephone us out of this?" inquired Harold dispassionately. He and Gamadge each had Miss Prady by an arm; as they walked down the dark lane she occasionally bent her head to get at the handkerchief in her hand and wipe her eyes with it.

"I'm going to drive us out of it," said Gamadge. "I have my car."

"You certainly left me on the outside of the case this time."

"Outside? You had the worst job of all. And how were you going to install Mrs. Gregson's radio for her without glowering, if you knew she'd just killed Benton Locke?"

"I still don't see how she worked it."

"Good heavens, she was probably off the place by the time we'd begun lunch; I went up afterwards and looked complacently at a sign on an empty room. Locke telephoned her on Tuesday night after I saw him, and told her that if she was manufacturing evidence of attempted murder against him, Cecilia Warren, or Mrs. Stoner, he'd publish the fact that she was in possession of a tube of morphia with a corner missing from its label at the time of her husband's death."

"How'd he know she had it?"

"When dependents are uncomfortable and unhappy, Harold, they forget their obligations to their benefactors;

they prowl, they snoop and they conspire. Mrs. Stoner's only crime from first to last was in warming and feeding her young friends at the expense of their miserly patron; but Benton Locke, a lonely, penniless, restless boy, no doubt explored the house for want of something better to do. He found the tube of morphia among Mrs. Gregson's possessions; she had kept it ever since the days when she had seen or even helped her aunt in the struggle to cure Cecilia Warren's father of drug-taking. Benton Locke knew nothing of its source; he told nobody about it; but when Gregson died, and that tube was found, Benton knew very well that Mrs. Gregson had killed him. Those tubes of morphia with their serial numbers missing were known to Cecilia Warren too."

"And they both kept quiet about it."

"Mrs. Gregson never dreamed that Locke knew of its existence. She was a woman of infinite resource, where her obsession was concerned, and when he telephoned she assured him that she didn't suspect *him* of wanting to kill her; but that she could tell him and Mrs. Stoner why she knew that Cecilia Warren was guilty of the attempts against her life. She said she didn't know where Five Acres was, but that he could follow us up here on Wednesday in his car, and wait along the road. He could drive her to Pine Lots, and she would present them with the evidence against Miss Warren.

"Locke pretended to agree; but he telephoned Cecilia Warren, advised her to be in on the conference, and perhaps suggested the presence at it of Paul Belden. He drove up here as arranged, picked her up as requested, and I suppose then informed her that Cecilia Warren would be present at the conference to speak for herself. That would have been an excuse for her to insist on a private word with him. She got him to stop at——"

Here Gamadge stopped himself.

"Made him drive up that road," supplied Miss Prady, bending to her handkerchief.

"And shot him with the gun that everybody knew he carried in his car. She left him there, say at a quarter past two. She posted the anonymous letter in Burford—the letter to the police, incriminating Cecilia Warren. It would take her an hour and a half to get to the Smiles apartment in New York, and plant the gun. Two hours back to Five Acres; that brings us to about five forty-five. She ran Locke's car along this lane and hid it in the woods; she was in her room long before I telephoned from Pine Lots and you reported on her. I suppose she had no hat on when she came back from that stroll?"

"No, she just had her knitting bag on her arm. I can't believe it now."

"You can believe that she had a hat in that knitting-bag."

"I don't know how you had the nerve to leave her loose and travel up to Omega." Harold was aggrieved.

"My dear boy, that's just the point—she wasn't loose! She had no car! I had been careful to separate her from her own, and Locke's was of no use to her. She wouldn't dare drive it again, much less take it to a filling-station; I checked on the mileage, and she must have used up all but a few gallons of petrol, even if Locke had it filled after he left New York on Wednesday."

"She ran that car into the gorge while she was supposed to be out walking to-day? She was crazy; that's all."

"No, she wasn't. Perhaps not quite human."

Harold felt a slight shudder. He said after a pause: "Anybody half-human would show something, after all that."

"You forget that Mrs. Gregson was obsessed. She had killed Gregson for the kind of life she wanted; she had been cheated of her reward by Cecilia Warren's ingenuous remark about a laugh; she had had three years to brood in. The Mrs. Gregsons are immensely concerned for their reputations; jealous of small social privileges and social position. This Mrs. Gregson was also without affection or imagination, with a terrific ego and an indomitable will."

Miss Prady said: "Benny told me she was so cruel. She was so jealous of Cecilia Warren. She liked to make her sleep in that little top-floor room in Bellfield."

"Yes. She shouldn't have indulged that fancy," said Gamadge. "It was the ruin of her, when Miss Warren moved down to the guest-room. What a risk she took, when she planted that gun at the Smiles apartment! But it was the only evidence she had, the only evidence which she could connect directly with Cecilia Warren. I dare say she was amused when poor Colby—how I hate to think of his horror when he hears all this—when he explained to us both on Tuesday how easy it is to get a duplicate key made. She had one to the Smiles apartment, no doubt had had it a long time. She knew when Miss Warren would be out, and what was the right time to go there. Well, Miss Prady, I gained your confidence by rather unorthodox methods; but thank goodness I did gain it, and you did most sportingly agree to meet me to-night and drive up here in the Gregson car. I made poor Cecilia Warren give me a key to it."

"What was that about blackmail?" said Harold. They had turned out of the lane, and were walking up the highway; faster, now.

"Miss Prady and I worked it out before we started up here. She telephoned to Mrs. Gregson and told her that she knew all about the tube of morphia from Locke. She said she needed money—"

"And that's true!" said Miss Prady.

"So Mrs. Gregson invited her to come up and get it. Really, Miss Prady showed extraordinary nerve; but she was really quite safe."

"You try it," said Miss Prady, "and see if you feel safe."

"Here we are," said Gamadge. "Miss Prady, my car's just up the road, as you know; get into it and wait—we shan't be long. Harold, as soon as we get into Five Acres go and put that knife where it came from—a kitchen drawer, I suppose. Then hurry out to your room and pack, and join Miss Prady in the car."

Three minutes later Gamadge and his assistant were standing on the porch, and Gamadge's finger was on the night bell. After some delay Mrs. Tully opened the door. There was cream on her face, her hair was wired for the night, and she wore a pink cap, a pink woollen dressing-gown, and large pink slippers adorned with pompons. She was ill-pleased.

"What's all this?" she demanded. "What are you doing here, Gamadge, and what's your young man doing out of bed?"

"I'll explain, Tully." Harold slid past the pink mountain, and made for the east wing. Gamadge backed Mrs. Tully towards the lounge. "Just go up and rout Miss Lukes out, will you? I want to talk to you both."

"I will not wake Lucy Lukes up! She's as tired as I am. More so. Do you know what time it is?" Mrs. Tully spoke in a hissing whisper, in order not to wake the lodgers. "Do you want a room? What's the matter with you?"

"I don't want a room. I want to telephone, and then I want to talk to you both, and I have no time. You go and bring her down, like a good girl."

Gamadge made for the booth. Mrs. Tully, casting a truculent look after him, turned and lumbered up the stairs.

Gamadge found his party after a long wait. Durfee's voice barked: "What is it?"

"Gamadge speaking. I wanted to say that I had a hunch about Locke's murder—"

"Do you have to drag me out of bed at this time of night to listen to a hunch?"

"No; I followed the hunch, and I know who did it and where his gun is and where his car is."

"What are you talking about?"

"I want you to get the credit, Durfee; you can call up the Westchester people, or the Cold Brook sheriff—"

"Cold Brook?"

"—and leave me out of it. Because I want to get home to bed. I've been working on this case for you all day."

"Very kind of you. Who killed him, for instance?"

"Mrs. Gregson."

"Who?"

"Mrs. Curtis Gregson. The one that killed her husband three years ago. I wasn't able to hold her for you—she drove herself into a ravine, and there isn't a hope that she's alive. But if you want to make sure, you can get wreckers on the job right away. The ravine is on a lane just below a sanatorium called Five Acres, not far from Cold Brook. Anybody there can direct you. Left-hand side of the route as you come up," said Gamadge hurriedly. "You can't miss it."

Durfee had difficulty in articulating. Then he said: "Where in the devil are you?"

"Here at Five Acres. Mrs. Gregson was staying here under the name of Greer—I sent her here." Gamadge heard a kind of snort behind him, which came from Mrs. Tully. She and her partner were just outside the booth; he felt beleaguered.

"For God's sake——" began Durfee.

"She hired me—for camouflage," said Gamadge. "I found it out, and came up to see her about it. She wanted a private talk, but they lock the place up; so she crawled out of a window. We went to this lane, in her car. When she knew I knew she'd killed Locke she attacked me."

"With Locke's gun?"

Gamadge coughed. "Attacked me, jumped into her car and drove it over into this ravine. The gun's in the car, all right."

"If you'd have the plain, ordinary, God-forsaken common sense to tell me these things you dig up, Gamadge, people wouldn't get away from you and get killed. You stampeded her. Wait there——"

"I had to stampede her. I couldn't get proof you could use without stampeding her. Now you have the gun, and Locke's car, and his murderer. What a scoop!"

"This doesn't make good sense. Wait there. I'll be up——"

"Can't wait. I'm leaving."

"Are you crazy?"

"No, and I'm not crazy enough to go home to-night, either. I'll see you to-morrow morning at half-past nine, and not a minute before."

Durfee said in measured accents: "You stay there. You're a material witness. I'll call up and have your car stopped."

"*You're* out of your mind if you so much as mention my name. I'm nothing but information received, you poor idiot. I don't come into it at all." He added: "Did I let you down the other time? I'll see you to-morrow; and don't you go waking Clara up to-night—she hasn't a notion where I am or what I've been doing."

He rang off. As he came out of the booth a pink fury, wide as a door, barred his way.

"You can't do this to us, Gamadge!" Her whisper was ferocious. "You got us into some kind of a mess. You can't go off to-night and leave us battling with a lot of cops."

"I wouldn't go a step, Tully, if I could do a thing for you. Much better for all of us if I go. They won't bother you here—they'll just go over her stuff and quit. You didn't even know who she was."

"You've ruined the place. You sent a murderess to us under a false name."

Miss Lukes, whose dark hair was brushed severely off her face and braided into a short tail, and whose red flannel robe was far from picturesque, now stepped forward and confronted her partner. "We wouldn't have the place at all, Florence Tully," she said, "if Mr. Gamadge hadn't put up all the capital. I guess we can help him out now."

"Don't take that into consideration, Miss Lukes," begged Gamadge. "I'm as sorry as hell about all this. I don't blame Tully for bawling me out."

"I do," said Miss Lukes. "She's acting very selfish. How did this Mrs. Gregson, or Greer, or whoever she was, get hold of a car?"

"You don't know a thing about that, Miss Lukes. Somebody must have driven it up and left it. I don't see why anybody should ask you about that."

"If they don't, we won't mention it."

"You needn't mention Harold, either; he's going back with me to-night, and I don't think any of your guests will miss Mr. Thompson."

"We'll say he left."

"Anything else we can do for you?" Mrs. Tully stood with folded arms, glaring at him; but suddenly she burst out laughing, and gave him a sledge-hammer clap on the shoulder. He staggered under it.

"Get out while the going's good," she advised. "Drive straight up the hill and turn right. You needn't hit the route till you're beyond White Plains."

Bless you both. I'll telephone." Gamadge fled out of the house, down the drive, and to his car. He found Miss Prady extended on the back seat with a rug over her, and Harold in front, holding the door open. The engine was running. Gamadge sprang in, and they were off.

"Get out the map," he said, "and read me how to get away from this region without hitting any town within ten miles." He drove up the hill, turned right, and struck a high, level road running south. Harold, the map jiggling under his eyes, read out directions that sent the car swerving around corners and into byways, through sleeping settlements, over and down a hill like a switchback at a fair. Miss Prady, extended, with her knees up, her feet braced and her eyes closed, bounced silent in the rear.

But they entered New York City sedately, and first drew up in front of Miss Prady's rooming-house. Gamadge escorted her to the vestibule, and waited while she fumbled for her key; at last he took it away from her and unlocked the door.

"You've been a wonder," he said. "Clara's looking forward to seeing you again and often."

Miss Prady's head lolled. "Wanted to catch her; didn't

know what it would be like," she mumbled. Gamadge restored the key to her bag, gently pushed her into the house, and closed the door after her. He hoped she would not sink to sleep on the stairs.

By the time he had reached the Biltmore and surrendered the car to its personnel he was almost asleep himself. Harold stood blinking beside him in the lobby, uncertain as to his immediate future.

"We're here for the night," said Gamadge. "Let's have a drink."

They had the drink, and then Harold registered and they went up to Gamadge's suite. He felt as if he had been out of it a year. When he got Clara on the telephone, he regretted the impulse that had made him wake her up.

"Darling," she murmured.

"I had to know how you were. I'll be home in the morning."

"For breakfast?"

"No, but Durfee'll be there, or I'm much mistaken. Be nice to him."

"I was—when he called me an hour ago."

"Damn him."

"I told him I didn't know where you were. How was Omega?"

"Horrible. It's sickening of me to have waked you."

"I'm glad you did. I—was—very—much—worried."

"You sound that way. Go back to sleep."

Gamadge rang off, and sat down with a long sigh to take off his shoes. He remembered just before he sank into bed to ring the office and leave a call for eight o'clock.

XVIII

Harold Does Very Well

"Leave the bags here until later," said Gamadge. He and
Harold had breakfasted, and now stood in the Biltmore
lobby; it was a quarter past nine o'clock. "Go up to the house
by subway," continued Gamadge. "Watch your chance, and
get in by the basement door. Be in the laboratory; and
remember, you haven't been away."

"Won't Theodore spill it?"

"Theodore will say nothing. Durfee isn't interested in
your activities, and won't ask about them—we hope."

Harold said, rather awkwardly: "You don't have to keep
me out of it."

"I have to keep everybody out of it. I'm not doing you
any favour."

Harold walked off. Gamadge left by another door, got
his car, and drove it to Park Avenue; he went northward
and then east, arriving at his house on the stroke of
nine-thirty. When he entered he whistled; the whistle
brought Clara flying down the stairs, and Durfee out of
the office. Gamadge addressed the latter over Clara's
head:

"Excuse reunion ceremonies, will you, old man? I'll be
right with you."

Durfee, leaning against the jamb of the door, watched
them stonily. At last Clara released the traveller and went
upstairs. Gamadge said, getting out of his coat, "Delighted to
see you. Where's the other one?"

"What other one?"

Gamadge hung his coat up in the hall closet, and then
turned to smile at his visitor. "The one in uniform. The one

that's going to help you take me to jail. I won't go quietly."

Durfee cleared his throat. "No harm in talking it over first."

"That's what I thought." Gamadge led the way into the office, pushed up a big chair for Durfee, sat down at his desk, and got out a box of cigars. He offered one to Durfee, and when it was peremptorily refused, lighted it for himself.

Durfee sat forward, his hands clasped. He said: "They got the two cars and the woman out this morning early. Those people at Five Acres identified her by her clothes."

"Bad as that? I thought it would be."

"Stuff in her handbag identified her as Mrs. Curtis Gregson. The automatic, one bullet missing, was in a rear pocket of her car."

Gamadge looked amiable. Durfee studied him; his face never had much colour in it, but this morning it was ashy-looking, and his eyes were dull. But he seemed at ease, leaning back in his chair with his knees crossed, the cigar in his fingers.

"I didn't care for the way you tried to bribe me last night," said Durfee. "I didn't know I'd made that kind of an impression on you."

"My dear man! Such a thing never entered my head."

"Bribing me to keep you out of the case; that's what you were doing."

"I solemnly assure you that all I wanted was to get away from that place last night and get some sleep. I had had a long day."

"You can't stay out of the picture, Gamadge; those two women at Five Acres are telling everybody you sent Mrs. Gregson to their place. It's in the papers—or will be."

"I don't expect to be out of the picture. I kept out of it last night because I'd been running my legs off solving the Gregson case, and I didn't want to sit up all night talking to a lot of small-town officials and state police, and having my photograph taken. I thought you'd do me the favour of letting me have a few hours' sleep. As a matter of fact, though, I really don't understand why I should be pushed into the limelight. I'm a private citizen."

"If you don't like publicity, why do you risk it by going into these cases and getting people killed? Locke——"

"Locke got killed because he tried to acquire a fortune by withholding evidence against Mrs. Gregson three years ago."

"Why not tell me that the day before yesterday?"

"I had no proof of it. There wasn't even any proof that Mrs. Gregson was working up a case against Cecilia Warren. Let's see that letter she sent you people."

Durfee, gazing fixedly at him, drew a grey envelope out of his pocket. Gamadge compared its enclosure with the one which Mrs. Gregson had given him. "There you are," he said, "like as two peas. Only this one really means business." He read aloud:

> *"The murderer of Curtis Gregson is still at large. Ask Miss C. Warren, Care of Mrs. J. Smiles, where the pistol is that killed Benton Locke."*

Durfee studied the other communication. He asked: "You say Mrs. Gregson wrote these?"

"Yes. It's certain."

"But the second one clears Miss Warren of writing the first, then. She wouldn't write a letter incriminating herself."

"I think Mrs. Stoner was supposed to be responsible for those letters. They sound rather like the kind of thing a Mrs. Stoner might think up if she were trying to be portentous. Mrs. Gregson intended them to sound so."

"I thought Mrs. Stoner was a friend of Mrs. Gregson's—lived with her all these years."

"I think Mrs. Gregson had cast her in the rôle of secret persecutor. Not avenger—that was the rôle Miss Warren was cast for, as you shall hear. Mrs. Stoner was grateful to Gregson, you know; she might be supposed to cherish animus against his wife. She might be supposed to have given Cecilia Warren the idea for several alleged attempts at murdering Mrs. Gregson. Mrs. Stoner's position was dangerous; it would have become more so," said Gamadge, thinking of the stump lot, "if Mrs. Gregson had succeeded in planting evidence at her door."

"But if Mrs. Stoner was supposed to have it in for Mrs. Gregson, why should she supposedly write a letter incriminating Miss Warren?"

"Oh—because Miss Warren had supposedly killed Benton Locke, whom Mrs. Stoner greatly loved."

Durfee got out a handkerchief and mopped his forehead. "Mrs. Gregson was actually hiring you to get up a case against them, drag them both into it?"

"Even Mrs. Stoner, her best friend."

"And you could have saved us from going and searching that apartment, could you?" Durfee's eye was baleful.

"You pretend that I, or anybody except the Commissioner and the District Attorney, could have prevented you from searching the Smiles apartment?"

Durfee said, after a pause: "They were quite polite about it. Mrs. Smiles—peculiar type."

"Very."

"Said we must follow the pattern, whatever that meant, and would we have some coffee."

"And Miss Warren looked over your heads."

"I would have picked her for the person responsible for Gregson's death if I'd seen her at that time. Cold-looking woman."

"Her defence against a rather cold world. I shall now, Durfee, tell you the story of Mrs. Gregson; which includes a flight of cellar stairs, a poisoned mackerel, a gas oven, and a Boone fruit cake with six grains of arsenic in it."

"I'll be glad to hear it."

Gamadge told the story, explained his reactions to it, and recounted his interviews with Locke, Cecilia Warren, and Mrs. Stoner. "But I knew the attempts at murder were fakes," he said, "and I knew she'd killed Gregson. I knew it when she refused to change that will. I knew she was out to rehabilitate herself by incriminating somebody else; and that must be the most promising suspect, her next heir."

"Why did she leave money in her will to Locke and Cecilia Warren? Why did she buy Mrs. Stoner that annuity?"

"She left Miss Warren and Locke money in her will to provide herself with suspects; that was her first and best reason. But she also left them money, and gave Mrs. Stoner the annuity, so that they shouldn't tell the real story of life in the Gregson house; her hatred of Gregson, and the general unsatisfactory state of things at the time of the murder. That's what I suppose, anyway."

"You supposed a lot of things."

"I didn't *suppose* that Locke knew about that tube of morphia."

"Locke and who else? What did you find out in Omega?"

"That Cecilia Warren's father wasn't a drinking man. Why did he crash, if not from drugs? Why shouldn't Mrs. Gregson have had access to them? She must have been about the Warren house often enough at the time."

"Cecilia Warren——"

"Cecilia Warren was about seven years old when her father owned that tube of morphia with the corner off the label. He owned it more than twenty years ago, Durfee."

"You certainly did a lot of guessing in this case. I don't see how we're ever going to tie these letters up to Mrs. Gregson." Durfee fingered them, scowling.

"Perhaps the income tax people will let *you* look at her returns. Perhaps there's a plant label, or a luggage tag, at Bellfield. Perhaps there's marked linen at Pine Lots. Any expert will tell you those letters were printed by the same hand. They're identical."

"And she hired you just as a first step to getting her story to the police?"

"That's it. To get it to the police without seeming to wish to get it there. Eventually I should have been able to persuade her that publicity was her best and only course." Gamadge clasped his hands behind his head and scowled. "I get madder every time I think of it."

Durfee, with a sardonic smile, said that he imagined Gamadge was a little peeved.

"A little peeved! Poor Colby."

"She took a risk with that arsenic in that mackerel. I suppose it had to be arsenic, in case the doctor wanted specimens?"

"Yes; she didn't give herself much of a dose, though. And how beautifully she had built up the stories! I could almost see her plunging down that cellar stair, and catching her skirt on the splinter."

"All to get herself acquitted of Gregson's murder by the people that mattered to her?"

"The people that mattered to her? Everybody mattered to her. I know very well how she became a woman of one idea, Durfee. She murdered a husband who had become intolerable to her, with the idea of getting his money and living a happy life; but through Cecilia Warren's evidence she found herself acquitted of the murder simply because the jury couldn't bring themselves to convict a woman with an unblemished reputation. Conventional morality made her a good woman to that jury; a love affair, just one, would have doomed her. She had no inner life; she found herself cut off from small social activities; she had only one thought to feed on."

"And you went up there last night and taxed her with all this, fondly hoping she'd confess and let you bring her down to headquarters and charge her?" Durfee's smile was one-sided.

"Certainly not. Fondly hoping she'd make the murderous attack she—er—did make. Then I could bring her down and give her in charge, as you say. Locke's car would have been found in that ravine, and whether or not she should ever be proved guilty of his murder, she wouldn't have been able to go on trying to get Cecilia Warren electrocuted for it—and perhaps for Gregson's."

"You know you ought to have come to me; if not at first, then the minute you heard Locke had been killed."

"I held off for two reasons."

"I bet they were good ones, too." Durfee gazed at him unwaveringly.

"The best. Would a cigar still poison you?"

Durfee slowly stretched out his hand and took one from the box. When he had it going, Gamadge went on: "I had to keep Cecilia Warren out of jail; it's easier to get in than to get out again, you know, Durfee; and plenty of people still think she killed Gregson. You did, yourself."

"It was just a theory."

"When police have theories, it's time to get a lawyer. Meanwhile, with Miss Warren still out of jail, I had to get some kind of proof against the wretched woman, so that she'd never be able to use faked evidence herself. I was deucedly afraid of her. You don't know what she was like, Durfee. I didn't know what she mightn't cook up. When I first met her, you know, I thought she looked like somebody who'd never got over the shock of a hideous surprise. I was right—it was the surprise she got when she sat there at the inquest and heard Cecilia Warren say that she used to come down on hot nights and sleep in the guest-room. From that moment she knew that her plans were ruined. She felt the ground open under her, Durfee. I suppose it never felt really solid to her feet again."

Durfee said: "One of your rigmaroles. How am I to get it in shape to hand in down-town, or send up to Westchester?"

"I'll have Harold type out a complete statement. Harold!"

At his employer's summons Harold came in from the laboratory. His white tunic was buttoned neatly about his neck, and he held a forceps in one hand and a piece of parchment in the other. He said: "I dried out most of that paper Martin et."

"Good. Harold, Lieutenant Durfee wants a typed statement from my notes on the Gregson matter. I'll give you some more this morning; you ought to be able to get the whole thing down to him by three o'clock."

"O.K."

"Three copies for Lieutenant Durfee, please, and—er—half a dozen for me."

"Don't you send anything to the papers," Durfee warned him, getting up.

"Certainly not. I have files; cross references, you know."

"I'll tell you one thing," said Durfee, as Harold turned to go. "It's lucky for you, Gamadge, that the woman's hands were still gripping the wheel when they found her in that gorge."

"Still gripping the wheel, were they?"

"I'm told it was hard to get them loose."

Harold had paused on his way back to the laboratory. Durfee went on, faintly smiling: "You have no witnesses to what did occur. Before you get through with this you may need an unblemished reputation yourself."

Gamadge laughed. He accompanied Durfee to the front door, and returned to find Harold standing where he had been, and looking morose.

"I wanted to say you had witnesses," he said.

"I should have strangled you before you got the words out. Nonsense."

"You might need them, at that."

"Absurd. Durfee's idea of a joke. Now don't spoil it, Harold." Gamadge patted him on the shoulder. "You did very well."

XIX

Home Work

At four-thirty Clara was serving tea; Theodore circulated among the guests with a tray and glasses, in case certain of them should prefer something stronger. Martin was having a light refection under the tea-table. Clara's chow watched him indulgently; he could not but make allowances for a creature who dined out of a saucer.

Gamadge had just finished reading aloud from a typed statement, copies of which were in the hands of all the visitors. Cecilia Warren and Belden sat together on the sofa, Schenck next to Clara, Mrs. Stoner beside Gamadge in a deep chair, and Miss Prady, attended by Harold, on a love seat which Theodore had drawn up to accommodate them.

"You will please take your copies of this thing home with you," said Gamadge, "and learn them." He looked up in hurt surprise when Paul Belden burst into uproarious laughter. "I see no occasion for levity."

"Neither do I," said Cecilia Warren. But her face glowed as she looked at Belden. "You ought to be crying with relief, Paul. You're very ungrateful, and you've spilled cocktail on your trousers."

"By heavens, I can't help it!" Belden roared again. "He's a genius, and some day he'll get hung. I've seen a man walk a tightrope before, but not with three people hanging on each side of him." He added, accepting a cocktail napkin three inches square from Clara, and dabbing at his trousers with it,

"Gamadge knows how I feel; darn him, he knew how I was feeling all along. He might have given us a hint that he was on the side of us angels."

"Oh, no, I mightn't," said Gamadge. "I didn't even tell my assistant or my wife. Somebody would have given the show away, and said something to somebody else; and somebody else might have warned Mrs. Gregson that her private investigator was investigating the wrong things. I'm not sure that Mrs. Smiles couldn't keep a secret out of her face, though." He glanced at a huge basket, twined with ribbon, which stood on a side-table. It was heaped with fruit, nuts, chocolates, and preserves, and topped with a small bottle of champagne. "Decent of her to send this along."

"She loves you," said Cecilia. "I thought you thought I might be going to murder her, too."

"Not after I found out that she had no property to leave you. If she gives many presents of this sort," and Gamadge looked again at the imposing basket, "she must live well up to her income."

Clara said: "You say the most ghastly things, darling."

"I'm light-headed. It's reaction."

Miss Prady, who sat with her feet close together, her shoulders and knees knobbily defined under her thin sweater and skirt, said: "I think Mr. Gamadge was wonderful to keep us all out of it, just wonderful. If he gets into trouble I'm going to tell everything."

"Oh, Lord, you'd have us absolutely in the soup!" Gamadge was horrified.

"I'll deny it," remarked Schenck. "I'll deny it all, on oath. Mrs. Gamadge laid herself open to a charge of prowling. You can't give her away, Miss Prady."

Harold observed in a paternal tone that Miss Prady wouldn't tell. He seemed to view her with favour; so far as Gamadge knew she was the only feminine creature, except Clara, whom Harold had ever noticed at all.

"You left out something in that confession." Schenck pointed with a long finger at the statement. "You never said anything about losing a cigarette case in the Bulliters' balcony. Suppose Durfee traces you to the Bulliters; you ought to have some kind of excuse for going there."

Cecilia Warren looked at Gamadge. "Is *that* what you did with that pistol that night?"

"Er—yes. So last night, between my return from Omega and my trip to Five Acres, I retrieved it."

Belden laid his head back against the cushions of the sofa to howl: "Oh, Lord, the Bulliters!"

"Mrs. Smiles was so wonderful with the police," said Miss Warren. "Paul, you will spill that cocktail again." She took the glass from him, and went on: "She insisted on giving them coffee, and she told them they were so wonderful, and that when she had had sneak thieves they got back her acquascutum."

"Where's Colby?" asked Belden. "Isn't he going to have to learn his piece too?"

"Oh, poor Mr. Colby is miserable," said Clara. "He's going south. He's going to take his vacation now."

Gamadge frowned. "I hated to have him in it," he said. "I tried to think of some way to keep him out of it at the last."

There was a silence. Cecilia Warren turned melancholy eyes on him, to say: "It's awful, Mr. Gamadge, but you don't know what it means to me—to know she's dead."

"I think I do know."

"Apart from all this last terrible thing, I mean. Mr. Gregson made her take me in, but I was so unhappy there. And after I said that—about his laughing—I was always so afraid of her. I knew she would never forgive me. I used to go and see her, just because I was so afraid. But I didn't know she would do this!"

Belden said: "We were all scared; except Mrs. Smiles, of course, who wasn't let into the secret."

"I knew she'd put that pistol in my room. I didn't dare say a word, I was so afraid she'd tell about the morphia. I thought she was safe herself, and wouldn't mind telling, to get me into trouble."

"You didn't realize that she'd never tell anything, if there was any chance that it would reflect on her," said Gamadge.

"No, I didn't."

Miss Prady said: "I knew when you looked at me, Mr. Gamadge, that you were going to find out who killed Benny."

Mrs. Stoner had sat quietly drinking her tea. She now put the cup down, and said: "I blame myself very much."

"You blame yourself, my dearest Minnie?" Paul Belden leaned forward and took her hand. "What for?"

"I should have told Mr. Gamadge that Benny thought Vina had done the things herself. But it seemed so unjust to her. I was so afraid he'd done them, and Cecilia was too. You looked so angry when you came to Pine Lots, and by that time——"

Gamadge coughed. Mrs. Stoner looked at him, and coughed too. She went on to say: "But I ought to have known that you were to be trusted."

"Well—I strained your capacity for trust in me."

"That pistol!" Cecilia Warren looked at Clara admiringly. "You were wonderful, and how I hated you both!"

Clara said: "It was just so the police wouldn't find it in your room, and so that Miss Prady would be willing to go up to that awful sanatorium."

"Awful?" Gamadge looked at her in reproof. "It isn't awful, and we'd better be polite to Mrs. Tully and Miss Lukes for the rest of our lives. They've had to do some home work themselves, don't forget that. In fact," he said glumly, "there are eleven people doing home work on this thing, and eleven's a good many."

"You said eight hundred people could keep a secret if each of them wanted to."

Schenck remarked that eleven was enough, and that he thought of going south himself.

Belden's long arm went round Cecilia Warren's shoulders. He said: "There isn't much use trying to tell you people how we feel about what you've done. I can't even begin to. This girl—she's all I ever cared about. The way she's stuck to me . . . I don't know whether any of you know what small-town gossip is like, or how much super-abundant energy the ladies of all ages can put into breaking up a love affair between unpopular people." He took his glass back from Cecilia and drained it. "To the women of Omega, young and old; God bless 'em!"

Cecilia smiled at him. "You were too popular, Paul! That was the trouble. They all wanted you." She addressed the others rather shyly: "I don't know what I should have done without him. He was always there, and he was such fun. But

I wasn't going to be a burden on him, and then the trial came, and I couldn't bear——"

"She couldn't bear the way her pictures came out in the newspapers," said Belden. "Gamadge, I wish there were something we could do for you. Do you want your backyard landscaped? Does Mrs. Gamadge need a part-time secretary?"

"I can make very nice apple butter," said Mrs. Stoner. "Poor Curtis liked it. Of course," she added, "I can't keep that annuity."

"If you think Curtis Gregson would have wanted you to give up that annuity," said Belden, "you're greatly mistaken. Besides, you're going to live with Cecilia and me, and you won't have to make apple butter. We're going to keep whatever the law lets us keep. I mean it, though, Gamadge—whatever we can do, now or in the future—"

"You can do something now," said Gamadge. "All of you. Just read the statement over once again, out loud. Perhaps you don't quite realize that it's important."

Papers rustled. Harold, looking at his copy, observed that he wanted to ask a question first.

"Question? What question?" Gamadge regarded him suspiciously.

"Well, I don't quite understand the time-table here; I mean, there isn't any." He added; "Except for Mrs. Gregson's trips."

"Why should there be any, except for her trips?" Gamadge scowled at him.

"It would be clearer if there was a time-table for your trips. On Wednesday, now; I know when you left Five Acres—I saw you go. You must have been at Pine Lots in a little over half an hour at latest; but you don't seem to have reached home until——"

Gamadge said in a slow, menacing drawl: "Have I got to sit down and work it out just to indulge your passion for detail?"

"No, but——" Harold met his eye, and stopped. Mrs. Stoner said primly: "I don't know when Mr. Gamadge came to Pine Lots." Clara remarked: "I don't know when Henry got home."

"Nobody knows, and nobody cares, if you don't." Gamadge shook the typed pages in his hand. "All ready?"

The class came to attention.

"Then," said Gamadge, "please repeat after me."

A chorus rose; Belden's *r*'s rolling richly, Mrs. Stoner's pipe lagging behind the rest: "On Tuesday afternoon, November the twenty-fifth, at four o'clock . . ."

ABOUT THE AUTHOR

ELIZABETH DALY was born in 1878 in New York City. The daughter of a judge and niece of the famous playwright and producer Augustin Daly, she grew up immersed in the world of literature and the theater. Miss Daly received her B.A. from Bryn Mawr College in 1901 and her M.A. from Columbia the following year. She later returned to Bryn Mawr as a reader in English and remained there for two years, adding to her duties the coaching and producing of amateur plays. Although she began her literary ·career at the age of sixteen and published light verse and prose in various magazines, she did not write her first mystery novel until she was past sixty. In 1940, *Unexpected Night* was published and marked the first appearance of Henry Gamadge, her famous bibliophile detective. Miss Daly considered the detective novel at its best a high form of literature and didn't seek to write any other kind of fiction. Elizabeth Daly was a very popular writer in the United States as well as England, where Gamadge was dubbed "the American Peter Wimsey." One of her greatest fans was the grande dame of English mystery herself, Agatha Christie.

Murder Most British

With these new mystery titles, Bantam takes you to the scene of the crime. These masters of mystery follow in the tradition of the Great British crime writers. You'll meet all these talented sleuths as they get to the bottom of even the most baffling crimes.

Elizabeth Daly

☐	24883	THE BOOK OF THE LION	$2.95
☐	24610	HOUSE WITHOUT THE DOOR	$2.95
☐	24267	SOMEWHERE IN THE HOUSE	$2.95
☐	24605	NOTHING CAN RESCUE ME	$2.95
☐	24616	AND DANGEROUS TO KNOW	$2.95

Margery Allingham

☐	25102	TETHER'S END	$2.95
☐	25214	BLACK PLUMES	$2.95
☐	24548	PEARLS BEFORE SWINE	$2.95
☐	24814	THE TIGER IN THE SMOKE	$2.95
☐	24190	FLOWERS FOR THE JUDGE	$2.95
☐	24852	DANCERS IN THE MOURNING	$2.95
☐	25411	DEADLY DUO	$2.95
☐	25412	FASHION IN SHROUDS	$2.95

Dorothy Simpson

☐	25192	SIX FEET UNDER	$2.95
☐	25292	CLOSE HER EYES	$2.95
☐	25065	PUPPET FOR A CORPSE	$2.95

Prices and availability subject to change without notice.

Buy them at your local bookstore or use this handy coupon for ordering:

THE THRILLING AND MASTERFUL NOVELS OF ROSS MACDONALD

Winner of the Mystery Writers of America Grand Master Award, Ross Macdonald is acknowledged around the world as one of the greatest mystery writers of our time. *The New York Times* has called his books featuring private investigator Lew Archer "the finest series of detective novels ever written by an American."

Now, Bantam Books is reissuing Macdonald's finest work in handsome new paperback editions. Look for these books (a new title will be published every month) wherever paperbacks are sold or use the handy coupon below for ordering:

☐ SLEEPING BEAUTY (24593 * $2.95)

☐ THE MOVING TARGET (24546 * $2.95)

☐ THE GOODBYE LOOK (24192 * $2.95)

☐ THE NAME IS ARCHER (23650 * $2.95)

☐ THE BLUE HAMMER (24497 * $2.95)

☐ BARBAROUS COAST (24268 * $2.95)

☐ BLUE CITY (22590 * $2.95)

☐ INSTANT ENEMY (24738 * $2.95)

Prices and availability subject to change without notice.

Special Offer
Buy a Bantam Book
for only 50¢.

Now you can have an up-to-date listing of Bantam's hundreds of titles plus take advantage of our unique and exciting bonus book offer. A special offer which gives you the opportunity to purchase a Bantam book for only 50¢. Here's how!

By ordering any five books at the regular price per order, you can also choose any other single book listed (up to a $4.95 value) for just 50¢. Some restrictions do apply, but for further details why not send for Bantam's listing of titles today!

Just send us your name and address and we will send you a catalog!